Blackfriars Gate

A DCI Shaftoe Mystery

JJ Thomas

ISBN 978-1-9163141-0-8

To Mam

TABLE OF CONTENTS

Chapter 1

Neil Thomson gave out a long deep sigh as he stood at the door of the restaurant which he frequented, with his friends, every Thursday night. He'd left them moments ago still engrossed in their conversation but an important early morning meeting with some Chinese businessmen had prompted him to leave now. He suddenly remembered that he hadn't told Rob about a phone call he'd had that day. It could wait. As he looked out at the rain coming down in sheets, intermittently blasted by the wind, he was tempted to re-join them. But he was just putting off his stay of execution; he'd left his coat in the car and so he was going to get wet whatever he did. A cloaked figure moved across the modern Gothic archway opposite. It's too early for Halloween, he thought, so it must be a woman wearing a burqa.

Well there was nothing for it. He opened the restaurant door and made a dash across the road. He walked into the passageway between two modern Gothic arches, one opening out onto Stowell Street and Chinatown, and the other into Blackfriars Court and a blanket of darkness. He shook the water from himself like a long-haired dog. Of course, the restaurant gave out most of the light into the court at night, and it was closed for refurbishments. He could see movement at Blackfriars Gate and the outline of a dark figure. Then it was gone. It must be the woman wearing the burqa.

He stood for another moment in the shelter of the arch. Nothing for it. He moved quickly to the first set of steps, guided by the light from the flats, as a sudden blast of wind stung his face with needles of rain. He shivered. Halfway along the path he stopped. He pushed his hand in his pocket and retrieved his phone to switch on the light. Damn. The battery was dead. He looked towards Blackfriars Gate. The passageway was in blackness and there was very little light coming from Friars Lane. He'd have to be careful so as not to break his neck in the darkness. Should he go back onto Stowell Street and the long way around to the car? No. He would get soaked.

He walked towards the first gate with his arms outstretched, like a blind man, shuffling his feet which slapped on wet stone paving. There was a sudden crash and then a clatter. He jumped. There was a pain in his chest and he held his breath. He turned and realised someone must've smashed something in one of the flats. He breathed out and sighed. He glanced up, but there was no moon and only the sound of wind and rain: the buildings buffered any sound from Chinatown and Friars Lane was always quiet, especially now the restaurant was closed.

He shuffled again slowly towards the first gate and stretched out his arm. He could feel cold wet stone on his palm. He shivered. He felt the uneven flagstones under his feet. As he entered Blackfriars Gate darkness overwhelmed him, but he knew his eyes would adjust to the light and so he gingerly took another step which echoed on the stones in the tunnel. He took two more steps into the passageway and stopped. Was there someone else there? He could sense a presence. Or was he just imagining it? His heart raced.

"Hello." Nothing.

He moved another step forward. A bright light blinded him and he put his left arm up to his eyes. A cloaked and hooded figure stepped forward. There was blackness inside the hood where a face should be. One arm was raised above its head and there was a flash of metal in its hand. He saw the hand with the metal come down towards him. There was a thump to his chest and then a sharp pain. He breathed quickly. The figure raised its arm again. He tried to scream; nothing came out but a croak from the back of his throat. There was another sharp pain. His knees started to buckle. He put his hand to his chest and then moved it away: he stared at the blood on his hand. He was falling. He could see his wife Sarah, and his children, Ashley and Lucy, smiling at him. Then darkness.

***

DCI Alex Shaftoe parked her car around the corner from Stowell Street, at the end near the red-dragon Chinese archway entrance. Her phone had rung moments after she'd got into bed, so she'd quickly dragged on a pair of jeans and a baggy jumper. She looked dishevelled and her make-up had come off before she had gone to bed: enough to 'frighten the bairns', as her mam would've said. She sighed because she'd only just got off the plane from her holiday in Spain that afternoon. It had been a late holiday, in October, because her daughter Lisa hadn't been able to go at any other time. A blast of wind straight from the North Sea hit her face on and she shivered. "That's brought you back to earth…no more balmy Andalusian nights," she muttered to herself. "Time to think seriously about the early retirement you were talking to Lisa about," she continued. But in her heart of hearts she knew she was stuck whilst her mam was alive – she couldn't leave her. She shook her head again and sighed a second time. If she gave up work now, she'd be just kicking her heels around the house, in between visits to the nursing home.

There was a hum of voices, and the wind carried a waft of aniseed and ginger through the air as she turned into Stowell Street and Chinatown. She breathed in and then out through pursed lips. Human nature's fascination with the awful never ceased to amaze her, not to mention the time the police had to spend getting rid of nosy people from crime scenes. The scene that greeted her was more like the celebration of Chinese New Year without the firecrackers. Curiosity about the commotion on the street had emptied the restaurants and casino of their customers, despite the chill wind. The neon lights of some of the restaurants, blue, red and green glared garishly, silhouetting the large number of people on both sides of the pavement all the way up the street. She shrugged. It could be worse, she thought, it might've been a Friday night instead of a Thursday. She caught sight of the familiar silhouette of Dave Bell, his stout figure in profile, showing the full extent of his growing belly which hung over his trouser belt. She pushed her way through to him.

"What ye doing here?" His sheep-shaggy eyebrows shot up in surprise. "I thought ye weren't due in till the morrow."

"I got off the plane a couple of hours ago." She rolled her eyes. "I was phoned just as I got into bed." She took a deep breath. "Tell me," she said to Dave.

"A gang fight broke out about an hour ago. Knives. Four people hurt and on their way to hospital now. All knife injuries. Another one ran off." He nodded up the street. "The lads are interviewing people who witnessed what happened."

With no one dead, little wonder he'd been surprised to see her. An obvious cock up because they'd thought she was due back in work today rather than tomorrow. He could easily handle a gang fight without her needing to ruin her beauty sleep. As her eyes moved up and down the street, she saw three uniformed police officers with their notebooks out. But at this time of night, and with this type of lighting, how reliable were the witnesses going to be? "How many were involved?" she asked as she continued to survey the street.

"We think five with the one that got away."

Standing in the middle of Chinatown she asked the obvious question. "Any Chinese?"

"Na. But we're not sure about the one that got away."

The street was finally clearing as people went back into restaurants, encouraged by the uniformed police officers. "Any initial thoughts?" she said, although she had already guessed at his answer.

"Drugs," he said without hesitation. His phone rang.

***

Sarah Thomson was sitting on a bar stool in her kitchen twisting her wedding ring around her finger. She glanced at the clock – it was nearly midnight. Neil had never been this late before. What if he'd had a car crash or an accident? No, she was being neurotic. She rubbed the back of her neck. The car might've broken down? But he would've rang her if this had happened. She stood up and fingered her necklace. And then she picked her phone up from the kitchen table. She'd tried and tried to phone Neil for the last hour, but his phone had switched onto answer. She would phone Rob.

"Hello, Rob, it's Sarah. Did Neil leave Chinatown at the usual time?" she rattled out in one breath. She'd woken Rob and could hear it in his slow response.

"Yes. Just after ten. Hasn't he come home?"

She looked at her watch again. "No, and I'm worried. Did he park in the usual place?"

"Yes. Have you tried the breakdown services?" A hint of concern now in his voice.

"No. I phoned you first," she said anxiously.

"Maybe he's broken down and his phone battery is dead. It happens to us all," he suggested.

She hadn't thought about that.

"Sarah, are you still there?"

"Yes," she muttered.

"Let me know if you need any help."

She phoned the breakdown services next – nothing. She phoned the three major hospitals in Newcastle and after each call her stomach sank; she'd have to go to their accident and emergency wards herself. She glanced at her watch; the police wouldn't be interested in a man two hours late home. There was something wrong, she just knew it, so she called up the stairs to her son, "Ashley."

Twenty minutes later, Ashley pulled her car into Blackfriars car park next to Neil's car. He'd insisted on driving when he'd seen the agitated state she was in – she knew he'd been right. Her knees felt weak as she got out of her car and peered through the window of Neil's car where she saw his jacket lying on the passenger seat. But what was his jacket doing in the car in this weather? And was his phone inside his jacket pocket? Maybe that was the reason they hadn't been able to find him on the phone? Her hands were shaking as she rang his number again. Nothing. She glanced towards Ashley who had just finished checking the last of the car doors – they were all locked. "We'll retrace your dad's route through to Chinatown and then we'll go to the hospitals." She could hear the quiver in her own voice. There was something very wrong; she'd sensed it for the last hour.

She moved towards Blackfriars Gate and Ashley moved to her side. As she turned sideways, he pulled his phone out of his jean pocket because the entrance was in blackness. Then a burst of light from his phone torch lit up the tunnel and Neil lying on his back across the flagstones. She stood for a moment, staring at Neil and then rushed forward. She bent down and put her hand on his chest.

"Neil! Neil!" she shouted. She sat down beside him, lifting his shoulders and pushing her arms underneath him so she could allow his head and upper body to rest over her legs. She could feel something sticky on her hands so she opened them and her eyes widened – it was blood. "Neil, Neil " she whispered as she stroked his hair and kissed his forehead.

Ashley crouched down beside her, tears running down his cheeks as he said, "Mum, he's gone."

Neil's eyes, unblinking, stared at her. They were the same brown eyes that had looked at her so often over more than twenty-five years. "No, he hasn't son. He wouldn't leave us."

"He's gone, Mum," he whispered again as he focused on Neil's dead eyes.

Ashley was right but she couldn't take it in. When was the last time she'd told Neil how much she loved him, or that she couldn't imagine life without him? When was the last time she'd told him what a good man he was and a good provider? What a good husband and father? She hugged his head to her chest. She didn't want to say 'goodbye' to him, so how could she regret not saying, 'goodbye love'.

Ashley stood up and made a phone call, then sat down beside her, one of his arms around her shoulder, the other outstretched holding one of his dad's hands. He was quietly sobbing. Then everything became a blur as silhouetted figures moved around in bright lights. She just held Neil. Someone bent down, trying to move her but she resisted and pushed them away. Then a woman crouched down beside her. She looked up and saw kind brown eyes and felt a hand on her shoulder.

The woman spoke gently. "I think you'd better let us take care of your husband now," and then carefully moved her arms away. "Come and stand beside your son."

Ashley took her hands and pulled her to her feet. She stumbled because she couldn't feel her legs – they were numb. She huddled against his shoulder as the woman with the kind brown eyes came to speak to her.

"I'm DCI Alex Shaftoe," she said as she signalled to another policewoman who came across to lead them to a car.

***

The following morning, Alex got out of the jeep she'd parked on Friars Lane. She opened the car boot and kitted herself out on automatic pilot in protective overalls, shoes and gloves and then bent underneath the blue and white police tape. She yawned; it had been a late night and her unpacking was going to have to wait. Welcome home, Alex. Here's a murder for you to sort out. The area was cordoned off and a uniformed police officer was on guard at the entrance. At Blackfriars Gate, John Robertson, dressed in white overalls, was waiting for her; he headed up the CSI team – Crime Scene Officers – but had once been one of her DCs. He'd shown a flair for forensics and she'd encouraged his move to CSI. He smiled at her and then almost immediately shook his head.

"This is a right buggers' muddle." He stared at the stone flagstones inside Blackfriars Gate.

A faint smirk crossed her lips because he'd picked up that expression of speech when he worked for her. A Scot, he had followed his Geordie girlfriend to Newcastle, settled in the city and married her. A tall redhead with a close-cropped beard, he was a Prince Harry look alike and turned the odd head because of that.

"It's one of the worst forensic messes I've seen," he continued.

She'd expected as much because Sarah Thomson had been sitting hugging her husband's body, with her son beside her, when they arrived on the scene. John was going to have to eliminate their DNA first, then hope that they hadn't destroyed any other evidence.

"It's going to be difficult. And the heavy rain outside last night has made it worse." He ground out his exasperation as he put his hands to his head.

"Have you got anything at all?" She tried not to let concern creep into her voice. She'd never seen him looking this worried; he usually worked his forensic magic with ease.

"We've got a woman's footprint at the end of the gate." He pointed. "The sole of the shoe had blood on it. Whoever it was went back through Blackfriars Court."

She darted him a glance. "Have you got anything on Friars Lane?"

"Nothing so far that would help. The rain was heavy and we'll have to eliminate the wife and son." Chagrin twisted John's mouth. "But as always, I'll do my best." He pulled a face.

She stepped further into the passageway between the two gates, her eyes roaming and tracking the scene in daylight. The alcove where Neil Thomson had been lying was very deep, much deeper now in daylight than it had seemed in the dark last night. There were old stones lying against the wall which must be from the original medieval building, or at least she assumed it was medieval. Above her, thick gnarled wooden beams ran along the roof of the passageway, and there were traces of blood there too. The killer must've had blood on them because there was blood everywhere. She walked into the alcove.

"The killer must've been waiting in here," she muttered as much to herself as to John. She pressed herself against the back wall; it was deep enough to hide in the dark, even if someone else had come along. She stared down to the bloodstained flagstones where Neil Thomson had been lying, worn smooth by centuries of footfall. His phone battery had been dead, they thought, so he'd walked across the court and into the passageway in the dark. "It would also have been dark for the killer. But there must've been light when the attack happened, otherwise the killer wouldn't have been able to see what they were doing." She paused. Surprise. "The killer must've switched on a torch which blinded him and struck while his eyes were adjusting," she muttered on. That made sense.

"But the killer couldn't have known Neil Thomson's phone battery was dead, otherwise he would've had light going through the passageway between the two gates," John interjected, disturbing her thoughts.

She went back into the alcove. "The police surgeon was sure it was a frontal assault on Neil Thomson. I'm going to have to come back in the dark and see if it would've been possible to surprise him if he'd had a phone torch and hadn't been walking in the dark."

She left John behind at the gate puzzling over his messy forensics, and walked through the passageway, and then into the court which for the most part was grassed over. She noticed a plaque which meant she could indulge in an interesting historical interlude from the crime scene, so she walked up some stairs to it. Members of the CSI team were doing a fingertip search across the grass. In white overalls with their heads covered in white hoods, on hands and knees, they looked like a row of baby polar bears. She studied the plaque. In front of her was the old monastic refectory in time-worn sandstone, licked by centuries of wind and rain. There were two wings on either side. The central building, now a restaurant, had the passageway where the murder had taken place running through it. The whole complex had been a rectangular configuration with a church, now long gone, making up the fourth side.

She read on. The passageway where the murder had taken place was called a 'slyle', the architectural term for a covered passageway in a medieval monastery or church. The large stone alcove where Neil Thomson's body had been found had once been a stone staircase leading to the monastic dormitory. So that was why it was so big. She turned around to the modern flats behind her which looked down onto the court: all three floors had Gothic-arched windows in cream sandstone. It was an attempt to keep them in context with the monastery. But had anyone in the flats seen anything? That was probably their best hope; that and Chris Laidlaw, the pathologist, being able to give them some leads.

She walked through to Stowell Street. She glanced across at the restaurant where Neil Thomson had eaten last night, and then up the street towards the area which had been cordoned off and where the gang fight had broken out. Neil Thomson might've been unlucky and got caught up in the gang fight as he'd cut through Blackfriars. It would all depend on which way the gang had come into Stowell Street. She turned her head to her right. If they'd entered through the Chinese archway from the direction of St James' Park or from Newgate Street, they were unlikely to have killed him, unless they followed him into Blackfriars and had attacked him from behind. But it had been a frontal assault according to the police surgeon.

She then turned to her left. But if they'd come to Stowell Street from Friars Lane end, it meant someone may've been lying in wait at Blackfriars Gate. This meant that whoever had killed Neil Thomson might've made a mistake and thought he was a gang member. She sighed. But then the gang fight had broken out an hour after Neil Thomson had been murdered and that was based on the time that he'd left the restaurant and confirmed by the police surgeon. She turned her head up Stowell Street and spotted two uniforms walking to the entrance to the flats which overlooked Blackfriars Court. She walked towards them.

"We're just about to interview a woman in one of the flats, ma'am," a young, slim, fair-haired constable said as she approached them. "She says she saw something in the courtyard last night."

"I'll join you," she said because she'd already reckoned that the flats were the most likely location for witnesses. She noticed the constables both dart each other a nervous glance. "Don't worry. I'll lead the interview," she volunteered. "You just take the notes." They both struggled not to sigh in relief. She always tried to put uniform at their ease, but then, rank made some of them nervous.

Two flights of stairs later, they arrived outside the front door of a top-floor flat. The door was opened by a young, petite Chinese woman with long straight, black hair and a perfect complexion. "Hello, I'm DCI Alex Shaftoe." She opened her warrant card." I gather you reported seeing something last night. And you are?"

"Sam Smith." She gestured to them to follow her inside and led them into a front room which overlooked Blackfriars Court.

"Could you tell us what you saw?" Out of the corner of her eye she saw both constables dutifully open their notebooks.

"I went to the windows at about ten." Her eyes strayed to two small Gothic-arched windows which overlooked the court. 'I noticed a cloaked figure walking through the courtyard. There was a hood over his head."

"You say 'he'," Alex said. "Are you sure it was a man?"

"Well, I can't be sure." Her eyebrows furrowed. "But from the way he walked, I assume he was a man. And he was tall."

Alex moved across the room to one of the windows and peered down onto Blackfriars Court. "Can you tell us what the cloak was like?"

"It was black with a hood."

"And was it a light material or heavy?" She asked as she moved to the other window which faced the court, trying to imagine what it must have looked like, in the dark, from this spot. It was difficult to judge what could be seen in the dark.

"It seemed to be heavy." Sam Smith said. "Probably wool." She raised her shoulders and shivered. "I called my husband to have a look."

"Why?" Alex turned to her.

"Because I thought it was the ghost of a black friar." Her eyes surveyed Alex and the two constables to gauge their reaction. "I had heard there is a ghost of a monk around here…And it was wandering through Blackfriars Court." Her voice rose slightly to try and justify her assertion.

"And did your husband see anything?"

"Nothing. It had gone before he arrived at the window," she said apologetically.

She wondered if it had been a trick of the light in the courtyard last night. Then she remembered the Chinese tradition of ancestor worship and considered if that had anything to do with the Chinese woman's assumption that it had been a ghost. "And did you see anything or anyone else?"

"No. After my husband had a look out of the window and saw nothing, he closed the curtains."

Chapter 2

As Alex walked into the incident room, she saw the broad frame of DI Dave Bell, his back to the room exposing his bald patch, as he scribbled on the new glass board. He'd set up a Major Crime Investigation and as usual, he was her Deputy Senior Investigating Officer – SIO. The glass board, like the whole office, was new and she surveyed the room with its new desks, clean carpet and freshly painted walls as if it belonged to someone else – no doubt, she'd get used to it in time. The office was a hum of activity with the rhythm of tapping on keyboards and voices on the phone. At one desk to the right, staring into a computer screen, was a young woman she didn't recognise. She looked a bit like a goth – an earring through her nose, a red streak through her black hair and dark eye make-up. She watched her, mesmerised for a moment, as she chewed gum, her jaw moving first one way and then the other, her head not moving from the screen.

At the back of the room were a group of uniforms, the PCs who'd be doing the leg work. Some of them had already been out in Chinatown last night and she could pick them out from the tiredness on their faces. She believed in including uniform in her briefings, which wasn't the done thing, and she'd been challenged about it by the ACC, Damien Sutcliffe. But the uniform appreciated their inclusion in a Major Incident Room briefing, and it made sense that they knew what was going on before they trod the streets interviewing.

As she moved next to Dave at the glass board everyone swivelled around in their new chairs in a choreographed sweep. Gone were the days of a rugby-style huddle around an old white board "Tell me," she said.

Dave took a deep breath. "Aye. There's loads. The witnesses from Chinatown have identified the four that went to the hospital. They're denying everything, of course," he said sarcastically and then nodded at the young woman who looked like a goth. "Debbie's been going into their background."

Debbie's head moved up from the computer screen, her eyes surrounded by dark eye make-up fixed on Alex. "Three of them have been picked up for drug crime before. Nothing serious. Just small-time drug dealing."

She smiled at Debbie, whose name was at odds with her goth look. "Welcome on board. I take it you're our analyst." The police had been using civilian analysts for a long time now, called in on a need basis because of their skill set. She turned back to Dave. "What about involvement by the National Crime Agency – the NCA?"

"Not at the minute, but they want to be kept informed. And the rest, I suppose, depends on what we find." He rolled his eyes.

She rubbed the side of her cheek. Centralising specialised resource for crimes like drugs, modern slavery, cybercrime, rape and serial killers made sense. She agreed with it. But the national police forces now had to interface with the NCA which at times could feel like interference. And, of course, the brightest and the best were going to work for the NCA.

"And the four lads we caught in Chinatown are denying they'd anything to do with the Blackfriars' murder," Dave added with a shrug of frustration.

Her brow furrowed. "Have we had further confirmation that Neil Thomson's attack was a frontal assault?"

"Chris thinks it's a frontal assault, like the police surgeon last night," he piped up, "although he was at pains to say this is only based on the initial analysis."

This was to be expected; pathologists were cautious until they'd the opportunity for a thorough examination and analysis.

"Chris is up to his eyeballs in work," Dave continued. He's trying to see if there's a DNA match with the gang members in the Stowell Street trouble and Neil Thomson's murder at Blackfriars. He's analysing the knife wounds. He's got a dead body and four injuries in the Royal Victoria Infirmary – RVI. His lass is going mad about him having to work weekends again."

She surveyed the room. "Have we got any witness evidence about the way the gang entered Stowell Street?"

"Aye, they came in t'uther end to Friars Lane," Dave volunteered. "They were seen coming down from the St James' Park area."

"That means they're unlikely to be responsible for Neil Thomson's murder." She scrutinised the faces in the room to see if anyone disagreed with her. If they did, they said nothing.

"Aye. The witnesses say that the gang fight broke out at eleven. We know that Neil Thomson left the restaurant at about ten. The police surgeon thought he died at about ten or thereabouts." His lips quirked. "And the wife discovered Neil Thomson after midnight."

"We've got a connection between Neil Thomson, the man killed in Blackfriars, and the Chinese. His personnel recruitment company was doing business there," Debbie said whilst continuing to stare at her computer screen. "The NCA is looking to see if he has any connection with drugs."

She nodded and then turned her attention back to Dave. "What about CCTV?"

"Absolutely nowt. The one that got away…the fifth one involved in the gang fight seems to have disappeared into thin air. The lads have done door to door at Blackfriars." He raised one of his bushy eyebrows, flecks of grey mixed with the brown. "I see that you interviewed the resident at Blackfriars who claims they saw a black friar walking through the court at about the time of Neil Thomson's murder." He pulled a face. "We might have our first murder by a ghost."

"You're sure it isn't Darth Vader going to a fancy dress?" She suggested.

"Mebbees the monk from the Dolce Vita has moved since it shut down."

The grins around the room which had greeted her mention of Darth Vader turned blank at Dave's comment. She knew the Dolce Vita, a night club in town, but it had closed down long before any of the youngsters in the room had started going into town at night.

"You haven't heard of him?" Dave said rhetorically. "He used to go dancing on the floor and was seen by loads of customers and staff." He started to shake his stiff hips from side to side and most of the room started to smirk. His moves were more rigid and not as athletic as the David Brent dance in *The Office*, but he was running a close second in the 'naff factor' stakes.

"*Strictly Come Dancing* eat your heart out," she sniggered and then moved the conversation back to the case. "It seems like that may be our murderer and it's a good disguise. You can easily take off a hooded cloak and completely change your appearance," she muttered.

"We've got someone else in Chinatown at the time of the trouble who's been done for aggravated burglary. We are questioning him right now," Dave said.

"Why, was he part of the fight?" She asked.

"Na. But we are wondering if he might have done-in Neil Thomson."

"What about Neil Thomson's friends?"

"Anaya and Ian are taking statements from them. They seem to have left the restaurant at about 10.30 p.m. That's about half an hour after Neil Thomson was murdered. That's been confirmed by the restaurant and the credit card statements. They all had their cars parked near Newgate Street or St James'. The opposite direction to the way Neil Thomson went. And they'd left before the gang fight broke out."

"Anything else?"

"Not at the moment. We're hoping that forensics and pathology might give us some leads."

***

Dave followed Alex from the Incident Room through into her office.

"I've been looking into the four gang members in the RVI. Three of them have been picked up before for petty crime and small-time drugs –"

"And the fourth?" She interrupted.

"I think he may be a 'county-line' kid."

They all knew that these were youngsters who were recruited or coerced by drug dealers, groomed and offered money to sell drugs in rural areas. It was a nationwide problem and the NCA had set up an initiative to tackle it.

Dave continued. “I’ve been on to the NCA. You know they’ve set up a new unit in Birmingham to deal with the ‘county-line’ problem across the UK?”

She moved across to her coffee machine as she listened to him. She hadn’t had a drink since breakfast and she was feeling parched. “Do you want a cup?”

“Na. I’ve just had one,” he answered. “One of the lads we’ve picked up is as clean as a whistle. No form at all. And he’s young. Only fifteen. The NCA reckon Adam Vickers, that’s his name, was just about to be used as a drug mule. Probably to go up into Northumberland – Morpeth, Alnwick and maybe Wooler and Berwick.”

They already knew, like most police forces, that the ring leaders operated mobile hotlines to market the drugs with young mules, like Adam Vickers, conducting the sales. The ‘Adams’ of this world were unlikely to be caught by the police and, if like Adam they’d been in no previous trouble, they faced lenient sentences if they were caught. “What do we know about him?”

“Not much at the moment.” He opened the palms of his hands as they rested on his knees. “He lives in the Byker Wall with a single mother. She works. No other siblings. We’re not sure if the mother has a bloke on the scene.”

“Do you think it’s worth a try?” Whenever they could, they tried to set youngsters back on the right path. They saw this as as much a part of policing as catching hardened criminals. And, of course, it would help resolve the gang fight quickly if they could persuade Adam Vickers to turn police witness.

“I think so.” He moved his right hand to his jaw. “I’ve spoken to his mam on the phone. She seems a nice lass. She was very worried and upset about what’s happened to Adam.”

"Then one of us needs to go the RVI in the morning. A day will give him some time to think about the mess he's in and consider his position…and then go to speak to the mother." She was reluctant to let one of the younger officers go because they hadn't yet watched Dave or her in action.

"You go," he said. "I've got a lot of interviews to run through."

"I was supposed to be going to the opera tonight. It was booked months ago," she said ruefully.

"Then go. There's nowt here for you to do tonight. The forensics and pathology aren't going to be through. And if anything happens, I'll phone ye."

"If I go to the opera tonight and get a good night's sleep, you'll have to have a night off tomorrow." They'd done this for the last five years. As they'd both got older, they'd realised that a good night's sleep actually helped when dealing with a major investigation. But she was conscious that he was usually first in and last to go because since his divorce, he had a city-centre flat, close to the station. She felt a pang of guilt as she thought about the breakdown of his marriage. She knew that his wife had claimed that he spent more time with her. And when she'd thought about it, she'd realised that his wife had been right. She wasn't sure what his kids had said; he'd been tactful and had never said anything. They were a good team, the two of them, an unholy alliance of opposites who complemented each other. "Okay. Let the uniform on guard at the RVI know I want the other three suspects moved. I want to speak to Adam Vickers on his own tomorrow morning."

He nodded and left the room.

CHAPTER 3

Alex clutched the driving wheel more tightly; she was dreading seeing Sarah Thomson again. Sarah Thomson, with heart-wrenching grief so deep it had brought back to her the memory of Daniel's death. She drove through Darras Hall, to the north of Newcastle, with the drone of an aeroplane coming in to land in the distance, and the image of a smiling Daniel before her. She could feel tears welling in her eyes. She guessed she was roughly the same age as Sarah Thomson whose life now had been shattered in middle-age. She'd been young when she lost Daniel and to a bomb rather than a knife. In nearly twenty-five years of policing, she'd had her share of murder and death and although she'd never become hardened to it, she'd learnt emotional detachment. But not to a woman losing her partner – that was too close to home. Her chest tightened as her grief resurfaced again; maybe it was because she'd never found anyone else after Daniel died.

A car hooted. She jumped, pulling the steering wheel to the left because her jeep had started to wander to the centre of the road.

The houses at Darras Hall all jingled with money and most hid behind high fences and high hedges, but some were more palatial than others. As she pulled into the drive of Neil Thomson's house, it was not one of the largest or grandest on the Darras Hall estate. Most of the police knew the estate because its affluence made it a target for burglaries. The door of the house was opened by a young man in his early twenties, middle build and dark haired. He'd been crying. He was the same young man who'd been with his mother at Blackfriars last night. She smiled softly.

He spoke to her without a Geordie accent which came as no surprise to her. She expected that, like her, he'd gone to a private school because a lot of the children in Darras Hall did. She didn't speak with a Geordie accent because of school and despite the fact that both of her parents had heavy accents. She smiled as she remembered her dad saying to her 'you'll never be an officer in the British Army if you speak like me'. How things had changed with Geordie, now a trendy accent in the UK, helped along by celebrities like Ant and Dec. She was led towards the smell of lemon cleaning fluid and a high-end kitchen, in black and white, with sliding doors along one wall opening out onto a well-kept garden beyond. Sarah Thomson was sitting on a stool, shoulders hunched up, elbows resting on the breakfast bar, her hands hugging a mug. An attractive bob-haired blond and, like her, she guessed in her fifties. Sarah Thomson turned towards her with bags under her eyes and dishevelled hair from a sleepless night and tears.

"Hello Mrs Thomson. I'm DCI Alex Shaftoe. We met briefly last night. Do you feel you could talk to me?" She smiled softly into Sarah Thomson's eyes as she sat down next to her. She put her arms on the breakfast bar and mirrored Sarah's body language to signal the overwhelming empathy she felt for her. "We're trying to get a picture of your husband's movements. Some information about who he was with and where he was. Are you able to help me?" They already knew that Neil Thomson had been eating in Chinatown with a group of friends. As she glanced to her left, a middle-aged woman with dyed dark hair, sat at a white marble table surrounded by black leather chairs.

She attempted to smile at Alex with a face pained in grief. "I'm Hannah Scott, Neil's sister."

She nodded and returned her smile. There were streaks of water on the black marble floor and a mop and bucket propped against the table. Perhaps something had been dropped, or maybe cleaning was a sign of Sarah's stress?

There was a long silence, and whilst she waited, she scanned the white cupboards of the kitchen with their black marble work-tops. Then Sarah began to speak. "Neil was in Chinatown eating with some friends... he has known for years. They meet up every Thursday night after work. I mean the men... we do socialise as couples as well." The composure was gone and she sobbed. Ashley moved across the room and put his arm around his mother's shoulder, and Alex waited until she'd calmed herself again.

"Mrs Thompson, can you give me the names and addresses of all your husband's friends?" Her team had already checked with the friends who had been in Chinatown last night, but she now wanted to broaden out the research. She'd a bad feeling about the cloaked and hooded figure that had been spotted at Blackfriars. It seemed bizarre and macabre.

Sarah's head was bowed and she talked to the breakfast bar. "Yes, Ashley will be able to give you the names and addresses."

"Is there anyone you can think of who might have done this to your husband? Absolutely anyone at all?"

"No. I've been lucky and I know it," she croaked. "Neil was a good husband, father and friend. We've led very ordinary lives and this sort of thing just doesn't happen to people like us."

She wasn't sure the house in Darras Hall could be called 'ordinary'. Her stomach started to sink as she considered Sarah's response to her next question. "I'm sorry to have to ask you this, but was your husband totally loyal?" She couldn't think of a more tactful way of saying it.

Sarah, her mouth wide open, sat bolt upright, her back as rigid as the bar stool she sat on. Alex's stomach churned; was she going to scream? But then she looked towards family photos on one of the kitchen walls, and her shoulders started to relax.

She spoke softly. "Ah, Chief Inspector, we had a happy marriage and shared everything." She stared at a photo of her husband. "I'd have known if Neil had been unfaithful to me. And I never had to worry for a day about that. Neil was a loving husband and father."

She sobbed again and so Alex waited. The scene at Blackfriars last night came back to her mind and how she'd cradled her husband in her arms. "And what about any professional rivalries?" she continued as Sarah's body stilled from the sobs which had been racking it.

"There wasn't any." She was calmer. "What you must understand is that Neil was a charming, considerate man... he was honest and didn't play any dirty tricks... everyone liked him."

She questioned whether anyone in business was that clean, but then she remembered her own father who had been all of the things Sarah had just described. "Do you work, Mrs Thomson?"

"No, not since I had my family." Her voice was a barely audible whisper.

She looked Sarah in her tear-stained face, "And what did you do when you did work?"

"I was a secretary... and that's how I met Neil." Her eyes moved to the window and the garden beyond.

"And how many children do you have?"

She continued to stare out into the garden. “Two. My daughter is living and working in London. She’s on her way here now.”

“Mrs Thomson, where were you last night?”

“I was here at home.”

“Is there anyone who can corroborate that?” She doubted, having seen her at Blackfriars last night, that she’d had anything to do with her husband’s murder, but nonetheless she needed an alibi. Most murders were committed by people close to the victim – family or friends. It was a statistical fact.

“One of my friends was here until about nine.” She turned her head towards her son. “Ashley was in the house all night.”

She was relieved that Sarah had answered her questions calmly and wasn’t indignant at being asked for an alibi. “And Ashley accompanied you to Blackfriars?”

“Yes, that’s right.” She paused. “After I’d spoken to Neil’s friend, Rob, and rang around the hospitals.”

“You seem to have got concerned very early on about your husband’s late arrival home?”

“It was unusual for him to be late. And if there was a problem, he would’ve rung.”

“Thank you, Mrs Thomson. I’m sorry I’ve had to trouble you. However, we’ll need you to formally identify the body, probably tomorrow.” It was a waste of time as the poor woman had already identified the body at Blackfriars, and it was likely to intensify her grief again, but police procedures hadn’t been written with the widow finding her husband’s body in mind.

She moved her head towards Ashley who was sitting at the dining table opposite his aunt. “Can you get me the names and addresses of your dad’s friends Ashley?”

He nodded and left the room.

Chapter 4

A weight pressed down on Alex's chest and she breathed heavily as she took the steep incline from the banks of the Tyne up Dean Street at a pace. It helped release some of the build-up of adrenaline which was the inevitable consequence of a murder investigation. She often went for a power walk when she wanted to think things through during an investigation. As Dean Street turned into Grey Street, her breathing eased off on the gentler incline. The sweep of the grand sandstone buildings greeted her like an old friend. A nineteenth-century build, Grey Street had been voted the best street in the UK by Radio Four listeners. At the top stood Earl Grey on a column. Though not as tall as Nelson's column in Trafalgar Square, it had been created by the same sculptor and like Trafalgar Square, was a natural focal point for the meeting of a number of streets in the centre of the city. The statue honoured Charles Grey who, as Prime Minister, introduced the 1832 Reform Bill, and began the slow march to democracy. She smiled at the statue because she'd always felt that he should be holding a tea bag, or better still a teapot, because Earl Grey tea bore his name. Although more recently he was better known for his affair with Georgina, Duchess of Devonshire, immortalised in the movie *Duchess*.

Happier memories washed across her, like the tide on one of her beloved Northumbrian beaches, and a visit to Howick a couple of years ago with her mam. That was before dementia had put her in a nursing home. Near Craster on the north Northumbrian coast, Charles Grey's home at Howick was not the grandest stately home by a long stretch, but the afternoon tea had been good, and served with Earl Grey tea, of course.

She stood at the top of Grey Street near the Theatre Royal and looked about her for the tapas restaurant where she was meeting her friends. A quick glance at her watch told her she was late again. She saw the restaurant and walked across, pushed through the door and was immediately assailed by Mediterranean cooking – herbs, olives and tomato. There was the low hum of voices and background strains of classical Spanish guitar. Her mind reeled back to the holiday in Cordoba with Lisa: balmy Andalusian nights, the smell of jasmine and the glorious bougainvillea growing up the side of houses with a profusion of pink, purple and white flowers. Her stomach sank. She'd been struggling to get herself back into the groove at work since her holiday in Spain. Then she saw her friends and moved towards them, smiling, last again, and for the usual reason that a case at the station had held her up.

The only vacant seat at the table was beside a stranger; she tried not to show the shock she felt at the eye candy before her. He was a George Clooney look-alike, with a full head of short grey hair and grey designer stubble around his jaw line. His blue eyes twinkled at her as he said in a melodious voice,

"Hi. I'm Ewan."

She held out her hand to him. "I'm Detective Chief Inspector Alex Shaftoe." She could feel her cheeks burn with embarrassment as soon as she'd uttered the formal introduction she used when working. Ewan chuckled at her, his cheeks dimpling and laughter lines forming around his eyes. She sat down next to him and tried to manage it in a dignified ladylike manner after the gaff she'd just made. She stretched out a hand for the bottle of white wine, but Ewan beat her to it.

"I'm told you are an archaeologist and historian like me. I work at Durham Uni," he said as he poured her wine.

She stopped her mouth from falling open, but the twinkle in his eye made her realise that he'd registered her surprise. He hardly cut the image of an archaeologist with his well-tailored grey suit, open-neck white shirt and a sandalwood aftershave which was just the right side of overpowering. Even TV archaeologists tended towards the hippy or outdoor look. She couldn't think of a single one from all the series, except Simon Schama, who was an historian rather than an archaeologist, who was as well turned out as this.

"And what did you study?" Ewan continued.

She watched him topping up his own glass of wine. "Roman history and archaeology."

He raised his eyebrows and then smiled. "And you didn't want an academic career?"

"There weren't many jobs back then and I'm sure it's still the same now," she stuttered out. Her reason was a bit more complicated, but she wasn't interested in going into that tale, particularly with a stranger.

He stroked the designer stubble on his chin. "It seems a strange career move from history and archaeology to the police?"

She studied her wine glass to avoid eye contact "Not so strange. You're often digging up the past in police work and investigation... academic discipline helps." She was going to have to pull herself together. She was behaving like a teenager who'd met their favourite celebrity pin-up boy. She put some tapas onto her plate and only then realised how hungry she was, and as she did so, she glanced at Jo who was at the other end of the table. She was the only member of the 'opera group' who wasn't an academic. The group had been convened some years ago, by Jo, to take advantage of the Opera North season at the Theatre Royal: the other two regular members had philistine wives who didn't like opera. It was a bit odd how the other three hadn't asked her how her holiday had gone but were engrossed in their own conversation. She looked at Ewan's left hand and could see he wasn't wearing a wedding ring. Was this the latest conspiracy by the gang of 'three' to get her 'fixed up'? The 'opera group' did this from time to time, and chief conspirator was her friend, Jo. It was probably no accident that the only vacant seat put her next to Ewan who just happened to be a specialist in one of her great passions – archaeology and history. "And what's your area of expertise?" she asked.

"Anglo-Saxon archaeology." His eyes were smiling at her again.

Her love, as a child, of the history of Anglo-Saxon Northumbria had been the reason she'd studied history and archaeology in the first place. Alex glanced up, caught Jo's eye, and gave her a knowing look across the table. "So, you work at Durham University?" She'd stated something he'd already said and could have kicked herself for her clumsiness.

"Yes, that's right. I'm part of the team working on Holy Island. You know about the recent work there?"

At least she was on safe territory talking about archaeology and history. She was more used to people trying to quiz her about her police work. "Only what has been reported in the press, but I'd be interested to hear what's going on." She looked up and smiled, took another mouthful of tapas and prepared to listen to something interesting.

"You know about the excavation at Green Shiel, on the north side of the island, where they found a stone-built early medieval farmstead. The only one in Northumberland."

She nodded, her mouth full.

He continued. "We've recently found what seems to be one of Britain's earliest churches, built after the mid-seventh century. We think the church was built, at least partially, of white sandstone which would've reflected the light. It would've been visible from the royal palace at Bamburgh." He took a sip of wine. "We've found a signalling tower at the same place; the promontory where the cliff is. We reckon it was for signalling messages to Bamburgh. Of course, this was before the first Viking raids."

"I'm surprised there haven't been more excavations on Holy Island," she said, and out of the corner of her eye she caught Jo signalling. "I think it's time for the opera."

As they stood up, he said, "I was in Chinatown last night when a gang fight broke out. I gave a witness statement to the police." He raised his eyebrows. "Is that one of the cases you're dealing with?"

She looked him in the eyes and nodded.

"I was having a meal with a businessman, Peter Dodd," he said in a matter of fact way. "He's showing an interest in helping fund the excavations on Holy Island."

***

As they sat down in their box at the Theatre Royal for the performance of *Carmen*, Alex's eyes were drawn to the box opposite where a grand entrance was being made by a blond woman, hair up in a chignon, wearing a long red dress and matching gloves which came up to her elbows. She couldn't see her facial features from across the theatre, but the woman had a stunning figure accentuated by the waist-hugging sleek dress. She was maximising her entrance by standing for a long-time, feigning conversation with the others around her. This lady was expecting to be admired. A lot of people in the stalls and circle were looking across at her, whispering to each other, and obviously wondering if she was someone famous or well-known? Jo shook her head at Alex because she didn't recognise the woman. Eva Peron, in the *Evita* musical, sprang to Alex's mind. The scene where Eva was on the balcony greeting the crowd and singing *Don't cry for me Argentina*. At least the woman hadn't started waving to the audience in the theatre.

She was jolted out of her thoughts by Ewan who was sitting in front of her in their theatre box. She'd decided to sit at the back, just in case she needed to leave, and had her phone on her knee so she could feel it vibrate if anyone called her. She leant forward as Ewan turned around to speak to her.

"The blond woman there in the other box, I'm sure she was in Chinatown last night. And I'm sure she was interviewed by the police." He smiled. "She's not the type of woman you'd forget."

Alex could feel her mobile vibrating on her knee. She quietly got up, sneaked out of the door of their box at the Theatre Royal, and into the corridor just as the *Toreador Song* had begun. It was their pathologist, Chris Laidlaw. "Hi. You got some news for me?"

"It's not necessarily good," Chris said. "We haven't been able to match Neil Thomson's DNA with any of the knives used in the gang fight in Chinatown... although the knife used to kill him is the same or similar."

"You're absolutely sure?" It came out of her mouth on automatic pilot. She knew Chris would be sure or he wouldn't have phoned her. "One gang member got away."

"I know," Chris said. "Is that singing I hear in the background? I didn't know you had taken to playing music in the office?"

"Thanks, Chris."

***

Alex glanced sideways at Jo as she drove the car out of the car park and asked, "What did you think of the performance?"

"I thought it was one of the best I've seen of *Carmen*. I didn't have to suspend my disbelief because they were young and energetic, and so it made the story believable. The singer playing Carmen was brilliant... a good actress and soprano. The matador was rippling muscles... as well as a good tenor voice."

She smirked at her friend. "You're turning into a dirty old woman, Jo. I'm surprised you didn't comment on his pert buttocks."

"You didn't give me a chance. Nothing wrong in admiring beauty.... How was your holiday in Spain? You look tanned and relaxed."

"It was lovely spending time with Lisa. We haven't been in that part of Spain for years, and I'd nearly forgotten how lovely Cordoba is."

"I've never been to Cordoba."

"You've missed a treat. It's not overrun with tourists like the coast. It's still very Spanish. Flamenco dancing, classical Spanish guitar. The Mezquita is one of Europe's most glorious buildings."

Jo puzzled, "What's that?"

"It's a tenth-century mosque. But later, after Ferdinand and Isobel had destroyed the multi-cultural nature of the area, a church was built in the centre of it. It was an act of vandalism, but somehow it works. There is a huge forest of columns and then a church in the centre."

"Sounds fascinating." Jo rolled her eyes.

She smiled at her friend who didn't share her love of history. "The old Juderia, the Jewish quarter, is wonderful. It's full of my favourite Mediterranean houses. A narrow street with a small door, and then into a fountained courtyard with three-storeys of rooms surrounding it. Beautiful."

"And Lisa?"

"She's got an American boyfriend and it's been my main worry about her working in America." She could feel her stomach knotting. "If it gets serious, she might decide to stay there permanently... it's a long way to travel to see any grandchildren." She sighed. Children gave meaning to life even if most people didn't stop to think about it much. The driving force behind most parents' lives was to provide for their children: they kept marriages together, drove ambition for promotion, dictated holidays and house choices. Without children, life would be like navigating to the north pole without a compass, floundering around in a barren waste without a clear idea of where north was. She hadn't expected Lisa to go off to America. She'd been very unsure about what to do after she'd left Cambridge, and had eventually plumped for a job in publishing because she loved books. But there were few publishing houses now because of the move to e-books and the 'Amazon revolution', and so she'd ended up moving to New York to take up a job there.

"Well you could live there," Jo said optimistically.

She always looked for the positive solution in any situation. There were only two countries Alex had ever been able to envisage living in – the UK and Greece. "I'm too British and too old to change."

"Lisa isn't married yet." She paused. "What about Ewan?" she grinned. "He's quite a dish... divorced for a while now.... It's about time you got a life. Nothing wrong in having dinner with him and seeing how things go. You can even talk history to each other."

She gave her a bemused smile. "That's your idea of foreplay?"

Jo laughed. "No, but it's yours."

"And how do you know he wants to take me to dinner?" She'd already guessed at the answer to the question.

"Because he told me, but he didn't want to seem pushy. Why don't you give it a try? You might get on. Failing that, you could have a few nights of unbridled passion."

"I've got used to being on my own, Jo. I don't know what I'd be like trying to compromise with another human being. I've tried in the past." Briefly, she remembered the two police officers with whom she'd had a fling and which hadn't worked out.

"Yes, but they were policemen," Jo protested.

"But it's the way we live. It takes another policeman to understand. Unsociable hours. Having to cancel at the last minute. Obsession with a case." She could have gone on but she didn't. It was too many years since Daniel had died to claim he was still there with her, but he was because no one since had measured up to him. Everyone she'd gone out with, including Daniel, she'd met in a work context, and she'd known them for a while before the relationship started. And then there was her. She'd never been able to put her finger on it, but she'd never been immediately attractive to the opposite sex. She was physically attractive, she knew that because she'd been told often enough, but something else was missing. Chemistry. She didn't flirt because she was shy and always had been, and because of that she gave off an air of aloofness. She'd been anything but a 'come hither' female. At university she'd heard someone refer to her as an 'ice maiden'. When men had pursued her, it had been for all the wrong reasons with the exception of Daniel. But then for a moment, she wondered if she was working at her own isolation because of the demands of the job.

Jo's eyes were pleading as she turned to her. "It's time for a change, Alex, or you'll turn into a crusty old thing."

"I know. But I'm not prepared to think about radical change while my mam is still here.... After that, I may even leave the police force."

"All the more reason to give it a try. Look at you in a skirt showing off your legs and your tan... relaxed... you look years younger than your age. It's no wonder Ewan's interested."

"I'm suspicious, Jo. He seems too good to be true. He's got an easy charm which you'd expect in a lady's man. Someone like that would normally be looking for a younger model, not someone in their fifties. And anyhow, he's just told me that he's been interviewed as a witness for the Stowell Street gang fight last night. Now wouldn't be the time to consider dinner with him."

CHAPTER 5

A white flash of light streaked across the room as Alex sat bolt upright in bed. Her eyes split open as she kicked her legs free of the knotted duvet, slowly untangling herself from the dream. Her heartbeat was thrashing her ears as she swung her legs out of bed then blinked. She blinked again; the room was in darkness as her mind crept its way back to reality. Her hand moved automatically to the switch of the bedside lamp and she heard a click, then a burst of light. She surveyed the familiar scene of her bedroom as realisation crept in with full waking consciousness. An old nightmare and one she hadn't had for years. She puffed out a deep breath.

She was glad to draw back the curtains exposing the misted glass, and glad to see the light glance off the walls above her bed. The wallpaper made it look like her bed rested in a forest of trees. For a few moments she breathed in deeply. Her love of trees and woods slowed her heartbeat as she imagined she was walking through a wood in the early morning light. The sanded and varnished oak wood floor touched her bare feet and she looked across at the photo of Daniel and her as they'd been more than twenty-five years ago. It had been taken not long before he died in a blinding flash of white light. They were both smiling, with Daniel's arm around her shoulder. "Good morning love".

Time had stood still for Daniel, but not for her as she focused on the young Alex, and then at the mirror and the middle-aged Alex. Her hair had been dark brown, and although the same length as it had been back then, it was now highlighted to hide the grey. Her brown eyes were more worldly now. She looked at the photo of their daughter, Lisa, who Daniel had never known, but who had his eyes, hair and the same shaped face. She smiled and then sighed as she looked at them both in their two photos, in two different times.

Coffee. This was her parents' house and it was decorated in her mother's chintzy style. As she padded down the stairs, she promised herself again that she must get the place redecorated. But she didn't have the heart to change things – at least not yet. The house was haunted by happier times, before her dad had had a massive stroke and died, before her mam had got dementia and eventually had to go to a nursing home, and before Lisa had set off for America. Nothing like a nightmare to make you feel miserable, she thought, and an empty house shouting its silence to make it even worse. Much of her life had been written in the bricks and mortar of this house, but she hadn't meant for that to happen. She'd had no choice as a young widowed mother with a job in the police and its unsociable hours: grandparents to look after Lisa, a grandmother to share the mothering and a grandfather to help compensate for the loss of Daniel.

As she pushed open the door of the kitchen, she was greeted by out-of-date yew cupboards surrounding three walls – her mother's favourite wood – the base units topped with black marble. It all needed renewing, but it was a link to happier times when there were four people sitting down to breakfast. Her stomach knotted – she missed Lisa. She put on the coffee maker, a trendy machine in steel with a steam nozzle which she'd bought a few months ago, and which stood incongruous with the rest of the kitchen. She opened the fridge door where a carton of milk stood lonely in an otherwise empty fridge. Her row of alternative medicine pills, potions and aromatherapy bottles were gathered together on one kitchen worktop, and she grabbed some pills from a couple of the bottles.

The uneasy feeling wouldn't go away. Back to bed with her coffee to read something to take her mind off things. She had more than one book on the go, as she usually did, because what she read depended on her mood: a novel, a psychology book on sociopaths which Jo had recommended, or a biography of Peter the Great?

***

A whiff of disinfectant followed Alex along the hospital corridor, as unappealing as the bland taupe walls on either side of her. She turned right, and into the sound of raised voices at the end of the long hospital corridor. She squinted, and not for the first time wondered about an eye test, but she could just see a blue police uniform dodging between people and equipment. There was someone running towards her with a police officer chasing them. The gang from Chinatown; who else could be trying to escape a police officer? She stuck her foot out just as a young man was about to run past her. He fell flat on his face on the hard corridor floor. She bent down and momentarily felt a pang of guilt. "Don't move." He was rubbing his left shoulder and not the right one which was in a sling. She was relieved she hadn't damaged him. "Are you alright?" she asked.

He flashed anger. "What d'you think?"

Her eyes widened. "How did you think you'd get away? We know who you are and we'd have found you." She pointed at his nightshirt. "How far do you think you'd have got in hospital green?" She just stopped herself from saying 'pillock'. Her nightmare hadn't made for a good start to the day.

He looked down at the floor as a breathless 'bobby' arrived.

"I'll deal with him now ma'am... this one tried to escape when he went to the toilet."

She continued to walk up the long corridor, turning into a ward where the young men from the gang fight in Stowell Street were being kept under guard. Dave had rung and arranged for the police to remove three of the four gang members they had under hospital arrest, because she wanted to speak to one boy alone. They didn't know what had caused the fight in Stowell Street because the four of them in custody had been tight-lipped.

She'd been told that the boy's name was Adam Vickers, and according to the uniform who had been guarding them, he hadn't shown any of the cockiness of the other three. She stood at the door and could see the boy lying in the foetal position, facing a blank wall. He'd been brought up in poverty by a single mother. They lived in a maisonette in the Byker Wall, high above the banks of the Tyne at the east end of Newcastle.

"Hi, I'm DCI Alex Shaftoe," she said quietly. The boy didn't stir. She moved a chair so she was in his line of sight and sat down. He neither moved nor flinched. "Adam, I want to help you. We know you haven't been in trouble before with the police. We know you've been trapped by the gang into carrying drugs for them. But if you continue down this road you might end up hurt again or dead." She spoke quietly and with an even voice. There was a bandage around his left hand, a souvenir from the gang fight. She shook her head." I can protect you, if you will let me. I can make sure the gang doesn't get to you again."

He moved and looked at her. "How?"

"We'll move you and your mam and give you police protection." She knew the drug gangs often coerced the kids by threatening their family.

He shook his head. "They'll get me or my mam."

"They've already got you." She tried hard not to allow impatience to creep into her voice; it had never been one of her virtues. "I suppose it depends on whether you want to be honest or not? They may get you, if you give me information. But other kids in your position have been helped to get away. We've got a good record on that." She held eye contact with him and smiled. "Let's help you or you'll ruin your life." Her concern gave her voice an edge as her eyebrows furrowed.

Fear etched his face. "It's already ruined."

"No. It's not. But it will be if you continue with this. Far better try to be brave and move on. Can I leave you to think about it, Adam?" She'd try again when he'd been moved into custody and separated from the other three suspects. "The other three don't know I've been speaking to you," she said and got up from the chair she'd been sitting on. Her team would have to sort out the gang fight, but the NCA would be interested in any information they might have about the drug supply chain. The four would be charged for the fight, but they hadn't found any drugs on them which was surprising. She shook her head, moved the chair back, then left the room.

***

Alex had vague childhood memories of the Byker where her father had been born and where he had set up his first shop near St Peters, on the banks of the Tyne. In her dad's youth, it had then been a world of nineteenth-century brown brick-built terrace houses with grey slate roofs, row after row running down the steep banks of the Tyne. She shut her jeep door and looked up at the exterior of the Byker Wall, built in the 1970s to replace the Victorian slum dwellings which had housed the workers for the heavy industry on the Tyne. It was curved and the brick broken up with bright coloured balconies in red and green. She had left the Royal Victory Infirmary – a name long abbreviated to RVI or 'the infirmary' in the north-east – and made her way straight to Adam Vickers' home in Byker. Her jaw tightened as she remembered Adam lying in the foetal position in the hospital; she was going to do her best to get him out of this mess. Her body tensed at the thought of the drug gangs and the shattered lives scattered across their path, but many of them were also victims. At least, at the beginning. She surveyed the Byker Wall in bewilderment and paused to consider how she was ever going to find Linda Vickers' maisonette.

She knocked on the door and was relieved when she heard someone coming to answer it. She'd started to regret not bringing someone with her, but they were all busy with the two cases they had. She'd had to stop two people to ask where to go as she tried to navigate the Wall. She pulled her warrant card out of her bag. "Hello Ms Vickers, I'm DCI Alex Shaftoe. Can I come in." She followed Linda Vickers down a passageway and into the main room. The furniture was shabby and there were cracks in the faux leather settee, but the room was clean and she breathed in the smell of bleach. "I'm here to have a chat with you about Adam."

Linda's face had a drawn, gaunt look and the black rings under her eyes spoke of sleepless nights.

"Would you like a cup of tea or coffee?" she asked in a whisper.

"No thanks, I had a cup just before I left the station." This wasn't true, but when she glanced around the room and at how little Linda had, she felt guilty about accepting anything. It reminded her of what her dad had said about the dignity in poverty which had been the hallmark of Byker during her grandparents' generation. "I've already seen Adam at the RVI. He's not in any serious trouble yet but he will be if he doesn't get away from the drug gang."

"Adam is a good lad; he always has been. I just don't understand how he has got involved in all of this?" Linda bit her lip.

Alex breathed out loudly. "The drug gangs prey on lads like Adam. To get them to carry drugs into the countryside for them, because they are unlikely to be picked up by the police."

Linda had tears in her eyes and rubbed under each one with her index fingers. "I asked him why he had done it," she said tearfully, "and he said for the money because we've got nothing."

She could feel the tension leaving her body. She wasn't going to have any difficulty persuading this woman to help Adam and the police. "I've spoken to Adam about getting out of trouble. But it will mean leaving here and settling somewhere else."

"But where?" She rubbed her temple and turned to Alex in bewilderment.

She leaned towards her and smiled. "That's what we need to discuss. Do you work?"

"I've got three part-time jobs but we still can't manage." Her eyes darted about the room as if she was looking for something to comfort her. "I pay the electricity bill one month, the council tax another month, and we're always in arrears with everything. I'm left with £100 to live off and that includes our food." She rubbed her hands together, her voice choked with panic and desperation.

Heat flushed across Alex's face and she struggled to keep her body language under control. She didn't want Linda to think she was angry with her, rather than at the injustice of what she had just heard. She knew there was a national issue about people who worked and were no better off than if they were on benefits, but she hadn't come across a case of it in her police work before today. The people they'd arrested in the past weren't trying like this woman. Empathy swelled and began to overwhelm her and she struggled not to allow it to turn into anger. "Do you have any qualifications?"

"I had Adam when I was sixteen." Her chin lowered to her chest and she stared at the floor. "It was one of those teenage mistakes. Although he is the best mistake of my life." She smiled softly at the thought of her son.

She watched her closely and calculated that this made her about thirty. Mid-brown hair and middle-build, with clothes that were cheap but clean. She wasn't wearing any make-up. "And your parents?"

"They threw me out when I fell pregnant and refused to have an abortion," she whispered to the floor.

She widened her eyes in a question. "And Adam's father?"

"We have no contact with him. He didn't want to know when I fell pregnant and wouldn't have an abortion."

"So, you get no financial help from him?"

"He's no better off than us." She glanced around the room.

"And Adam is your only child?"

She met Alex's eyes. "Once bitten, twice shy."

This was different from her usual experience of youth offending. The kids she'd dealt with were often one of a number of children with the same mother, but different fathers. "And what is Adam like at school?" The Incident Room team had so far only checked on whether Adam had a police record, and basic information like his address and parents.

Linda raised her chin. "He was doing well before all of this happened. I pushed him to take school seriously." A hint of pride in her voice.

"Would you be prepared to leave Newcastle?" She would need to ask the team to check with Adam's school about his track record.

She stared at Alex. "Yes. If it will help," she stuttered. "But what are you actually talking about here?"

Helping in these types of situations was as important to her as bringing criminals to justice. "I will need to discuss this with Social Services. But we need to get Adam away from the drug gang and so it might be easier if you were outside Newcastle. We will sort out a flat for you, we'll have a look at a good school for Adam and we can review your finances. Would you be prepared to look at getting some qualifications yourself?"

Linda couldn't have been more stunned if someone had told her she'd won the lottery. "You would do that for us?"

Yes, she would help, and so would Dave Bell. The two of them had a good track record of getting help where it was needed, and where it was deserved. It would take a lot of phone calls and if need be, she'd get the ACC on side. From his point of view, this helped the image of the police in the community and it was crime prevention, another statistic he focused on. She couldn't recall him involving himself in trying to help anyone for the sake of it, even when he'd been a young police officer, but he was essentially a decent man, she reminded herself. He was ambitious but not a self-serving careerist; she'd know him for years now and she knew that much about him. "Yes, I would. But I need Adam to tell me what he knows. He's frightened not only for himself but for you."

"And what sort of protection can you offer us?" Her head jerked up.

"If Adam agrees to help us, we will move you somewhere safe temporarily."

Her head turned suddenly. "But what about my jobs?"

"You'd have to leave them. We'd arrange finances for you and we'd look into helping you get on your feet until we've moved you somewhere permanently. But I need you to persuade Adam to help us."

Her lips trembled. "I'm afraid. This is a drug gang."

"I know. But there'll be serious problems if he doesn't get away from them. Adam could be arrested, seriously hurt, end up on drugs himself which often happens... and he'll end up with no qualifications. This is a gang of youngsters and not any of the big boys. If we get you away from Newcastle that will put you out of harm's way."

There was a pause as Linda rubbed her hands together and stared out of the window. Then came the words she'd been hoping for.

"Okay. I'll speak to him."

She handed Linda a card with her phone number. She admired her for trying so hard in difficult circumstances. She'd only been sixteen when Adam was born and she wondered why she hadn't agreed to an abortion? And why her parents hadn't stood by her? To go ahead with the pregnancy was a brave decision for a sixteen-year-old to make. "Would you mind if I have a look at Adam's bedroom before I leave?"

Alex was led up the stairs. The room was shabby, like downstairs. A single bed with a threadbare duvet was pushed against the blue wall which badly needed a lick of paint. The few clothes Adam possessed were hanging on the door, and apart from the bed, the only piece of furniture in the room was a chair. Her heartbeat slowed, and she could feel an ache in her throat. This boy had nothing, and the temptation to get some money from the drug gang must have been overwhelming. She despaired that an underclass existed in what was one of the richest countries in the world. There were people who wanted to live like this, but not this mother and son. She was going to ask Linda if she could look in draws for anything to do with the drugs gang, but there were no draws to look in. "Do you mind if I look under the bed and check Adam's pockets?"

Linda nodded.

There was nothing under the bed but a tatty pair of trainers.

***

Alex stood in the dark, her back pressed against the wall of the stone alcove in Blackfriars passageway. Like the Three Musketeers, Chris Laidlaw and John Robertson stood either side of her with their backs pressed to the wall. She had a stick in her hand to act as a knife. She'd decided to reconstruct the night of the Blackfriars murder. DC Luke Richardson was now making his way across Blackfriars Court in the darkness. She could hear him approaching, his footsteps moving across the stone paving, echoing loudly in the silence of the court. Luke stopped at the first gate. She held her breath and had her phone ready. She waited. The footsteps were slower but getting closer. She waited for another footstep. She jumped out of the alcove and switched on her phone torch. Luke automatically raised his left arm to his eyes. As he did so she struck with the stick once and then again. Luke feigned to fall to the ground. She looked at Chris. "What do you think of that?"

"I think that's how it happened. Luke was using his right hand to guide him along the passage wall and so using his left arm to shield his eyes was natural.... And, of course, this exposed the left side of his chest and his heart." Chris stared down at where Luke was lying. "But Neil Thomson's head was pointing towards Friars Lane and the second gate."

"Do you think the killer pushed the body into the alcove?" she said, surveying the flagstones.

Chris bent down over Luke's prostrate body. "I think they must've done... but we can't be sure... the body had been moved by the widow before we got here."

"If the killer left the body lying across the passageway, they took the risk of perhaps being caught before they got away," she said.

Chris turned towards Blackfriars Court. "So, we're working on the basis that the killer went back through the court and into Chinatown?"

"We don't know. We've got no witnesses." Frustration in her voice.

Chris turned his head to the second gate. "Friars Lane would be easier."

"Yes. I know. But if you think about it, it's safer to walk back through Blackfriars Court and then out into Chinatown through the Gothic arch. It would attract less attention than walking out into Friars Lane. There's a restaurant at the end of the street and someone may have seen them."

"Unless, of course, the gang fight had already broken out on Stowell Street?" Chris suggested.

"Neil Thomson left the restaurant at about ten. The gang fight broke out at about eleven. It's unlikely." She turned to

John. " What about the forensics? Are they any help in indicating which way the murderer left the scene?"

John shook his head. "There are men's footprints at both ends of Blackfriars Gate. I've been able to eliminate the son's footprints and Neil Thomson's..."

"And what about the woman's footprint?" she butted in before John had finished his sentence.

"It's not the wife. I've eliminated her. The only other clear print is at the opening into Blackfriars Court." He shone his torch and pointed to the area. "That doesn't mean that there weren't other prints which have been destroyed when the wife and son messed up the forensics," he ground out.

"So, it means if it is the murderer's footprint, they left through Blackfriars Court," she muttered almost to herself as her mind shifted up a gear.

"Aye. But the shoe was a stiletto heel. It seems a strange pair of shoes to wear to commit a murder."

"Can you reconstruct the shoes, to see if it's possible to commit murder when wearing them? I mean the right angle and height for the stab wounds?"

'Aye. I'll have a go," he smirked." And like Cinderella, we'll have to see whose foot matches the slipper."

She turned her head down to Luke who was still lying obediently on the stone paving. "Okay, let's do it again, Luke, with your phone torch on." The killer couldn't have known Neil Thomson's phone battery was dead."

Alex pressed herself against the wall of the alcove, Chris and John followed suit, as they waited for Luke's approach for a second time. Luke's footsteps were much faster than last time because he wasn't walking blind. She waited until he entered the gateway and then jumped out, shining her torch in his eyes. He put his left arm up to shield his eyes because he had his phone in his right hand, and she struck. It was possible to commit the murder, even if Neil Thomson had had his phone torch on. The element of surprise was there. “Luke, you couldn’t see us in the alcove now you had a torch with you?”

“No. It’s too deep, ma’am.”

Chapter 6

Dave Bell opened the door of the interview room where Linda and Adam Vickers were sitting on two chairs. "Hello," he said, and smiled at them as he entered the room. He'd spoken to Linda Vickers twice on the phone, but this was the first time he'd met either of them. He decided, on past experience, it was best to put them at their ease straightaway. "We've spoken to Social Services and we think that the best thing is to move you to Alnwick."

"But will we be safe there?" Linda's eyes darted around the room as though checking for a hidden assailant. "This is a drug gang we're dealing with."

"They're bairns not many years older than Adam." He gestured with his right hand towards Adam. "I think you'll be safe enough. You'll have police protection." He was thankful that neither of his two kids had ever got involved with drugs. He'd been out for a pint with his son last night. The force had destroyed his marriage, as it had destroyed a lot of police marriages. But his kids had been grown up by the time his marriage had shattered to pieces. They didn't seem to blame him, although his daughter swore she'd never marry a policeman. But he knew he should've spent more time with them when they'd been young.

"I'm frightened." Linda looked like a rabbit caught in a car's headlights.

"We're offering you protection. We've found you accommodation, Adam, a good school, and you a job." Dave fingered the file in his hand. He was eager to get back to the Incident Room. But when he saw Linda's fear, he felt like going over and giving her hug – politically incorrect these days. He looked directly at her. "We'll take care of you. We've got a good track record of that. And Adam is more likely to have trouble if he stays with the gang."

She nodded her head.

He opened the file which contained photos of youngsters who had previous in drug crime. He spread the photos across the table. "Do you recognise the one who got away on the night of the Stowell Street fight?" He asked Adam.

Adam hardly looked at the photos before he said, "No."

"That was a quick look," Dave said.

"He's not there because he's Chinese." Adam placed his bandaged hand on the table.

"Chinese?"

"Yes. But he's tall for a Chinese person," Adam volunteered. "I mean, I know there are tall Chinese people these days. I read that it was something to do with diet. They eat less rice. But it's still unusual."

"And have you ever seen him before?" Dave asked. "I mean before the night of the gang fight?"

"No," Adam said.

"And did he know the other three who were involved in the fight?"

"Not really... except one of them, I think."

"Which one?" He pointed at the three photos of the gang members.

"That one." Adam pointed his bandaged hand to one of the photos.

"So, what was he doing on Stowell Street?"

"I don't know but he started the fight... He started pushing him." He gestured towards the photo of the gang member he'd just identified, "and claiming he was stealing money."

"And was he?" Dave scratched his balding head.

Adam shrugged. "I don't know."

"So, what exactly happened, Adam?"

"He started pushing that boy and then pulled out a knife... and then the others pulled out their knives... I was the only one who didn't have a knife."

"And then what happened?" Dave rubbed his jaw.

"Everyone started fighting..."

He gave Adam a look that said, 'go on'.

"He ran off."

They'd found nothing on the CCTV cameras and this was unusual because there were so many in the town. They'd have to have another look to see if they could spot a tall Chinese man. "Which way did he run?"

"Up Stowell Street towards the Chinese arch."

That was the way the gang had entered Stowell Street. "Do you know his name?"

"I heard him being called Johnny."

Dave rubbed his jaw again, "So we have a Chinese man... a young man... who started the fight... pulled out a knife... is called Johnny... who then ran away... and is taller than your average Chinese man?"

Adam nodded.

"What was he wearing?"

"Jeans and a hoody."

Dave glanced towards the photos on the table. "We are going to need a photo-fit. I'll send our man down to talk to you. He'll try and get you to help him design a picture of the Chinese man." He stood up. "They do it on a computer these days." He directed his next comment to Linda Vickers. "I'll send him down here now... before we take you home."

***

Alex walked out of the Incident Room and turned right. A bit further down the corridor, a middle-aged man, grey hair thinning on top, wearing a good navy suit was standing. As she approached, she stretched out her hand. "Mr Patterson, I'm DCI Alex Shaftoe.' He took her hand in a firm grip, grief marking his countenance. "I think you have some information for me?" She opened the door of the room they were standing outside.

As they walked in, Rob Patterson said, "Yes. I'm afraid I forgot about it the other night when I was being interviewed by one of your officers," he breathed out heavily.

"It's easily done," she said. "We find people often remember things that they forgot to mention – later on."

"You see when we were having the meal in the Chinese, Neil told me that he'd seen Peter Dodd, a Chinese man and a younger Chinese man on Stowell Street."

She raised an eyebrow and waited for his explanation.

"We knew Peter Dodd when we were students at Newcastle University in the eighties." He gave his brow a weary rub. "The older Chinese man with him was also a student at Newcastle University at the same time as us."

"And the younger Chinese man?"

"Neil recognised him because he'd just recruited him for a company here in the north-east. He was a scientist... a chemist, I think." He paused. "You see, Neil hadn't realised that the Chinese chemist had anything to do with Peter Dodd or Wang Wei Li. They certainly didn't feature when they were doing the recruitment."

"And he was concerned about this?"

"Yes. You see, Peter Dodd and Wang Wei Li were involved in drugs when they were students."

"What do you mean by involved?"

"I suppose you could say they were involved in supplying drugs."

"And did Neil intend doing anything?"

"No. He was curious... that was all. That Peter and Wang Wei Li were still friends and that they knew the Chinese scientist. Though I suppose the Chinese community is close-knit."

"Excuse me a moment, Mr Patterson." She got up and left the room. She went into the Incident Room. "Debbie," she said to their goth analyst, "can you get up on screen photos of known middle-aged Chinese men involved in drugs?"

"Yes, ma'am.' She said, still chewing her gum.

"And follow me, please." She returned to the interview room with Debbie following behind her, clutching her laptop.

"Debbie, show Mr Patterson the photos."

Rob gave Debbie a startled look. No doubt because of her appearance, and particularly her make-up-blackened eyes. He was probably puzzling about whether she was a police officer.

Debbie sat next to Rob Patterson so he could see her laptop screen.

A few minutes later, Rob said, “That’s him.”

Debbie looked up from her screen and Alex gave her a slight shake of the head. Rob had identified a well-known Chinese Triad Chief. Debbie picked up her laptop and left the room

She continued. “And did the three men see and recognise Neil Thomson?”

“Yes, they did. They were walking down Stowell Street, in the opposite direction and on the opposite side of the street.”

“They didn’t acknowledge each other?”

“No, Neil said they looked away when they saw him.”

“And what was Neil doing on Stowell Street?”

“He had been on some business in that part of town. He had parked his car at Blackfriars.”

“And did he often park his car there?”

“Yes. If he was in that part of town. He did a lot of corporate business in the restaurant... entertaining clients... so they let him park there... whenever he needed to.”

“So exactly when did this happen?”

“The day before we were all in the restaurant.” He paused and his brow furrowed. “Wednesday afternoon... but I’m not sure what time.”

“And did Neil think he might’ve been followed after this happened?”

Rob’s eyes widened inside his rimless glasses. “He didn’t mention that to me... I think he would’ve done... and I think he would’ve come straightaway to the police.”

“Can you remember anything else, particularly about Peter Dodd or the man you have just identified.”

"Not really."

"And Neil hasn't mentioned seeing either Peter Dodd or the Chinese man... before Wednesday?"

"Not to me." He paused. 'You don't think this has anything to do with Neil's death?" His voice rose anxiously.

"Mr Patterson, I'm fact finding. I'm not jumping to any conclusions." She got up from her chair. "Thank you for your help." She walked towards the door. "If you think of anything else, let us know." He got up from his chair and she escorted him from the room.

***

Alex walked across to Debbie's desk in the Incident Room. She wanted an update on the Chinese Triad Chief and the Chinese chemist who Neil Thomson had seen in Chinatown, the day before he was murdered.

At her approach, Debbie's make-up-blackened eyes raised themselves from the computer screen. "Have you got anything for me?"

"Yes, ma'am. I've got the file for Wang We Li from the NCA straight after he was identified by Mr Patterson. He's involved with the Fourteenth Triad."

She knew that they were one of the three Triads active in the international heroin trade. They had a long pedigree stretching back to the opium wars of the nineteenth century. "Has he ever been arrested?"

"No, ma'am."

She wasn't surprised at that. He would be careful that nothing led back to him. "Do we know where he sits within the Triad organisation?"

"No. The NCA haven't got a handle on that... apart from the fact that he's a chief."

The Chinese Triads had numeric codes to distinguish ranks and positions within the gangs. But she wondered how well this worked in the modern world and the spread of Chinese influence? She wasn't an expert on Triads, she had no need to be. "I take it the NCA would expect potential drug links for this man?"

"Yes, ma'am. But the Triads are involved in money laundering, smuggling, prostitution, counterfeiting goods. You name it."

Alex paused and considered if there might be something other than drugs going on between Peter Dodd and Wang Wei Li? She'd asked Anaya Patel to look into Peter Dodd's business activities. And it might be clear what was going on when they knew more about Peter Dodd. "Where is Wang Wei Li based?"

"London, mainly, it seems. This is the first time he's been known to have visited Newcastle. But, of course, that doesn't mean that he hasn't been visiting regularly and we don't know about it."

"The Chinese Triads tend to centre on a Chinese cultural club or a martial arts centre and have a presence in most UK cities. Have the NCA been monitoring anywhere like that in Newcastle?"

"They didn't say, ma'am. But if they have, they haven't picked up Wang Wei Li."

For a moment she considered if this meant that Wang Wei Li stayed with his 'friend', Peter Dodd, when he came to Newcastle. But they'd only establish that by monitoring Peter Dodd. "What have we got on the Chinese chemist?"

"His name is Li Qiang. He's been studying for a PhD at Newcastle University."

"So, what has he got to do with Neil Thomson's recruitment company?"

"A Chinese company operating here advertised, and he applied."

"Even though he's doing a PhD?"

"Yes. A lot of students work at the same time as studying these days."

She kept forgetting that. It wasn't common in her day; then, students got grants to go to University. ' I think we need to check him out thoroughly. Has he got any Triad connections, or have his family got any connections? It will be worth asking the NCA if they've got any broader intelligence. The Chinese Triads are global. And just because we don't know about him doesn't mean someone else doesn't know."

"Okay, ma'am."

"And what do we know about the company?"

"I'm looking into it at the moment, ma'am. But it seems legitimate on the face of it. And Neil Thomson was to have a meeting with some Chinese businessmen involved with this company, the morning after he was murdered."

It was important to distinguish between legitimate operations and what might be dodgy. And at this stage they couldn't rule out that what Neil Thomson had seen was innocent enough. Peter Dodd might've stayed in touch with Wang Wei Li without knowing he was involved with the Triads. And the young Chinese scientist might have nothing to do with anything illegal. But was it all just a coincidence? And where did the cloaked figure fit into all of this? Was it just another coincidence and had nothing to do with Neil Thomson's murder?

Dave Bell walked across to Debbie's desk and she turned to him.

"The county-line boy, Adam, has just told us that the gang member who got away was a tall Chinese man," Dave said. "We've just been re-checking the CCTV. Nothing. He seems to have vanished into thin air."

***

Ian Turner knocked on the door of the Thomson house at Darras Hall. "Mrs Thomson?" He showed his warrant card.

"No. I'm Hannah Scott, Neil's sister."

She led him through a light wood-floored hallway which was airy, bright and had a number of doors leading from it. It was the type of house he aspired to own. He'd got to know Darras Hall estate since he'd become a police officer. He wasn't from the north-east and had been sent to the area when he'd joined the police fast track. He wondered if the Chief Constable owned a house like this? Probably not, it would be beyond his salary; it was probably beyond the salary of most senior police officers unless they were bent. And then he walked into a black and white luxury kitchen.

A blond woman was sitting at a white marble table. Her eyes were glazed and encircled by deep, dark rings. "Mrs Thomson?" He waited for her to look up from the table. Her head turned and her eyes gazed at him blankly. "I'd be grateful if you could help us." He sat down beside her, although uninvited to do so, and pulled out photos he had in a brown envelope. He spread them on the table in front of her. "Mrs Thomson, do you recognise either of these two men?" He had a photo of the Chinese Triad Chief and another of Peter Dodd. Sarah Thomson shook her head.

"Are you sure"

"Yes." She stared out towards the garden.

"Mrs Scott, could I ask you to take a look at these photos?" It had just crossed his mind that she was Neil Thomson's sister; she might know these men.

"I don't know the Chinese man," Hannah said apologetically. She looked more closely at the photo of Peter Dodd. "But I think I recognise this man... I think he knew Neil when they were students."

"And you haven't seen him recently?"

"No. It was years ago."

He turned his attention back to Sarah. "Mrs Thomson, can I run you through events on the night your husband died. We do this routinely. Sometimes people remember things they forgot at the time."

"You were at home with your son. You had a friend here with you until nine. You became concerned about your husband's late return." He glanced down at his notebook.

"That's right," she said, her face expressionless.

"You then rang your husband's friend, Rob Patterson, who confirmed your husband had left the Chinese restaurant at the usual time. You drove to Blackfriars with your son, where you found your husband."

"Yes."

"Is there anything that you might have forgotten to mention to us?"

"No."

Hannah led him to the front door. "You'll have to forgive Sarah," she said. "She's in a state of shock. You see, they were very happy together. The doctor has had to give her some sedatives. And I had to go and identify Neil's body. It was too much for her."

"Mrs Scott, you have our contact details, if any of you remember anything." He put his hand in his inside jacket pocket to take out a card.

She put up her hand up to stop him. "DCI Shaftoe gave us her card."

As he walked to his car, his annoyance returned because 'memsaab' hadn't sent the gorgeous Anaya Patel with him today. He reasoned with himself that they were very busy and it would be a waste of police resource sending two of them for a follow-up interview. But he'd been wanting to take out Anaya for months now. However, she was shy and not at all like the other girls he had known; not a meal out, a couple of drinks and a shag girl. He'd gradually been trying to win her over at work with help and kindness and a good aftershave. Lately he'd noticed the odd shy smile and then she looked away again. He thought she fancied him and he might've been able to test that out today, if she'd been with him.

***

Alex knocked on the door of the ACC's office. He was located in a large room on the second floor of their new building.

"Come."

She heard and went in. The office had two walls of windows; one window opened onto the River Tyne with a view of two of its bridges. They all had similar desks which got larger and a bit more elaborate depending on rank. Damien Sutcliffe's desk was a larger version of her own and he had a window directly behind him. There were filing cabinets along one wall and above them there were a few decent reproductions of the impressionists – Monet and Degas.

"Your cases?" He asked.

A sedentary lifestyle was showing on his midriff and one of the silver buttons on his uniform jacket was emphasising the point. The mid-brown hair he'd had when she first met him, many years ago, was grey. And he wore reading glasses over his brown eyes which he'd taken off when he'd started to speak to her.

"There's the possibility of a drug link. Particularly with the Chinese chemist involved."

"So, we might have drug manufacture?" He clasped his hands together on his desk.

They all knew that the chemical manufacture of drugs was now a big issue. The production of fentanyl was a problem in the States and it was now a problem in Europe. It was being manufactured in China and exported globally but its manufacture had moved beyond China. It was easy to produce and was a hundred times stronger than morphine, and you didn't have to grow fields of poppies to get it. "I don't know. But it has crossed my mind."

"So, what do you want to do?"

"I want to put Peter Dodd under surveillance."

"Okay. And we'll need to keep the NCA in the loop."

CHAPTER 7

Clapping echoed through the lecture theatre at Newcastle University and Alex, who was sitting in the back tier, joined in. Ewan Sinclair had just finished his talk about the excavations at Holy Island, and the lecture theatre was full because of the local interest in the subject. Ewan had invited her himself through Jo, but she wasn't here for social reasons; that was out of the question for the time being. She'd only caught the last twenty minutes of the lecture because she'd arrived late.

She stood up and moved towards the aisle, and as she did this, Ewan excused himself from some people, who had come over to speak to him, and made his way up the stairs towards her, smiling. "That was interesting, Ewan," she said. He was wearing a smart pair of navy slacks which looked new and a brilliant white shirt open at the neck. There were some grey chest hairs protruding and he smelled of sandalwood.

"Thank you.... Although I think you missed the beginning, I saw you come in. But I can't take the credit. It's the material that's interesting... I wonder, would you like to have a bite to eat with me?"

"I'm afraid I can't, Ewan" She saw disappointment momentarily flash across his face. "I'm here on police business." She opened her bag and pulled out a photo of the Chinese Triad

Chief. "Did you see Peter Dodd with this man when you had dinner with him in Chinatown?"

He bent over the photo in her hand. "Yes, I did."

"And he wasn't with you when you had your meal with Peter Dodd?"

"No." He looked down into her face. "He came across when we were finishing our meal. I got the impression that they were old friends. He said he would meet Peter for a drink in the casino after we'd finished our meal."

"And you weren't invited?"

"No. He came across. Shook my hand when Peter introduced us. Said he would meet him in the casino. And then left the restaurant."

"What time was that?"

"Before the gang fight started," he said without hesitation.

She wondered for a moment what Wang Wei Li had been doing in Chinatown on the night of Neil Thomson's murder? That is, if he'd anything to do with it. She'd have expected a Chinese Triad Chief to be well away from any trouble. But then he probably wouldn't have been short of witnesses and alibis, if needed.

"What time did you meet Peter Dodd for the meal?"

"It was at about nine... late for me... I usually eat earlier than that. Still, getting some money for the excavations is worth a bit of indigestion."

"And you were in the restaurant from nine until the gang fight at eleven?" She saw him nod. "And Peter Dodd was with you all of the time."

"Yes."

"Anything else you can think of?"

"No. The rest of the evening I spent talking to Peter Dodd about the excavations at Holy Island." He smiled. "Trying to charm him into giving us some money." He paused. "I realise you're busy at the moment, but can I take you out to dinner another time?"

"Not while you're a witness in an investigation I'm leading," she said, surprised that he hadn't worked that out for himself.

"But surely you don't think I've had anything to do with all this?" His eyes widened.

"No. I didn't mean that. But you're a witness." She waited to see if the penny dropped.

He looked thoughtful and then gave her a broad smile. "Can I take you for dinner once your investigation is over?" His lips quirked. "Once, of course you have proved me an innocent man."

"As long as you talk Holy Island to me," she smiled.

"Your wish is my command." He feigned a mock bow.

"And I must dash." She headed for the door. Jo would be waiting for her at the Civic Centre, and as she'd twisted Jo's arm to come with her to the event in the first place, she didn't want to be late.

***

The hum of voices reverberated around the large room as Alex scanned the scene and reckoned that there must be a couple of hundred people. Out of the corner of her eye she spotted the Chief Constable, Andrew Fellowes, and saw him point a man over to her. She forced a smile as he approached: a rotund middle-aged man, thin on top, wearing glasses, and a good quality suit from which peeped highly polished shoes.

"Good evening, ladies." He held out his hand. "I'm Frank Elliot. I've just been speaking to Andrew and he tells me you are investigating the murder of Neil Thomson."

Alex took the hand offered and noticed that he didn't make the mistake, that many men made, of gripping a woman's hand too tightly and nearly cracking all the bones in the fingers. "That's right, was he a friend of yours?" The ACC had coerced her into coming to this charity event because he had to attend a conference. And she'd asked Jo to come along with her because she thought she'd be bored witless. It was hard work making small talk with strangers and although some people were gifted at it, she wasn't one of them. It was too superficial for her. She was only at ease talking about a subject she found interesting – history, literature, music. And avoiding talking about investigations at social gatherings was usually a problem, because once people knew she was a police officer, they usually asked her questions she wasn't at liberty to answer. But tonight was different. Many of the members of the business community were gathered here, so it gave her a chance to ask questions about Neil Thomson and Peter Dodd.

"Yes, we were friends in the business world. He did some work for me, recruiting staff. In fact, his company are currently recruiting some IT staff for me in China." He sipped some wine from the glass he was holding.

"Yes, we were told about that. Were you with him in Chinatown on the night he died?"

"No, I wasn't. As I said, we were business colleagues." His voice was nasal as if he had the start of a cold.

"And what was he like in the business world?" she pursued.

His eyes widened.

"Once police officer, always a police officer," she said in her own defence. "I'm trying to gather as much information as possible about him."

His head twitched into a wary nod. "He was a charming man and very honest in his business dealings. He will be missed very much by the business community in Newcastle. Neil was always trusted. He had superb interpersonal skills and he always stayed calm in a crisis. I'm not sure what will now happen to his company because he doesn't have a natural successor." He sighed. "I'm so sorry for his wife, Sarah, as they were very happy together and a good match." He shook his head sadly.

She asked her obvious next question. "And do you know Peter Dodd?"

She saw momentary irritation flash across his face. "I don't think I do. Is he connected with Neil Thomson's death?"

"No. But we think they were friends."

She looked around the room. "Is there anyone here who might know Peter Dodd?"

"I'm not sure. He didn't frequent charity events, otherwise I'd know him. I'm not certain that he had much contact socially or otherwise with the business community." He pointed to a group of people to their left. "I think David Cunningham may be your best bet."

She smiled hopefully. "Would you mind introducing me?"

They walked towards an older man in his sixties who had wings of white hair and was heavily overweight.

"David, allow me to introduce you to DCI Alex Shaftoe. She's in charge of the investigation into the murder of Neil Thomson. She was wondering if you know Peter Dodd?"

"No, I don't," he said without hesitation for thought and looked around the room. "In fact, I don't think any of us know him. But Neil Thomson will be missed. He was highly regarded in the business community. A lovely man with a lovely wife."

It would seem that the only philanthropic activity Peter Dodd was involved with was archaeology. That is, if he intended to help fund Ewan's excavations at Holy Island. Maybe, like her, he was interested in archaeology and there was nothing more to it than that.

Alex and Jo drifted off towards a waiter who had a tray of drinks and then a second waiter bearing a tray of canapés. Alex's eyes were drawn to a group of men. Standing centre stage, amid this admiring group, was a blond woman with her hair resting at shoulder length, wearing a sleek black dress nipped in to show off her waist and ending at her calves.

Jo turned to her. "Isn't that the woman from the box at the Theatre Royal the other night?"

"Yes, you're right. It's the hair that's different. She had it up in a chignon at the opera." She looked stunning and the Byron poem came to her mind, *She walks in beauty like the night Of cloudless climes and starry skies; And all that's best of dark and bright Meet in her aspect and her eyes.*

Jo's eyebrows nudged up. "She seems to thrive on admiration and being the centre of attention."

Alex could see the Chief Constable, Andrew Fellowes, trying to catch her eye and they moved across to where he was standing. He was a rangy man, with salt and pepper hair, and piercing green eyes which darted about like a gust of wind. He excused himself from the group he was talking to and headed in her direction. He must want to talk to her about the progress on Neil Thomson's murder.

"Hello Alex and Jo. I was wondering how things were going with Neil Thomson's murder?" He looked at Alex and smiled. "Any leads?"

She shook her head. "None, except a possible Chinese connection."

He met Alex's eyes for a moment. "That means you're not convinced."

"No. The MO for the murder, and the gang fight, seems to be different." She studied Andrew Fellowes' reaction for a moment. Although they'd known each other for years, their paths rarely crossed these days because of Andrew's elevated position, and for a second or two she considered whether she'd made a mistake not pursuing promotion. Then she looked around the room: too much time spent on PR, stats and finance and too little time involved in solving the cases. She would've been bored. She'd gone out with Andrew for a short while after Daniel's death and after his divorce from his first wife. It hadn't worked for either of them and Andrew was now happily married to Beth. She searched around the room, but she couldn't see her here tonight.

He heaved out a breath. "Well, we'll be under pressure shortly because he was a respected businessman."

She noticed an edge to Andrew's voice which hinted that he was already feeling the pressure; another good reason for not pursuing promotion beyond DCI. Her consideration was not about Neil Thomson's respectability as a businessman, but that a human being was dead – she would've definitely got herself into trouble if she'd gone higher up the ranks. It was then that the woman from the opera approached and put her hand on Andrew's shoulder.

He turned and beamed at her. "Hello, Helen."

"I hope you're not talking shop, Andrew?" Helen's voice was like honey from a jar where it had hardened and turned to sugar.

"I'm afraid we are." His countenance now more serious, he said, "it's not often we have the murder of a prominent businessman."

Alex saw Helen's eyes widen into a question as she looked at Andrew.

He picked up on her body language. "So, you haven't seen the press or the news?" His voice displayed a note of surprise.

She looked him anxiously in the eyes. "No. Why? Is it anyone I know?"

"You may do – Neil Thomson."

Her feet shuffled. "No. I don't think so."

"Do you know Peter Dodd?" Alex interrupted the flow of the conversation.

There was a quick flash in her eyes before she corrected herself. "No. I don't think I know him either. They haven't been involved in any of my charity work." She smiled sadly at Andrew.

"Have you met Alex Shaftoe and Jo Johnson?" Andrew Fellowes asked.

"No, I don't think so." Her smile was as false as her nails as she flashed her dentist-white teeth.

"This is Helen Carter. She basically runs a lot of the charity work in Newcastle."

"I think that's a bit of an exaggeration, Andrew." She simpered as the flattery hit its mark.

She extended her well-manicured hand with its diamond encrusted ring, too big for the finger it sat on, and squeezed Alex's extended hand, the diamond nipping her palm. She continued to smile innocently, as Alex determined to show no reaction. The nasty bitch.

Alex studied her closely. She must've been stunning when she was young: blond hair now dyed, big blue doe-like eyes, and perfectly shaped lips which naturally pouted. Men, no doubt, had fallen for her many charms over the years. Helen Carter stood, back straight with one leg slightly in front of the other, as if she'd had deportment classes or trained as a model. It reminded her of one of the newscasters on TV who always stood in that posture when the camera took a full body shot. But there was a grey pallor to her skin, and dark rings around the eyes which even expensive make-up couldn't conceal. And the slender legs and well-turned ankles were marred by a plaster above the right ankle. She could smell Mitsouko by Guerlain, but what was that other smell? She'd smelt it before. Yes, it was the smell that had come from her dad when he was dying. It was the sweet smell of living decay.

"Alex is the Detective Chief Inspector who is leading on the murder... and this is Dr Jo Johnson, a clinical psychologist who lectures at Newcastle University, and works for the police when we need her."

Alex could see Helen physically scanning them and measuring them up against herself. Her lips and eyes showed a flash of distain before she recast the artificial smile on her beautiful face. She did not like this woman. "What type of charities do you help?" She asked.

"I do all types of charity work, big fund raisers with the local business community... down to flower displays at my local church. I do love flowers and making things look beautiful." She looked again with a hint of disdain at Alex and then Jo. They were threatening her and Alex guessed why. She smiled at

Helen. "And do you have a career?" She saw a flash of anger in those summer-sky eyes.

"Charity work has been my career." Her voice had lost its sugariness and she whined like a blast from an air-conditioning unit in mid-winter.

Jo smiled sweetly, too sweetly. "So, you're dependent on your husband?"

Alex sensed the anger rising in Helen Carter who didn't reply. She smiled pleasantly as she looked Helen Carter in eyes that had turned Robin-egg blue, as if the frost had touched them.

"Did you go to university?" Jo asked with an innocence which matched Helen Carter's posturing.

Alex stifled a quivering giggle; Jo didn't like Helen Carter either.

"I must go and mingle, Andrew." Helen's voice was low again and she gave Andrew a doe-like look in the eyes.

"And I must do the same," he responded.

"When I saw her standing in the box at the opera," Alex said as they moved off, "I thought of Eva Peron. It looked like the scene at the beginning of *Evita*, where Eva Peron is standing on the balcony waving to the crowds."

Alex saw Jo looking in the direction of Helen Carter. "Did you notice she looks ill?"

"Yes, I did. And she knew Neil Thomson and Peter Dodd. She wasn't very good at hiding her body language."

CHAPTER 8

Alex sat at her desk moving her swivel chair from side to side with a slight of her feet. She had a pile of overtime claims to sign off and an assault case that needed to go to the Crown Prosecution Service. Her new office had a beech veneered desk, a larger version of the desks out in the main office, but she was uncomfortable because of the glass wall which looked directly into the Incident Room and meant the team could look into her office. She'd stopped pacing up and down her office floor – something she wanted to do right now – because the team could see her. Nor could she loop her hair through her finger, something she did when she was thinking. She'd taken to stopping herself just in time and pushing her hand through her hair instead. She started in surprise as her mobile phone rang. "Hello, DCI Alex Shaftoe."

"Hello, it's Neil Thomson's sister, Hannah Scott. Do you remember me?"

"Yes, of course I do." She hoped she didn't want an update on the case.

"You said to ring you about anything that might help with Neil's murder. I'm not sure if this is nothing, but in today's *Northumbrian News* there's an article about a woman killed in a hit and run incident near Bamburgh yesterday. She was once a girlfriend of Neil's; they went out together for about a year. I don't know what happened but I do know it ended badly... I was too young to be involved. Her name was Helen Armstrong, although from the paper her married name was Helen Carter. I recognised her from the photo in the paper."

She could feel her heart jump. "Is Helen Carter a good-looking blond woman?"

"Yes. That's right."

"Is there anyone who could tell me about what happened between her and your brother?"

There was a pause at the end of the line. "The only one who might know is Neil's friend, Rob Patterson."

"Thank you, Mrs Scott. I'll look into it."

She closed the phone and looked through her glass wall into the Incident Room and her unsolved cases on the glass board. It was probably nothing because it was so long ago and some teenage romance. She walked through to the incident room. "Have we got a number for Rob Patterson?"

The blond head of Luke Richardson, always eager to please, bobbed up from his computer screen; a new constable in his early-twenties, fair-haired and slim-built. He wasn't the brightest bulb on the Christmas tree, but he was thorough, methodical and pleasant. She was watching to see how he'd fair next to the likes of Ian Turner who was bright and quick.

"Yes, ma'am. He's one of Neil Thomson's friends and he was with him in Chinatown the night he died."

She moved across to Luke's desk, took a piece of paper with the number written on it and then walked back into her office. She picked her phone up and hitched her hip onto the edge of her desk as she punched in the number. "Hello, is that Mr Patterson? This is DCI Alex Shaftoe. I'm dealing with your friend,

Neil Thomson's, murder." She'd met Rob Patterson when he'd come into the station to tell them about Neil Thomson seeing Peter Dodd, Wang Wei Li and the Chinese Chemist in China-town.

"Ah, yes. How can I help you, Detective Chief Inspector?"

"Could you tell me what you know about the breakdown of the relationship between Neil and Helen Armstrong?"

There was a humming silence at the end of the line. "But that was thirty years ago. Surely it can't have anything to do with Neil's murder." His voice incredulous.

"Possibly not. But I would like to know what you know about how the relationship broke down."

"You must be scraping the bottom of the barrel," he said sardonically. "It was a nasty business. Helen was pregnant. But at the time it wasn't clear if Neil was the baby's father. She accused Neil and two other people of rape and they split up. I think she had an abortion." There was a sharp edge to Rob Patterson's voice.

"Were the police involved?"

"No. And the allegation of rape was denied by all three men. They couldn't remember sleeping with her."

Her mouth dropped. "How come?"

"Because it happened at a party where there were drink and drugs," he said impatiently.

"Do you remember the names of the other two men she accused of rape?"

"Terry Marshall and Peter Dodd," he said without hesitation.

Her heart jumped at Peter Dodd's name. Another connection.

"You don't think this has got anything to do with Neil's murder?" His voice rose slightly as he asked the question.

"I'm fact finding at the moment, Mr Patterson. I'm not jumping to any conclusions. But thank you for your help."

"Chief Inspector, Neil Thomson was a good man. A good husband and father. It would be wrong to judge him on what happened with Helen Armstrong. We all make mistakes and regret them."

This connection was tenuous, but it was often unexpected threads which brought to life a pattern amongst the weave of a crime. She stood up from her desk and put her head around her office door. "Luke, can you get me the number for Jeff Brookes in Alnwick?"

Jeff Brookes was DI at the station in Alnwick. Dave Bell had told her earlier that morning that he was heading up the investigation into the hit and run, although she didn't know then that Helen Carter had been the victim. Luke scampered into her office with the number and she tapped it into her phone. "Hi, Jeff. It's Alex Shaftoe from Newcastle. I need some information from you about the hit and run at Waren Mill."

"It's a middle-aged woman called Helen Carter. The post-mortem has been completed at Alnwick. She died as a result of the injuries sustained by being hit by a vehicle."

She hadn't had much to do with Jeff, but on the occasions she had, they hadn't got on. She was sure it was because she was more senior than him. She didn't know enough about his background to know if he'd got himself into trouble, had been unfairly passed over for promotion, or if he'd been unwilling to come to Newcastle where there was greater opportunity for promotion.

"Why do you want to know? "

She could hear the prickles in his voice. "I think it might be connected to a murder I've got down here in Newcastle."

"You think," he said dryly.

"Can you tell me what you have?"

"Not much... I'm waiting for the full pathology report.... All I know is she already had terminal cancer and there was a dog bite on her leg."

"And what are traffic saying about the hit and run?"

"No witnesses. Nothing. Quiet country road early on a Sunday morning."

She remembered how ill Helen Carter had looked at the charity event at the Civic Centre and began to wonder if the hit and run had been suicide because of the terminal cancer. She sensed Jeff Brookes was being obstructive because he suspected the case was going to be taken from him. She could see no point in pursuing the conversation because it was going to get her nowhere. "It's okay, Jeff. I'll have a word with the ACC." With that, she closed the phone. He couldn't say she hadn't been in touch with him.

***

Anaya Patel focused her eyes on her computer screen. HMRC had just sent the accounts over for Peter Dodd's company. She looked at his tax return and then at overall profits. She then scrolled down to the previous five years and studied the profits and tax returns.

She then clicked onto property prices in the street in Jesmond where Peter Dodd lived. The houses cost millions. She looked again at the company accounts.

She picked up the phone to HMRC. "Hi, Stu. It's Anaya Patel again." She'd known Stu for a while now because, often as not, she did this type of research for DCI Shaftoe. She'd struck up a relationship with Stu although they'd never met because he was the liaison point for the police with HMRC. "On what basis do you investigate companies?" In the past she'd enquired about companies HMRC had already been investigating themselves, and therefore had not had a reason to ask about the criteria for HMRC investigations.

"It's risk based."

"And how do you work out risk?"

"It's complicated, Anaya. We focus on certain occupations – builders, 'rag trade', self-employed."

'So why haven't you investigated Peter Dodd's company?"

"His risk profile. He's paid his taxes on time. His accounts seem alright. He isn't involved in a trade we think is high risk."

"Thanks, Stu."

Anaya got up and walked towards DCI Shaftoe's room.

***

DS Anaya Patel knocked on Alex's door. She still wasn't used to hearing a knock on glass and being able to see who it was before they'd come through the door.

Anaya walked into the room, her black hair tied back in a ponytail. Her lips were pursed in concentration, accentuating her high cheekbones, as her large almond-eyes scanned the papers in her hand.

"Ma'am, I've been onto HMRC about Peter Dodd's business. He has a company selling fancy goods from China." She waved the papers in her hand.

"What d'you mean... cheap stuff?"

"No. A bit more upmarket than that. But his turnover isn't big enough to account for his lifestyle."

Anaya was good at figure work, as good as some of the forensic accountants they used from time to time. That was the reason she'd got her to do this research. She tried to vary the skill set on her team: Ian Turner was good at all matters IT. She'd been trying to encourage Anaya to fast track, without making it appear that she was giving her special treatment because she came from an ethnic minority. She knew the feeling of being patronised when she'd been one of the few women in the fast track – but that was years ago now.

"He's living in an expensive house in Jesmond. It must be worth a few million. And he has bought a house in Northumberland recently."

"Whereabouts?"

"It seems to be really remote." Anaya shuffled her papers and put a map on Alex's desk. It's out past Rothbury on the moors towards Otterburn. There's nothing else around." She put her finger on the spot on the map.

"I see what you mean. And HMRC haven't been suspicious about Peter Dodd?"

"They've had no reason to be. He pays his taxes and has given them no cause to investigate him."

"And there's nothing you can see to account for his lifestyle?"

"No, ma'am."

"Keep digging, Anaya."

***

Alex knocked on the ACC's door.

"Come."

His eyes moved from the papers on his desk as she entered the room. He removed his reading glasses and peered up at her. His thick mop of salt and pepper hair was unruly and he'd obviously been pushing his hands through his hair as he read. "Ah, good. I was just about to ask you to come up." He smiled at her without showing his teeth. "I've heard from the NCA. They want close involvement in both the Stowell Street gang fight and Neil Thomson's murder." He continued, "They were wondering if they can learn something from your technique in persuading the county-line boy to turn police witness. They've decided to investigate the casino on Stowell Street. You know what's been happening in Vancouver with the casinos being used to launder drug money."

"I can't see the casino in Stowell Street turning into another Vancouver." She sat down on the chair opposite his desk. Good news travels fast. Her success with Adam Vickers had reached the NCA quickly and she suspected that Damien might have something to do with it. But you can't teach compassion, she thought, as she smiled at him. "I'm here about the Neil Thomson murder. You know that Peter Dodd, the Chinese scientist and the Chinese Triad Chief were seen by Neil Thomson the day before he was killed?" He nodded so she continued. "It seems that Peter Dodd's company can't account for his lifestyle."

"Drugs?" he said.

She shrugged and then continued. "We're monitoring Peter Dodd. But we've discovered that he's recently bought a house in a remote part of the Northumbrian moors. Up past Rothbury and towards Otterburn. I want to monitor the house." She paused. He was keen on keeping on budget, and she always got consent first before surveillance operations because they were costly.

"And – "

"The house is close to the military camp at Otterburn."

"I'll get onto them, Alex. I'll have a word with them."

"I want to bring a body down from Alnwick. A woman, Helen Carter, has been killed in a hit and run at Waren Mill." She paused and looked him in the eyes. "Did you know her?"

"Yes. We met at charity events. A very pleasant woman."

She noticed a flash of unease at the mention of Helen Carter. "I've just found out that she went out with Neil Thomson when they were young. The relationship ended in allegations of rape against Neil Thomson, Peter Dodd and another man, Terry Marshall."

"But this all must've been a long time ago. It seems a bit tenuous." He spread his hands out on his desk, palms up.

"Yes. But there's a connection between them all. I've spoken to Jeff Brookes. He's being prickly about the hit and run because it's his case."

He frowned. "But what possible motive could she have for killing Neil Thomson? That he finished with her thirty years ago?"

"I don't know. But I intend to find out. That's if there is one." She pushed her hand through her hair. "I need you to sort this out and get the body down here... and the hit and run treated as part of my case. "She was relying on her track record in solving cases. Even if Damien didn't always agree with her methods.

"Okay."

"I'm going to need to talk to Helen Carter's GP, the oncologist, and anyone else involved. Can you get me a court order?" she rattled out and then gave him a knowing look. "I also want to put a watch on Terry Marshall's house." She waited to see how he would react, but he said nothing. That was a good sign.

"An oncologist?" he stared at her. "What's going on?"

"I don't know. But Jeff Brookes said she had terminal cancer. He didn't give anything else away. And quickly as possible, Damien. I don't want the trail to get any colder."

She stood up and walked towards the door. "And I'm going to use Jo. I think I might need a clinical psychologist on this one."

"Why?"

"It's not clear what's happened with the hit and run. It could be suicide since she had cancer." She shrugged. "We may need Jo to establish her state of mind." Clinical psychologists were used in court statements for the police as expert witnesses, but she'd started using Jo more widely in interviews over the past few years. Jo, of course, couldn't be involved in interviews under caution. But they'd had few people refuse to allow Jo into other types of interviews. Damien had worried at first and asked her if she'd been watching *Waking the Dead* or *Wire in the Blood*. But in the end, he'd agreed to it because he liked to be at the cutting edge of police techniques. He'd even talked about the results from using Jo in interviews at a police conference.

She left the room and closed the door behind her.

CHAPTER 9

It was a blustery autumn day, with the wind funnelling along the Tyne valley as Alex drove through the narrow streets of Corbridge. It had been a while since she'd been here and she was surprised at how busy the village was, especially as it was now autumn and the summer footfall to the Roman fort was over. She peered through the jeep window at an upmarket boutique and a number of tea shops, a butcher and a baker.

They'd begun to investigate Helen Carter in earnest since Damien, the ACC, had got Helen's body moved to Newcastle and the hit and run case transferred to her. She wouldn't be flavour of the month with Jeff Brookes in Alnwick.

She pulled up in an oval drive and got out of the car. The gravel crackled beneath her feet as she walked towards the front door and then knocked. A gust of wind sent leaves lashing around her legs and swept her hair into her face. The door was opened by a white-haired man, his red-rimmed eyelids drooping with fatigue, the skin darkened above his cheekbones. She pulled her warrant card out of her pocket. "Mr Carter?"

"Yes."

"I'd like to talk to you about the death of your wife." He turned into the house without a word or a backward glance, and as she followed, he led her with purposeful steps into a dark yew study which smelt of furniture polish and aftershave. The room was filled, from floor to ceiling, with bookshelves which at a glimpse covered a wide range of subjects. Four large computer screens dominated the space and were at odds with the otherwise traditional study. In one corner a running machine stood beside some weights. She regarded Alan Carter who was slim-built and whose bicep and leg muscles were clearly visible through tight-fitting clothes.

"Mr Carter, I appreciate this is a difficult time for you. But I need to ask you some questions."

He nodded and gestured with a hand for her to take a seat. She lowered herself onto a dark-red leather three-seater settee which felt hard and cold, as Alan Carter slumped down on a matching chair diagonally opposite her. There was a fireplace in between them but there was no cheery fire in the grate today. She cleared her throat. "How long have you been married, Mr Carter?" She could see him jolt himself back into the present.

"We had our twenty-fifth wedding anniversary last year."

"Mr Carter," she said softly, "did you know that your wife had been diagnosed with terminal cancer?"

He breathed out slowly, his face filled with despair. "Yes, I knew. We'd only just got the results back from the second opinion... it... it confirmed the original diagnosis." He took a handkerchief from his pocket and dabbed his eyes.

Her stomach clenched as she readied herself for the next question. "Do you think that your wife could have committed suicide because of her diagnosis?" She waited in silence for him to reply.

He shook his head firmly. "No way... Helen intended to fight on... and anyway, she left no suicide note in the house and the police didn't mention finding one."

She kept her voice even as she regarded him. "Mr Carter, suicide notes aren't as common as you might think. In fact, two-thirds of people who commit suicide don't leave a note."

He shook his head vigorously. "My wife loved life. She intended to fight on," he said emphatically.

"And you don't think that she might've wandered off into the road because her mind was on her cancer diagnosis?" she suggested.

"No. Helen had got over the shock before she was killed."

"We've established a link between your wife and a man murdered at Blackfriars, Neil Thomson. Were you aware they knew each other?"

He shook his head and immediately lowered his gaze to the floor.

She continued. "What about a man called Peter Dodd….or Terry Marshall?"

"Why should she?" he snapped short-temperedly and his shoulders slumped forward.

She found him impossible to read which was unusual for her. She couldn't make out whether the body language was grief or lies.

His gaze moved from the floor to Alex. "Were they involved in Helen's charity work?"

"No." She was sure about that. "We're still not sure yet if your wife's death was an accident."

"If it was an accident, why has the driver not come forward?" he sneered. "That's murder in my book."

"Mr Carter, I'm trying to establish events thirty years ago," she said. "I'm not sure at the moment if it's relevant, but I need to explore everything."

He shuffled in his chair. "Why? For God's sake, what's it got to do with Helen's death?" His face had reddened.

"Because that's when we think your wife knew these three men," she said quietly. She paused to consider if Alan Carter had calmed down. "I'm not sure if you knew your wife back then?" She waited for a response – nothing. "Or if you could point me in the direction of someone who did know her then?"

He buried his head in his hands, his elbows resting on his knees, and spoke to the floor. "There is her sister. Helen hasn't spoken to her for a long time. I met her for the first time at my mother-in-law's funeral a few weeks ago. Her name is Lorna Godfrey." He looked up and frowned. "What's this got to do with anything?" He put his hand to his neck and sighed. "My wife has a close friend, Jane Simpson, who she was visiting at Waren Mill the day she died. Helen has known her since they were young." His shoulders began to quake and his sobs were guttural.

She waited patiently for the worst to subside. He wasn't a handsome man and had a large nose and a thin mouth which looked incongruous next to his nose. He must be about sixty and at least ten years older than his wife. His face matched his age, his neck craning like a bird. Her eyes moved to the large computer screens, probably, she thought, because he spent too many hours in front of the screens. Yet from the shoulders down he had the lean muscular body of a much younger man.

He blew his nose. "I'm sorry."

"Don't worry about it." She could feel her stomach clenching and she took a deep breath. "I'm sorry to have to ask you this," she began softly, "but where you were on Sunday?"

His head snapped up and his spine straightened. His lips pulled back to show his teeth. "I was out of the country," he shouted. His shoulders were shaking and he looked down and put his face in his hands.

She understood his reaction. He felt guilty that he'd been out of the country when Helen had died. "Could you explain to me what you were doing?" She tried to keep her voice calm.

He glanced towards the screens. "I'm a computer expert. I fly around the world troubleshooting computer issues for governments and big companies."

"And what does that involve?" IT was not her forte; she left that to the younger members of her team. But Alan Carter's age meant that he must have been involved in IT at its beginning, before it really took off.

"Ethically hacking into systems. Looking at potential problems and getting fixes." His statements were clipped in a monotonic voice as if programmed in computer binary code. But his voice was incongruous with his body language which showed emotion.

"And are you abroad a lot of the time?" Why didn't they live near the airport in Ponteland? But then it was easy to cut up from Corbridge, onto the A69, and then on to Ponteland and the airport.

"Not all of the time." He drew in some deep breaths. "But I'm abroad a lot."

"Mr Carter, we may need to check your whereabouts on other days and I'll get a member of my team to contact you."

His face became stern. "Why? Am I a suspect?"

She waited for a moment before replying. "I need to eliminate you from my enquiries." She swallowed hard. "Mr Carter, I need to ask you the following question." She was struggling to get the words out of her mouth. "Was your wife having an affair?" she mumbled.

A storm broke. He clenched his fists and screamed, "No she was not." His spine straightened his shoulders shook. "Helen was the love of my life and if you think that I would harm a hair on her head..." His voice rose to a crescendo.

"Mr Carter, I'm not suggesting anything." She tried not to let the frustration show in her own voice. "But I need to eliminate you as part of my procedures. I realise this is a traumatic time for you and I hate asking you these questions." He seemed reassured and his shoulders relaxed and he let out a long sigh. She continued, "Can you think of anyone who might have wanted to harm your wife?"

His eyes widened in disbelief. "Everyone loved Helen. She did a lot of work for charity."

She doubted that the Helen Carter she'd met was universally well liked, but love is sometimes blind and this man loved Helen Carter. "You were away when your wife died. Is there anyone else who may be able to help us retrace your wife's movements on the day of her death?"

"My wife was murdered." He crashed his fist on the coffee table and the vase on the table shook.

She jumped.

He pinched the bridge of his nose between his thumb and forefinger. "It may be worth asking my daughter about Helen's movements on Sunday... she's married to a surgeon and my wife and her are often together in the evenings... and sometimes they go jogging in the mornings. She lives down the road in Corbridge but she's here at the moment." His eyes moved up to the ceiling.

"Your wife was up in north Northumberland very early on Sunday morning. Have you any idea what she was doing there?"

"My wife's closest friend, Jane Simpson, has a caravan at Waren Mill and she often visits her there." He had slipped into the present tense as if he still didn't believe Helen was really dead. "I told the other police officers this."

She changed the subject. "Do you own a red jeep?" This was the vehicle traffic were looking for in connection with Helen Carter's hit and run.

"No." His eyes questioned her. "Do you think that's the car that killed Helen? I do have a grey SUV. If that's what you mean... but it's not my wife's car."

"Would you be able to give me a recent photo of your wife?"

"I'm not sure but I'll have a look." He left the room and returned with a photo frame. "Will this do?"

He presented her with a silver frame in which Helen Carter was dressed in figure-hugging jeans and a baggy jumper. She was smiling at the camera, her hair drawn back in a ponytail. "Thank you. I know you will have been asked this already, but is there anything else that you think may help us with our enquiries into your wife's death?"

"No, I can't think of anything."

She stood up, waited for a moment, until Alan Carter realised she intended to leave. He showed her out of his study and to the staircase.

"Rebecca is in her mother's bedroom. It's the second door on the right."

"Mr Carter, I may need to take some of Helen's shoes with me for examination."

He nodded indifferently as he turned back into his study.

***

Alex tapped on the door before opening it. "Hello, I'm DCI Alex Shaftoe and I'm here to talk to you about your mum's –" The sentence wasn't finished before Rebecca burst into tears. "Can I come in?"

Rebecca nodded as she sobbed into a light-blue cashmere jumper which she was holding in her hands. She was perched on the edge of a king-size bed, covered in a black silk throw, shining in the morning light like a fine shroud. "I'm sorry for your loss." Again, a nod. She waited before continuing. She could smell expensive French perfume in the room, perhaps Chanel? She sat down on a black chaise longue upholstered with velvet-studded cushions which were surprisingly hard. "Did your mum ever mention a man called Neil Thomson to you?" she began. Black silk curtains hung on a rail, which split the bedroom into two halves and which separated the bed from the rest of the room. The floor in a varnished grey wood matched the grey marble on the wall behind the bed. Though black and grey were fashionable, the room felt cold and dark. She shivered, looked at Rebecca and waited for an answer to her question.

She raised her chin from the comfort of the jumper, then looked down and shook her head. "No, she didn't. I've never heard of him."

She bore an uncanny resemblance to her mother: same blond hair, same blue eyes and the same shaped face. "Are you sure?"

She nodded and clutched the jumper even more tightly. "What about a man called Peter Dodd?" Again, she shook her head. "Can you confirm whether your mum was here with you on Thursday and Sunday?"

"I can't remember," she screeched and then shuffled on the edge of the bed.

Her behaviour was child-like, but people reacted in different ways to grief, and she had just lost her mother. "We know you were with your mum in Chinatown on Thursday because you both gave statements to the police about the gang fight."

"If you say so," she answered petulantly.

She wasn't going to get anywhere with Rebecca whose grief was too raw. She was going to have to wait until she got over the initial shock before talking to her. "I need to take some of your mum's shoes with me." She waited a moment but there was no response as she continued to hug her mother's jumper. She went towards the wardrobe, helped herself to shoes, pushing them into a large plastic bag which she'd brought with her. She was now going to drive immediately to John Robertson and the CSI team so they could check the shoes against the bloody print they had at Blackfriars Gate.

***

Alan Carter heard the door close, but no steps going back up the stairs. The police officer must've let herself out of the house and Rebecca must still be upstairs in Helen's bedroom. He stopped his fingers gliding across the keyboard and wrenched his eyes from the screens.

He'd got over the initial shock about what Helen had done to Neil Thomson. She hadn't told him what she had done and he hadn't asked her? Sometimes it was better to leave things unsaid. He hadn't known about what had happened all those years ago at the student party, until Helen had told him after her diagnosis of cancer. After all, why should she tell him? It was irrelevant to them. He didn't know if she'd told Rebecca, but he wasn't going to tell her. Why upset her even more with something that was no longer important. But had Helen's death got anything to do with this murder? Was somebody on to what she'd done, or was it something to do with the other two men? He'd noticed money going missing from their account but £10,000 wasn't enough, surely, to fund murder. He couldn't imagine Helen doing it herself but how had she found out what to do? But then she met a lot of people through her charity work.

He hadn't gone with her to see the cancer specialists. He'd offered, but she'd asked him not to come: she wanted to face it alone. Both specialists had told her that the abortion she'd been forced to have had caused the cancer. He wasn't sorry that one of the three of them who had raped her were now dead. But how had the police found out about the connection between Helen and the three men – if you could call them men. It was nearly thirty years ago.

Tears filled his eyes and he wiped them with his sleeve cuff. He'd been surprised when Helen had shown an interest in him. Why would such a beautiful woman want him? He tried not to think about his failures, the potential parents who didn't want him and his other wives who'd got rid of him. But Helen had stayed with him and accepted his ways. And he'd let Helen do whatever she wanted to do and spend whatever she wanted to spend – after all, he earned enough. He was grateful she'd wanted him, had stayed with him and given him a beautiful daughter, just like her. It was more than he'd expected or ever hoped for. He didn't listen to what other people said about her; he was sure that some of it was women being bitchy because she was so beautiful. He knew she was no saint; she liked her own way and would throw a tantrum if she didn't get it. But he didn't care – he was grateful. She'd married him and given him a home and a family for the first and only time in his life. He took his handkerchief out of his jean pocket and blew his nose. And those bastards had taken it away from him. He clenched his fists in anger and pain. Who else was going to take him on? His family life was ruined. He banged his fist down on the desk.

Chapter 10

The ACC had managed to get Alex a court order in record time. She had to concede that the time he spent socialising with the 'great and the good' did produce benefits from time to time. She was now able to talk to the medical profession about Helen Carter. Her GP had been unable to tell her anything of any value, so she'd been pointed in the direction of the oncologist at the Freeman Road Hospital who'd been dealing with Helen Carter's case. She parked her car opposite the hospital because it was always easier to get parked there than in front of the hospital itself, then she crossed the road. She could remember the hospital being built in the seventies; it wasn't a concrete block but it still looked like a large office complex. Her eyes instinctively moved to the larger tower-like block in the same brown brick, broken up by horizontal strips of beige architrave, similar to the lower lying buildings around it. Her dad had died there of a massive stroke several years earlier. She shuddered. For five days she and her mam had kept a vigil around his bed until life had stopped with his heart and lungs; although in reality, he'd left them days earlier.

As she entered his office, the oncologist, Mr Stephen Bailey, was sitting behind a desk. She guessed he was in his late thirties with dark-red hair and dark-rimmed glasses. He looked down to the file lying on his desk. "I haven't had to do this before," he said as he stood up and offered her his hand. "I'm wondering how ethical it is to discuss private medical information, even with the police." He sat back down behind his desk.

She had dealt with this type of situation in the past; the medical profession was always reticent at sharing confidential medical information. "Mr Bailey, as I explained to your secretary on the phone, Helen Carter is now dead. We have her death and another, and we're currently trying to establish whether there's a link between the two. I need as much information as I can get about these two people. I have an order from the court and I've already spoken to Mrs Carter's GP."

He nodded and opened the large file in front of him.

"I know from the pathologist that she had cancer." She was talking to the top of his head as he bent over the file. "Can you take me through the facts, please?"

His eyes moved from the file and stared at her through his glasses. "She had ovarian cancer. This is a difficult cancer because, like pancreatic cancer, it is often symptomless until late in the day. In Mrs Carter's case, by the time it had been detected it had spread into the liver and kidneys and had become terminal. All we could offer was palliative care."

Her eyes widened. "You weren't intending any chemotherapy?"

He leaned back in his chair. "It was too late for that to be of any use."

"So how long did Mrs Carter have to live?"

"About six months," he said in a matter of fact way.

She thought about the charity event. It was little wonder that Helen Carter had looked ill. In fact, she'd looked good that night for someone with a six months death sentence. "Was there was anything unusual in your discussions with Mrs Carter?"

He frowned. "I'm not sure what you mean?"

"Did Mrs Carter ask whether anything may have caused her cancer, such as lifestyle, genetics, hereditary?"

His head moved back to his notes. "She asked me if an abortion could have led to the cancer. That was on the second occasion I met her. I explained that there was no proven link between abortion and ovarian cancer, but she didn't accept this." He shook his head slowly.

"But she said that she'd read a connection between multiple miscarriages and ovarian cancer on the internet. I tried to explain that there was a difference between miscarriage and abortion. But she was dismissive of the scientific research I discussed with her and felt that the link would be proved in the future." He breathed out loudly, frustration on his face. "I saw her again three weeks ago and again she raised the issue of the link between ovarian cancer and abortion." He met Alex's eyes. "It's not unusual for someone who has just been given a diagnosis of terminal cancer to look for something to blame. It's often part of the reaction to the shock."

She decided to push him. "Did she give you any idea when she'd had the abortion?"

He put his hands on his desk. "I'm afraid not."

She needed more than this. "Is there anything else you can tell me?"

"Yes. She was very aggressive. She shouted at me when I first gave her the diagnosis. By the second appointment she was screaming and refusing to accept she was terminally ill, and adamant that there was a connection between the cancer and the abortion. She said she wanted a second opinion."

His specialism meant that he must deliver bad news on a regular basis. So, his comment about Helen Carter meant that something was different about her reaction to the bad news. "Have you had other patients behave this way?"

"Not as aggressively as Mrs Carter. ' Surprise was written on his face. "And not persisting in making an unproved connection for the cause of the cancer."

"Do you know if she got a second opinion?" Alan Carter had already told her that they'd had a second opinion which had confirmed Stephen Bailey's diagnosis. But she wanted to know if he knew this?

"I don't know."

She was still puzzled why Helen Carter was persisting in making an unproven connection between the ovarian cancer and an abortion. "Have you had anyone else with terminal cancer try to make a link between ovarian cancer and an abortion?"

"No," he said. "It's more common for people who have in the past or do smoke... to try and make that link which is more scientifically proven."

To automatically make this link must mean that the abortion was still playing on Helen Carter's mind, even after all these years. Her right hand went through her hair. "It seems strange to come to this conclusion immediately after being given a diagnosis of cancer."

"It is," he agreed, "but people often act strangely when they're told they only have a few months to live." He paused. "It often prompts them to reflect on things that have happened to them in the past."

She frowned. "But this doesn't seem like a reflection… more a reflex reaction."

He looked at her directly. "But the abortion was clearly something which she hadn't ever resolved and so it was at the forefront of her mind. I had recommended she saw one of our counsellors after her second appointment with me."

She would need Jo with her if she was going to talk to a counsellor and she was currently at the university lecturing. "Do you know if she went?"

"I don't. But I can find out." He picked up the phone to his secretary and asked her to give Alex the information when she left.

"Do you think Mrs Carter may've been suicidal?"

He frowned. "I thought she'd been killed in a hit and run?"

"She was, but it wouldn't be the first time someone has thrown themselves in front of a car."

"It's difficult to tell." He clasped his hands in front of him on his desk. "We've had a few cases over the years where people have committed suicide. But they've been in the later stages of the cancer... and a while after the diagnosis."

She left Stephen Bailey's room. His secretary confirmed that Helen Carter had had one session with the counsellor, and that the counsellor was able to meet her in about an hour. She texted Jo to see if she could meet her at the hospital.

***

Alex sat at a table in the cafe of the Freeman Road Hospital sipping coffee, keeping an eye on the entrance for Jo who was going to join her for the meeting with the counsellor. She hadn't been able to tell Jo yet all that had happened when she met the oncologist – too long for a text. At least in the cafe there wasn't the sharp pungent smell of hospital disinfectant, although the smell of beans and chips wasn't enticing either, and not healthy considering it was a hospital. Then she saw Jo out of the corner of her eye searching the cafe for her so she raised her hand to wave. She was wearing a fitted black velvet hat hiding most of her grey hair and her signature earrings, long and dangling. Her black coat was open, exposing a dress in dark and light green, cut low at the neck. "Do you want a coffee?"

"No thanks. I had one at the university just before I left." She surveyed the café. "I really hate hospitals," She breathed out heavily. "They still remind me too much of Barry."

As Jo spoke, she could see the face of smiling Barry, Jo's husband, who had died of cancer in this hospital less than a year ago. They'd met when they were students and Barry, a physicist, had got a job at Newcastle University. They'd been lucky because Jo had also managed to get a job there as a clinical psychologist, once she'd finished her PhD.

Alex shuddered. "This hospital always gives me the creeps because it's where my dad died." She stood up and they left the cafe.

"You can walk for miles along these corridors. They feel longer than those in the RVI or the General Hospital. Maybe this is the way they keep the staff fit," Jo panted as they rushed to catch the lift.

They got out of the lift on the third floor and Alex, who had a terrible sense of direction, realised that they weren't far away from the Oncology Department where she'd met Stephen Bailey. The door of the office was opened by a smiling woman with honey-blond hair and an oval-shaped face. She fumbled for the warrant card in her pocket.

"Please come in and sit down," the counsellor, Maggie Russell, said.

She'd attempted to make the room more cheerful than the bland clinical rooms where the consultants sat behind desks to make diagnoses. There were no plants or flowers because they weren't allowed in hospitals now, but rather than the plastic chairs used elsewhere in the hospital, brightly coloured cushions had been scattered on the comfortable armchairs. There was a strong smell of perfume, and she wondered whether Maggie Russell was using it liberally to deliberately mask the smell of 'hospital'. "Thank you for seeing us at such short notice. I'm investigating the death of Helen Carter and I know from Mr Bailey, her oncologist, that she'd seen you at least once."

"She saw me twice," she corrected her.

Alex continued. "I know from Mr Bailey that Helen Carter was making a connection between her ovarian cancer and an abortion. Did she tell you the circumstances behind the abortion?" She took the Court Order out of her handbag and passed it over to Maggie Russell. She read it and passed it back.

"Yes, I know about the abortion and the rape which led to it." She shuffled in her chair. She was wearing a long brown ankle-length skirt and a white fitted blouse.

"We're interested in exploring this with you," she said.

She inhaled deeply. "If I start at the beginning." She looked at the file on her knee. "I think it's safe to say that she accepted that because of the circumstances of the pregnancy, she had no alternative but to have an abortion. However, she didn't feel that she received the support she should've had after the termination."

"By circumstances, you mean rape?"

"Yes."

"Can you tell us what you know about the rape?" She wanted to know if Helen Carter had been telling everyone the same story.

Maggie crossed her legs. "She said she was raped at a student party about thirty years ago."

This was the same at least. "Did she say who was responsible?"

"She said there was more than one man involved and she was too frightened to go to the police to report it." Concern crossed her face as she said this.

This was the first mention of Helen Carter being too frightened to go to the police. But it wasn't unusual. Many rapes were never reported. "And she didn't give you the names of any of the men who raped her?"

She shook her head. "No. I'm afraid not."

"You mentioned she didn't receive support?"

"Yes, that's right. Her family, and in particular she mentioned her mother."

Alex frowned. "Can you be a bit more specific?"

"She presented her mother as someone who didn't accept responsibility and had a tendency to panic. Her father took all the decisions and dealt with any difficulties. However, this was a time when she really needed a mother, another woman... and she felt badly let down. Her sister was too young and immature herself to be of much use."

"Go on," Alex said.

"She said that she ended up with depression and nowadays a counsellor or psychologist would've been involved, but back then there was a lot of stigma about seeking psychological help." She turned to Jo for corroboration, but none seemed to be forthcoming.

"Did she give you any indication of how her symptoms of depression manifested?" Alex asked.

"Yes, she said she had nightmares. She imagined the body of a baby in a bucket at the bottom of the bed. You see, she'd been over four months pregnant before she realised... and she'd had to go through a surgical abortion. The process is more complicated and involves dilation and evacuation and the whole thing can take up to a day. I think part of the problem was that they only put her under local anaesthetic and so she was conscious when it was going on.... It would've been better if they'd used a general anaesthetic." She breathed out. "She said she'd concentration issues and developed an eating disorder which today we'd probably recognise as bulimia. None of these symptoms are unusual following an abortion but the statistics depend on the source." She patted the file on her knee. "The conservative estimate is that about ten percent of woman suffer some form of mental health issue following an abortion. But that ten percent is linked to people who already had mental health issues... or who have religious scruples... or have been coerced into the abortion... or have received no support." She paused. "Of course, if you look at Pro Life statistics, the incidence of mental health issues is higher... I didn't get long enough with Helen Carter to explore some of these issues."

Alex noticed that Jo had been unusually quiet and hadn't asked any questions so far. Maggie's eyes moved in Jo's direction too. "So, she blamed her mother for not supporting her, and what about the men involved?"

"She was very angry with them." She placed her hands palms up on the file on her knees. "She felt that they'd ruined her life."

Alex's eyes widened slightly. "How so? She was married and had a daughter."

"She didn't present the marriage as particularly happy, although clearly the person she loved most was her daughter, Rebecca."

"Did she mention any extra-marital affairs?"

"No. Not to me." She leant back in her chair.

"And did you get the impression that she might seek revenge on these men?" Alex asked.

Maggie shot her a glance. "All she kept repeating was that they'd got away lightly and had gone on to have happy marriages and family lives."

"Did she tell you how she knew that?"

"No. I'm afraid not."

"But she continued to make a connection between the abortion and her ovarian cancer?"

"Yes, she did, despite my best efforts .. and the best efforts of Mr Bailey. She was a church-goer, as you probably know, and so I suggested she talked to her priest."

"About the abortion?"

"Yes, and about forgiveness."

"And so, you think she accepted this?"

She shook her head. "Not the last time I saw her."

"And when was that?"

She stood up and went over to her computer. "Three weeks ago."

"And do you think she was suicidal?"

"There was nothing to indicate that."

Alan Carter was sure his wife was going to fight on. "You got the impression she was going to fight on?"

"I couldn't say. You see her mind was totally in the past and what she saw as a ruined life. It was difficult to steer her away from that. My professional opinion is that she was a deeply troubled woman who had been haunted throughout her adult life by the events of one night when she was young." Sadness creased her face. "Perhaps if her marriage had been happy things might've been different. But even her love for her daughter didn't seem to be strong enough to heal the wound."

Alex turned her eyes towards Jo who still wasn't showing any signs of engaging in the conversation. "Is there anything else you think we should know?"

Maggie shook her head. "I'm just sorry I didn't have time to help her more before she died. I can only hope she saw her priest and he was able to help."

Alex smiled at her. "Thank you for your time."

As soon as they left the room, Alex turned to Jo. "What's wrong? I know I didn't get time to brief you properly before we went in, but we've winged it in more difficult circumstances."

"Let's go and have a coffee and a chat," Jo said.

"We're near enough to both our houses. Where do you want to go?" Alex asked.

"Let's go to my place."

***

Alex walked behind Jo, through the door of her house, located on the other side of Jesmond Dene from her own home. It was a lovely location on the east side of Newcastle. A steep-sided park, with the River Ouse running through it, established in the nineteenth century by Lord Armstrong. Jo's was a terraced house overlooking the steep-sided Dene. Her bike was propped against the wall in the narrow hallway; it was one of her two concessions to keeping fit in middle-age. The other was walking.

A lot of academics, like Jo, lived in Jesmond because of its close proximity to the university, and some of them, like Jo, cycled into work. Jo too, was coping with the emptiness of a house which had once been full. Barry was gone and her daughter, Emma, was now living in London: but she still had Bernie, her golden Labrador to keep her company. And the two of them, although on opposite sides of the Dene, could be at each other's houses with a brisk ten-minute walk across Armstrong Bridge, and that had been happening a lot over the past year.

She contemplated Jo's kitchen anew. She'd always thought it was large, because it was larger than hers, but after seeing the Thomson kitchen she came to the conclusion it was medium-sized. It was shabby-chic like Jo herself. A row of red pots and pans hung from the brick wall above the AGA cooker, and jars of different shapes and colours were strewn across a beech work-top. The kitchen smelt of spices – cinnamon and nutmeg. Unlike her, Jo was a keen cook and there were a number of cookery books lined up on one part of a bench.

"I had an abortion when I was an undergraduate in circumstances very similar to those of Helen Carter." Jo was hunched over the kitchen bench with her back to Alex.

She was taken aback. She sat down at the beech table in the centre of the kitchen. But then abortion is and was common even when they'd been young. She stopped herself from going into automatic pilot and questioning Jo, as she would a suspect. It was a professional hazard, as it was for Jo, who always asked how do you 'feel' when she posed questions deliberately evoking emotion. As Jo turned around, she could see her eyes were full and she was close to tears – she was more prone to tears than her. "I'm sorry, Jo. I didn't get the chance to brief you before we met the counsellor."

Jo placed two mugs of coffee on the table and then sat down opposite her. "There's really no problem, Alex. I've encountered this type of issue throughout my professional career and I've had to process my own feelings because of that. The circumstances of Helen Carter's abortion were very similar to my own. I got pregnant at a student party, didn't know who the father was, and I was in the middle of my degree.... And we were in the hospital where Barry died."

She'd started to feel guilty. "Do you think you came back to work for us too soon?"

"No... No. I'm fine really."

"Are you sure?" She frowned her concern. She hadn't faced anything like this before. In fact, Jo could be tough when it came to her attitude to suspects. When she'd questioned her about this, it became clear that it was the same mechanism which they used in the police. Emotional detachment. It was necessary when you were dealing with the worst side of human nature a lot of the time. You needed to protect yourself.

"Yes. I am. I'll be fine going forward." Her face mirrored her determination.

"I'm feeling a bit conflicted about Helen Carter." Alex put her elbows on the kitchen table and rested her chin in her hands. "Neither of us liked her when we met her at the charity event. But I'm beginning to feel sorry for her." She felt a wave of compassion sweep across her as she thought of the story which had unfolded so far. A terminal cancer diagnosis. A teenage mistake. Trauma. "The abortion seems to have haunted her through her adult life."

"But we don't know enough yet," Jo said. "The cancer diagnosis might've triggered the scenario about the abortion... the need to have something to blame... brought on by the shock. She might've rationalised the abortion before the cancer diagnosis and not thought about it again until recently."

Alex paused for a moment before she continued. "You had an abortion and went on to have a happy marriage. And as you've just said, you rationalised the abortion. I met Linda Vickers, the mother of the county-line boy, Adam. She was brave enough to go ahead with a pregnancy when she was only sixteen. Her parents threw her out. And she was deserted by Adam's father." She frowned. "And now we have Helen Carter who had an abortion in similar circumstances to your own... and yet doesn't seem to have rationalised it."

"Different personalities, Alex. People respond in different ways. Helen Carter may've been like her mother, not able to accept responsibility. Or at least what she told the counsellor, Maggie Russell, her mother was like. And that may be the reason why she had to blame something for her cancer."

Alex took her mobile out of her bag.

"Dave, can you get someone to check the private detectives in Newcastle and see if anyone has been hired by Helen Carter to look into Neil Thomson, Peter Dodd and Terry Marshall." She pre-empted Dave's obvious question. "We've just spoken to a counsellor who'd seen Helen Carter... and it seems she knew what was going on in their lives."

"Righty ho."

"Oh, and Dave, get the CCTV checked around their houses to see if Helen Carter has been following them.... And we'd better get uniform to do a door to door around the houses where the three of them live."

CHAPTER 11

The office of the private detective Helen Carter had hired was on the first floor, above some shops, on Grainger Street in the centre of Newcastle. The door was opened by a man in his thirties, smartly dressed in slacks and a shirt. She pulled out her warrant card. "Jason Bentley?"

"That's right." He held out his hand and smiled at her with dark brown eyes. "You must be DCI Shaftoe?"

She took his hand. "You've been talking to one of my officers about some work you did for Mrs Helen Carter." She followed him into a small one-room office and it became immediately obvious that he was a one-man show. He noticed her scanning the room.

"We do most of our work on this now." He pointed to his laptop. "I only have the office to meet clients. I don't really want them coming to my home."

She could see his point. The office was cheerful enough with a three-piece suite set around a coffee table. There was no desk, some pictures on the wall, and a coffee machine. "Can you take me through the work you did for Mrs Carter?"

He picked up the laptop from the coffee table, sat down and placed it on his knee. She sat on a chair opposite him. "She came to me because she wanted information about three men... Neil Thomson, Peter Dodd and Terry Marshall."

"Did she give you any reason why she wanted information about these three men."

"No."

She supposed that as long as the clients paid, and what they were asking wasn't likely to get the agency into trouble, he wouldn't be too concerned. "And you didn't ask?"

"No. Clients often volunteer information. It's usually someone suspecting their partner of cheating. . or trying to find a long lost relative... sometimes it's people who have been adopted."

She wondered how many of these ventures into the world of private detection led to violence. She doubted Jason Bentley would know. These agencies had been a fact of life for all of her time in the police. She hadn't had cause to cross swords with any of them and they'd always been willing to help when asked. It wasn't good for their business to get on the wrong side of the police. "Yes, but she wasn't asking you to find out about another woman. She was asking you to trace men. What did you find out?"

"Their names, addresses, telephone numbers, places of work, the companies they owned... wives .. children."

She thought about all the information available online now. "And she couldn't find this out herself?"

"It's surprising how many people aren't IT savvy. Particularly older people."

"Anything else?"

He harrumphed. "She wanted them followed."

Her eyes widened. "Did she give you a reason for this?"

"She said she wanted to know where it was best to find them."

"And you weren't suspicious?"

"I assumed she might've had affairs with these men... she was an attractive woman... and that was why she didn't want to contact them in the usual way. I might've been more suspicious if it had of been a man," he said to try and justify himself.

"Women do commit crimes, Mr Bentley," she said in her best school ma'am voice.

"I know. But if I'd got in touch with you about Mrs Carter's enquiries, would you have done anything about it? What with cutbacks, resource issues and fewer police officers. Not that I'm complaining. It helps my business."

She hadn't really thought about whether police resourcing issues was increasing the work for private investigators. But she had to concede he had a point. A middle-aged woman enquiring about three men in her own age group, wouldn't necessarily arouse too many suspicions. "So, you followed these three men?"

"No. I don't do that work." He tapped the top of his laptop. "And I'm not trained to do it. I have someone else who I get to do that work. When I'm asked."

"Who?"

"George Hall. He's a former police officer."

She knew George Hall; he'd been a contemporary and friend of Dave Bell's. "And he sends you a report?"

"Yes. He followed the three men and sent me a report. I then sent on the report to Mrs Carter."

"Can I have a copy of it?"

He looked reluctantly at her. "Mr Bentley, one of these three men has been murdered."

His jaw dropped as his finger hit the print button on his laptop.

Alex left his office with a copy of the report.

***

Dave Bell was propped against the bar of a pub in the centre of Newcastle, waiting for the two pints of beer he'd ordered. This was now his local, but it had been difficult enough to find a 'proper' pub near to his city-centre flat. He now lived down the Quayside not far from the station. He'd had difficulty finding a flat in a building that wasn't full of the young and trendy, and it had been a bit of a culture shock after a semi-detached in suburban Newcastle. His wife had stayed on there after the divorce. His daughter had helped him furnish the flat, but he still felt it was a bit too modern for him, although comfortable enough. "Here we go," he said as he placed the two pints down in a quiet corner of the pub, "proper beer. Not that trendy stuff." Opposite him sat a man, roughly the same age as him, with a shiny hairless pate and a beer belly to match his own.

"Here's to old times," he said as picked up his pint. "It's been a long time, Dave."

They had known each other since they'd been young PCs on the beat. "Aye. But you know what it's like when you're in the force," Dave said as an excuse which he knew would be understood.

George Hall had retired in his mid-fifties to save his marriage which had been heading for the police dustbin, like so many other police marriages, including Dave's own.

"This is not a social call is it?" George said as he lifted his pint from the table.

"Na. I need to ask you about some work you did for a private eye, Jason Bentley."

George took a sip of his beer as he listened. "Aye."

He had mixed feelings about retired police officers working for private detective agencies. "It's about some tailing you did for a client of his, Mrs Helen Carter... Do you remember it?"

"Aye. I thought it was a bit funny. Tailing three men. I thought she must've been having affairs."

He wondered for a second why George hadn't picked up the phone to him, but then would he have done that in the same circumstances. "So, what did you actually do?"

"I was trying to establish their routines. So, she could find them. I thought she mustn't have wanted to contact them directly because they were affairs."

"Aye. But three!" Dave had made his point to George as he picked up his pint from the table.

"Well, you never know these days, Dave. Why are you interested?"

"One of them was killed... And your client was there when it happened."

"Then why haven't you arrested her?" George said, his eyes widening.

"Because she's been killed in a hit and run."

George put his pint down. "Bloody hell."

"I need you to take me through everything you did and everything you saw."

"I need to have a fag first. You coming?"

"I gave up six months ago."

"I've tried a few times, but I just can't seem to do it," George said as he stood up and headed for the pub door.

As he waited, Dave tapped his fingers on the pub table. He was dying for a fag himself; it was always worse when he was having a pint, and all he had to do was go to the door and George would give him one. But the reason he'd given up was he'd been the only smoker in the station, and he couldn't keep going to the front door every half hour. Gone were the days of smoke-filled incident rooms and heavy drinking coppers. He glanced down at his growing beer belly. He'd taken to eating biscuits when he fancied a fag.

George returned to their table. "That's better. But I'm fed up of being treated like a leper. And it's murder standing outside in the winter."

"That's why I gave up," Dave said ruefully. "What can you tell me?"

"I put most of what I noticed in the report. It took me a couple of weeks because I was asked to specifically state their routines. It was easy with two of them. One went running in the Dene every morning with his dog at about six. The other one left for work at the same time every morning. It was more difficult with the third one... that is until I realised he went to Chinatown every Thursday night."

George must've made a packet following three men for a couple of weeks. "And you didn't notice anything unusual?"

"Na."

Dave took a photo of the Chinese Triad Chief out of his pocket. "Did you see him?"

"Aye. Once. Going into the house in Jesmond."

Dave took another photo out of his pocket, this time of Helen Carter. "Have you ever seen her?"

"Na."

CHAPTER 12

At Waren Mill on the north Northumberland coast, Alex and Jo floundered between the regimented forest of static caravans all the same standard, colour and size. They were in a sea of beige and green, on a sloped and undulating site, in a thick sea fret.

After twenty minutes of trial and error, they walked up some steps onto a wooden terrace and knocked on the door. They entered a small compact kitchen where there was a sink full of dishes and several dead flies on the windowsill. They were ushered, by Jane Simpson, to one end of the caravan which had a settee and chairs in brown, set around a coffee table strewn with mugs. Alex scanned the sitting area and she could see photo after photo of Helen Carter, most of them on her own, but there was one together with a smart-looking Jane Simpson, and another with her daughter, Rebecca.

"I'm investigating the death of your friend, Helen Carter." Jane Simpson hadn't shown any curiosity about Jo so she decided to introduce her. "And this is Dr Jo Johnson, a clinical psychologist who sometimes helps us with cases." She paused. "Can you start by telling us what happened on Sunday morning?"

Jane Simpson sighed. "I was expecting Helen for breakfast at about eight. But she called in earlier... it was before seven. She made herself a cup of coffee while I was still in bed. She then took her dog, Brian, for a walk before coming back to the caravan for breakfast." She exhaled deeply. "Just after seven I heard a dog barking outside the caravan door. I ignored it for a few minutes." She took a dirty paper handkerchief out of her jean pocket and wiped her nose. "Then I realised it was Brian's bark so I went to the door. There was no sign of Helen and Brian was barking like mad. So, I pulled my coat on over my pyjamas and followed him. He led me to Helen." She paused and wiped her eyes. "There she was, just lying there." Her voice was shaking. "I thought at first she was just hurt or had collapsed. I went across to her and I could see that her eyes were wide open. It was then I realised she was dead. I called the ambulance and police." She broke down in sobs.

Alex waited a few minutes and took a measured look at Jane Simpson. She had dishevelled hair streaked with grey and grease and no make-up on. Dirty black jeans and a long-sided grey cardigan failed to hide her bulging body. She'd expected glamour, like Helen Carter and her daughter, Rebecca, not someone who made Nora Batty look like a contender for the front page of *Vogue* magazine. She'd already checked up on Jane Simpson who'd been married and divorced, when still young, and had never remarried. She'd taken care of elderly parents until their deaths a few years ago at their semi-detached home in High Heaton near the Freeman Road Hospital, whilst working as a civil servant not far away at Longbenton. She was an only child with no close living relatives or friendships except for Helen Carter. "And you saw no one else when you found her body?"

She wiped her eyes with a paper tissue. "No."

"We need as much information as we can get to piece together the circumstances of Helen's death. I've spoken to Helen's husband and daughter already. And we know you were her closest friend throughout your adult lives. I'd be grateful if you could be candid with us. Helen is dead and so nothing can harm her now. Can you tell us about her?"

"She was a wonderful person who life had dealt a bad hand to." She stared out of the caravan window.

"How had she been dealt a bad hand?" Jo asked, picking up on Jane's words.

"Men!" she shouted.

Alex and Jo glanced at each other; the outburst had taken them both by surprise.

"You probably know already about Helen's past." She looked up and raised an eyebrow. "Her trouble began with Neil Thomson and that party. She was alright before then." She leant back on the chair and blew her nose loudly into a tissue.

Jane knew about Neil Thomson. But Alan Carter and Rebecca Gray both claimed to know nothing. Was it something Helen had confided in her a long time ago, long before she'd met Alan Carter, or Rebecca Gray had been born? And Alan Carter and Rebecca Gray's minds had been clouded with grief when she spoke to them yesterday. But she'd detected a flicker of recognition, or at least she thought so, from Alan Carter when she'd mentioned the names Neil Thomson and Peter Dodd. "So how did you become friends with Helen?"

"Oh, Lorna and I drifted when she went down south to university," she paused. "I had some 'man trouble', and with Lorna not around, I turned to Helen who'd always kept in touch with me after Lorna left."

Alex noticed criticism creeping into Jane's voice. She wasn't impressed with Lorna's behaviour and had blamed her for them drifting. "Are we talking about Helen Carter's sister, Lorna?"

Jane crossed her arms and tightened her jaw. "Yes."

It was certainly unusual for someone to start out as one sister's friend, and then end up best friends with the other sister. Another person she needed to interview. "So how did you find out about what had happened to Helen?"

"She told me everything, later on, and I'd already seen the change in Helen for myself, even though we weren't close at that time. Even I could see the difference in her."

Alex wondered about the role played by Helen Carter's parents in the abortion and whether they'd noticed the changes in Helen? And what, if any, action they'd taken? "Did Helen ever tell you the names of the people who were involved in the incident at the party?" She asked, half expecting an answer.

"It wasn't an incident. It was rape. And, yes," she said, "Neil Thomson and Terry Marshall. Peter Dodd supplied the drugs."

"Are you saying that it was Neil Thomson and Terry Marshall who raped Helen and that Peter Dodd supplied the drugs? Or did all three of them rape her?"

Jane folded her arms and her head jerked towards Alex. "Helen said it was all three of them."

"And where did this happen?"

"At a student party in Newcastle," she answered without hesitation, her arms still folded.

"When did Helen tell you about it?"

She gave Alex a look as if to say, 'stupid question'. "Back then, not long after it happened."

"And she hasn't discussed this with you recently?"

"No." She rubbed her nose. "Why would she?"

"Did you know that Neil Thomson was killed recently?"

Her mouth fell open in shock at the news and then she bared her teeth. "After what he did to Helen, he got what he deserved," she shouted.

"So, she hasn't mentioned Neil Thomson, Peter Dodd or Terry Marshall to you recently?" She could see that Jane Simpson hadn't realised where she was going with the questions, although her body language had shown surprise at Neil Thomson's death.

She stared at Alex. "Why would she?"

She wasn't sure if she was the type of person anyone would confide in. She seemed to just blurt things out without thinking and she revealed her emotions too easily. "Did Helen take drugs at the party the night she was raped?"

"She said she hadn't. Mind you, it might've been better if she had." She pulled her crossed arms more tightly. "Then she wouldn't have remembered what happened."

If Rob Patterson was right then this was a lie and Helen Carter had taken drugs. "Had Helen told you that she'd been diagnosed with terminal cancer?" Jane gasped and then the blood started to drain from her face. "I can see you didn't know."

She grimaced, her shoulders started to shake as she took her dirty handkerchief out of her pocket. "Well that's obvious," she snivelled.

"The diagnosis was made five weeks ago," Alex said. "Have you seen Helen regularly over the last five weeks?"

"Yes. I see Helen every week. We're close," she shouted.

Jo eye-signalled Alex that she wanted to ask a question. "Can you tell us what you feel about the breakdown of Helen and Lorna's relationship?"

Alex could see that Jo was trying to calm down Jane whose grief was as profound as that she'd seen from Alan Carter and Rebecca Gray. These were the three people who had loved Helen Carter the most.

"Jealousy," she shouted. "Lorna was always jealous of Helen because she is more beautiful than her."

"Did you believe that when you were friends with Lorna?"

Jane wrinkled her nose as she looked at Jo. "Things hadn't happened then to make me realise." She crossed her legs, her arms already crossed.

"So, what sort of thing happened to make you change your mind?" Jo asked.

"Helen told me she'd had problems with Lorna trying to take her boyfriends. She would try to push her way in when Helen brought new boyfriends home. She'd sit in the room with them and try to flirt with them."

"And did you witness any of this?"

She gave Jo a cold look. "No. But I believe Helen."

"Did Helen go to university?" Alex asked as she surveyed the caravan again and the photos of the dead woman. Jane's obsession with Helen Carter reminded her of the character of Mrs Danvers in Daphne Du Maurier's *Rebecca*. She looked towards Jo and wondered what she was making of Jane Simpson? Jo always cross-referenced people to the psychological types from the *Diagnostic and Statistical Manual of Mental Disorders'*, or DSM for short, because it was what was recognised in the courts. Was Jane Simpson obsessed enough with Helen Carter to be involved in murder? She sized her up again. She was a sad figure in many ways, and like Mrs Danvers in *Rebecca*, she seemed to be living her life through Helen. She made a mental note to check her alibi for the murder of Neil Thomson. But who would be able to vouch for her? She seemed to have no friends except for Helen Carter.

"No, but she should've," Jane said abruptly. "She was very clever. That party ruined everything. She found out she was pregnant. Then she had the abortion. It spoilt everything for her."

"What about afterwards? Didn't she consider going then?" Jo asked.

"She'd met Alan. And Rebecca came along quite quickly. I told her she should've gone." Her voice was getting louder.

"Was Alan the first man she went out with after the abortion?" Jo asked.

"No," she snorted. "She had a few boyfriends before him."

"What about Helen's relationship with her husband, Alan? Was it a happy marriage?"

"Have you met the miserable git?" She looked up for an answer. "Alan Carter is brilliant, mind you... his social skills, well –"she smirked, "he shows no emotion and doesn't talk very much. I told her she was marrying Mr Spock from *Star Trek*. She ended up having to get him help."

Alex smiled to herself about the comparison with Mr Spock and wondered whether the help had come from the Enterprise's surgeon, Dr McCoy. But Alan Carter had shown emotion when she'd met him and he was devastated at the death of his wife.

"What type of help?" Jo asked.

Jane frowned. "I think a psychologist."

Jo darted a glance at Alex. "Was he diagnosed with anything?"

Jane shrugged her shoulders. "Schizoid, I think."

"Were there any reasons given for this diagnosis?"

"His childhood... he was put up for adoption. His mother was unmarried. Two sets of couples adopted him... but then gave him back. They said he was too cold and didn't talk to anyone. And he was married before Helen."

She clearly didn't like Alan Carter. Her team were now researching the background of the Carter family, but she didn't doubt the information Jane had given her was accurate. It wasn't the sort of thing people lied about anyway. It was going to be difficult to establish if Alan Carter was diagnosed as 'schizoid' from the records available to them, particularly if it was a private diagnosis. And she needed to check with Jo what 'schizoid' actually meant.

"Then why did Helen stay in the marriage?" Jo asked.

"At first because of Rebecca. . and then later because it would've been too much hassle to divorce."

"Did she break up Alan Carter's previous marriage?" Alex asked.

"No. The marriage was already over when they met. I don't think Helen knew what she was getting into when she married him. I think she thought he was someone who was in control of his life."

"Did Helen have any affairs?" Alex asked, hoping Jane wouldn't shout the reply.

She shifted in her chair and twisted the side of her cardigan.

"Ms Simpson, your friend is dead and we don't know why at the moment? Holding information from us will only make it more difficult for us to find her killer, if that's what happened." This usually worked, the word 'killer' always brought a reaction even though it was only a suggestion.

"Yes, she did have affairs and who can blame her... married to Mr Spock," she muttered.

“That means more than one.”

“Yes,” she snapped.

“Why do you feel she was having affairs?” Jo asked.

“I always had the feeling that Helen was searching for someone and never found them. It was almost as if she was waiting for a man who never came.”

Alex wondered if it was it a case of Helen Carter had already found that man and lost him – Neil Thomson.

Jane’s eyes moved to the photos of Helen Carter. “Helen was the type of person who needed to find the right one straightaway. Like her daughter, Rebecca, someone to put her on a pedestal and look after her. She wasn’t someone who’d normally have had loads of affairs. She would’ve been loyal to one person, but Alan Carter was just not that man.”

Alex questioned that assertion about Helen Carter. Her greatest asset was her beauty, and she might’ve been tempted to have affairs because she could.

“Do you think she would’ve left him if she’d found someone who matched her expectations?” Jo asked.

“Definitely, because that’s what she was searching for.” Her eyes moved to the photos of Helen.

“And she never found anyone at all?” Jo’s voice rose slightly.

“Yes, she did, or thought she had, but he was married and wouldn’t leave his wife and kid.” She stared down at her hands.

“Could you give me his name?” Alex asked.

“Liam Gibson,” she mumbled.

She scribbled the name down in her notebook; another person whose life they needed to explore.

“Could you tell me who else she’d been having affairs with, particularly any recent affairs?”

"The most recent bucked the trend It was a youngster and I don't really know why she did it?" She muttered.

"A youngster. How young?"

"Seventeen or eighteen, I think." She looked across at the window, then at a photo of Helen and blushed.

Alex glared at her, finding it difficult to believe what her ears had just heard. The glamorous and sophisticated Helen Carter having an affair with a fumbling teenager. How desperate was she? "I take it his family had no idea?"

"I'd be surprised if they did." She snorted.

Even Jane was uncomfortable about this relationship and this was the nearest she had come to criticising Helen Carter. "How did she meet him?"

"She was walking the dog at Budle Bay before coming to visit me. He was on the beach with his dog."

"So, I take it he lives nearby?" Alex said. "What's his name?"

"Yes, Aidan Gibson."

She scribbled his name down. "Wasn't Gibson the surname of the man who wouldn't leave his wife and family for Helen? Is he related to the Liam Gibson you've just mentioned?"

"I've no idea. "She shrugged.

"Is there anything else you can tell us?"

"Helen left a box in my possession. It was locked and I don't know what she kept in it?"

Obviously, something she didn't want her family to know about. "We need to see this box as soon as possible. Where is it?" She looked around the caravan.

"It's in my house in Newcastle."

"I need to get the box straightaway... tomorrow." Would she need a warrant for it? This was unusual. Alan Carter had given her permission to take Helen Carter's shoes, but it was unlikely he knew about the existence of this box, otherwise why keep it with Jane Simpson. Perhaps Jane Simpson's permission was enough? She'd bounce it off Damien when she got back to the station.

***

Alex and Jo left Jane Simpson's caravan and walked back towards the car whilst trying not to get lost. When they were a safe distance away from the caravan, they both burst out laughing.

"She wasn't shy in coming forward," Jo said.

"She doesn't like men!" Alex commented. "She's obsessed with Helen Carter and she believed everything she said without question."

"But I think she was perceptive about Helen Carter's string of affairs. Although I also think there may've been an element of excitement in it for Helen Carter who was bored in her marriage.... She also seems to have Alan Carter weighed up."

"Tell me about schizoid personality disorder," Alex said as they continued to negotiate their way through the caravan site. It had an eerie feel because it was shrouded in the mist of a sea fret, and they hadn't seen a soul since leaving Jane Simpson's caravan.

"They're defined mainly because of their lack of interest in social engagement," Jo responded. "They're aloof and cold and they usually have difficulty establishing personal relationships or expressing feeling."

She raised her eyebrows. "Jane Simpson's Mr Spock analogy."

"That's probably the point... Helen Carter wasn't happily married to him, if what Jane Simpson has said is right. And I believe what she said."

Alex's eyebrows knitted together. "But he has shown emotion at Helen's death. Do you think he could be violent? He certainly had a temper when I met him."

"Being schizoid doesn't rule out violence."

Alex's mind shifted up a gear as she pondered scenarios. Had Alan Carter killed Neil Thomson? Had he found out about Helen Carter's numerous affairs and killed her? But then he knew she had terminal cancer, so she was going to die in any case. She was going to have to wait and see what alibis the team turned up for Alan Carter.

They got into the jeep and crawled down the country lane from the caravan site, driving in spectral white space with only a few feet of visibility because the sea fret had thickened. "The only good thing about this sea fret is the conditions are the same as the day of the hit and run," Alex said to Jo. They were making their way to the spot where Helen Carter had been killed. Chris Laidlaw, Mark Walker, the pathologist who had initially examined Helen Carter when her body was brought to Alnwick, and John Robertson from CSI, were waiting for her.

She parked the police jeep at the end of the lane, just before it met the B-road, which to the right led to Bamburgh and its iconic coastal castle. Below them was beautiful sandy Budle Bay and beyond, Holy Island. But today it was all veiled to the eye by the blanket of sea fret.

She left Jo in the jeep and stood at the edge of the road listening for traffic before she crossed to join Chris, Mark and

John. The three of them were studying the photographs taken by the forensic team on the day of the hit and run. As she joined them, Chris turned his head towards her and said,

"I don't think you've met Mark Walker, the pathologist who did the examination of Helen Carter's body at Alnwick."

She took Mark's outstretched hand. He had dark hair receding at the temples and was probably a decade or so younger than Chris who was about fifty. He was a couple of inches taller than Chris but not as tall as John Robertson.

"There's room to park a few cars here. And to swing a car around. Below is the track which leads to some buildings, holiday lets, I think, and beyond is Budle Bay." John Robertson had ignored the niceties of the introduction and was fully focused on the forensic evidence. He paced over to the area where Helen Carter's car had been parked and studied a photo. She followed him, leaving Chris and Mark behind watching them. John was in full swing, puzzling over the scene.

"To pull in here the driver must've either intended to go down to the bay or decided to turn his car around... Ma'am, stand over there where Helen Carter's car was."

She obeyed.

"Whoever was driving must've seen Helen Carter's car... even in a thick sea fret." He paused and surveyed the area again. "I'm going to bring my jeep over to where the vehicle must've been when it hit Helen Carter. Ma'am, would you stand beside the yellow plastic bin. That's where the body was."

John lined up the vehicle in front of her and nudged it backwards. He glanced at a photo he had lying on the passenger seat. He then looked through the rear-view mirror. "Crouch down, ma'am," he shouted through the jeep window. Chris stood forward and waved John backwards inch by inch. The jeep then stopped and John jumped out.

"I can't see anyone out of the rear-view mirror at this point," he said.

"The victim was killed because the spinal cord was severed and the skull fractured, causing a haemorrhage. It was caused by a bump to the right side of the head," Mark said as he peered down at Alex.

Chris nodded his agreement. "And we both believe that the vehicle was probably travelling at a low speed."

"But she'd have to be crouching down at impact?" Her eyebrows knitted.

"Yes," Chris said with confidence.

"So, what was she doing crouching down?" She muttered. "She had her dog with her so she may've been bending down because of him?"

"I might be able to help you there," John interjected, interrupting her thoughts.

"In her handbag there was £10,000 in cash but nee mobile phone."

This was news to Alex, but then Jeff Brookes hadn't exactly been forthcoming when she'd spoken to him. £10,000 was a lot of cash to be carrying around. Was Helen Carter being blackmailed or set up in some way? She certainly had a colourful past on the basis of what they'd just learnt. But equally it was unusual, in this day and age, not to have a mobile phone with you, at least most of the time. "So, you think she was looking for her phone?"

John inclined his head. "It makes sense."

"So, we think the hit and run may've been an accident?" Alex turned to the three men around her.

John moved to the yellow sand bucket and the two logs that were embedded either side of it. "If someone knew this spot, they may've thought that they'd hit the sand bucket or the tree stumps in the fret."

"But surely with all the coverage in the press, they must've realised by now that they'd knocked someone down?" Mark said.

"True. But a lot of people are frightened to come forward if they have killed someone, even if it was an accident," Alex said.

"I've got some good news and some bad news. Which would you like first?" John raised one of his ginger eyebrows.

She looked askance at John. "I think I'll have the good news first."

"We've identified a pair of Helen Carter's shoes as being responsible for the footprint at Blackfriars Gate."

Her heart skipped a beat, and then she waited for the bad news.

"However, we think it's unlikely that she was responsible for the attack on Neil Thomson." John darted a glance across at Chris.

Her jaw dropped. "Why?"

"Because the shoes are very high stiletto heels, and it's a wonder she didn't break her neck walking in them, let alone mount an attack on Neil Thomson." His eyes moved again towards Chris. "But I'm going to do some tests with Chris to be sure." He paused. "And I've identified a man's footprint in the mess of the forensics at Blackfriars Gate."

CHAPTER 13

In the drive from Waren Mill to Hexham, Alex lost the sea fret and drove west into a bright autumn day. Neither Alex nor Jo normally frequented charity shops. However, this afternoon they were visiting one in Hexham. The team had discovered that Helen Carter was involved with this particular organisation. She parked the jeep near Hexham House, and they then walked up the street towards the town centre.

"It's a long time since I've been in Hexham, and I hadn't realised how many charity shops there are," Jo said, peering across at a shop window.

"I know, but a lot of small businesses have been squeezed out of the market because of supermarkets and online shopping." Alex gestured towards the shops. "If it wasn't for the charity shops these might be boarded up."

Jo stopped and peeked into a charity shop window. "I see that, but Hexham used to be affluent. So, I wouldn't have thought there would be much of a call for charity shops here."

"The only other place I've been in a charity shop was in Edinburgh, in upmarket Stocksbridge where I went in thinking it was a boutique. So, they do exist in affluent areas. Maybe the market is from outside Hexham, with people coming in to buy at these shops because the goods are better?" She stopped outside a charity shop. A doorbell jangled as she opened the door. Immediately to their right was a counter, behind which were two elderly ladies, one with short white hair sitting knitting, the other tall, white haired and standing. "Hello, I am DCI Alex Shaftoe and this is Dr Jo Johnson. We're investigating the death of Helen Carter and wonder if she was known to either of you?" They both looked at each other and then at Alex. She could see that this was probably the most exciting thing that had happened to either of them in a long time.

"That's an awful business," said the white-haired old lady who was standing.

"Did she volunteer here?" Alex asked, noticing Jo heading for a rail of clothes.

"Yes," they piped up in unison.

"She was a lovely woman who worked tirelessly for the disadvantaged. She often helped in here behind the counter, or sorting through donations we get, didn't she Agnes?" She looked at the lady sitting knitting, the needles clicking in her hands.

"Yes, such a nice woman; always smiling. And she was really good with the customers, wasn't she Doris?" They were both nodding their heads in unison.

"She had a lot of time for the elderly and used to help them into the shop and got a chair for them," Agnes volunteered.

"She often gave us a lift home if we'd been working here in the shop. And she'd a lovely daughter, the absolute image of her mother. She used to call in sometimes," Doris added.

"Yes, a younger version of Helen," Agnes repeated.

"There's no justice in this world when a lovely woman like that is killed," Doris stated, whilst temporarily halting her knitting, as they both shook their heads.

She found it hard to believe that Helen Carter had been so good with the elderly. She would've expected her to have little patience with 'old dears'. Did she respond generously to being in a position of authority? Or did she like the self-image of being a good person? These elderly women weren't a challenge to her in the way that women like she and Jo were. "You said she did a lot for the disadvantaged. Can you give me some examples?" Alex asked.

"Oh, she helped run a soup kitchen here in Hexham. It's surprising how many homeless people there are, even in a place like Hexham." She shook her head and tutted. "She helped the church run a shelter for them. They set up beds in one of the churches when the weather is bad. Helen helped with the food and she helped provide the blankets. We're too old for that now," Agnes said while looking across at Doris.

"How often does the soup kitchen run?"

"Twice a week. I think Helen did a turn last week." Doris' brow furrowed.

"Did she ever donate anything?" Alex could see Jo out the corner of her eye. She'd been browsing some of the clothes whilst she'd been listening to the conversation. She was now holding up a dark pink Barbour padded jacket which looked immaculate and was moving towards the mirror with the jacket held up against her.

"Oh, yes, all the time," Agnes said as she hung some clothes on a rail.

"Have you got anything in here which she donated recently?" She knew it was a vain hope that Helen Carter had donated anything she'd been wearing on the night Neil Thomson had been killed, but it was worth a try. Even if John Robertson's hunch was right and Helen Carter hadn't mounted the attack on

Neil Thomson, she still might have the killer's DNA on her clothes.

"Yes, we have, let me see. "Agnes put the clothes she had in her hand on the counter and walked across the small shop to one of the rails. She turned to Alex. "No, I'm afraid not. Hardly surprising since it was always really good stuff.... No, wait a minute, she brought these pair of trainers in last week."

Alex saw Jo moving towards the counter. She'd decided to buy the Barbour jacket she'd been admiring in the mirror. "Can you tell me whether Helen Carter was working here on Friday?" She wanted to know if she had worked in the shop the day after Neil Thomson's murder. She would get the trainers she had donated checked for DNA.

"I'll have a look at the rota," Doris volunteered, putting her knitting needles down and leaning beneath the counter to bring out a book whose pages she then flicked through. "No, she didn't work on that day."

"Mind you, make sure you catch whoever did this to Helen," Agnes said. Doris nodded her head in agreement, her knitting needles still clicking as she said, "They deserve to be put behind bars and the key thrown away."

Alex paid for the trainers which Agnes had told her had been donated by Helen Carter. The doorbell jingled as they left the shop, Jo clutching a plastic bag with her recently purchased Barbour jacket inside. She hadn't had a hot drink since leaving home that morning. "Do you fancy a coffee?"

"Sounds good." Jo said.

***

They walked a little further up the street as it widened out into the Market Square, dominated on one side by Hexham Abbey and on the other by the fortified stone gateway of what had once been the bishop's residence. Alex s thoughts turned to history, it always did even in the midst of a case. She had questioned herself about this a long time ago and realised the distraction was helpful: it took her mind temporarily from a case and gave it a break. But she'd also realised she had a short attention span, unless the subject fascinated her, and it was one of the reasons she hated procedure. That was Dave Bell's forte. Her mind liked to roam; it was how she got her ideas.

She thought about the small crypt, part of the original Anglo-Saxon church and now beneath the more recent Abbey. It was built of stones from the Roman wall by the contentious and argumentative Wilfred, Bishop of Lindisfarne for a short while, and later of Hexham, Ripon and York. She'd always preferred Benedict Biscop, the unassuming scholar, and founder of the monasteries at Jarrow and Monkwearmouth. It wasn't that there was a great deal known about any of these characters, but she'd come to understand years ago in a moment of self-reflection, that it was whilst studying history that she'd developed an intuition about people which she used now to its full in police investigation. It was the reason she didn't like Helen Carter when they'd met her at the charity event. When she'd been young, she hadn't had the courage to follow her intuition about people, except when dealing with historical characters who were long dead. Now, experience had taught her to listen to her inner voice. She normally got an immediate feeling when she met someone – good, bad and sometimes indifferent, which usually meant that the person was neither good nor bad They crossed the market diagonally, to a street which also fed into the market square but was now paved and turned over to pedestrians. They then went through the door of a ubiquitous Costa Coffee Shop, on the right-hand side of the street.

She went to get the coffees and Jo set off to find a table. After she'd been served, she crossed the shop carrying two coffees and two chocolate chip cookies. Jo had already made her way to a quiet two-seater table near the window, and away from the tables where mothers and pre-school children chattered for a mid-morning break. As she sat down, Jo anticipated her question. "No, it doesn't come as a surprise," she said as she squeezed into the corner seat.

Alex hung her jacket on a chair. "But we seem to have two very different people emerging. We're now dealing with Helen Carter as Mother Theresa."

"Yes, but we don't know enough yet. What we are currently seeing is backing up the story in the *Northumbrian News*." Jo paused to sip her coffee. "So far, what we have is a potentially troubled woman... who possibly had unresolved psychological issues... which on the basis of the evidence so far has been triggered by rape and a subsequent abortion.... And probably brought on by the diagnosis of terminal cancer."

Alex placed her hands palms up on the table. "We've never faced this before; we've always been able to combine both the police evidence and the psychology. And the suspect has been alive for you to interview. I have a feeling that the psychology is going to be very important in unravelling this case."

"Then we need to get as broad a picture of Helen Carter as we can," Jo said, "since we can't interview her. And interview as many people as possible."

***

"I don't think I have ever been to Bywell," Jo said as they approached the hamlet. Not far from Hexham, they'd driven to Bywell on their way back to Newcastle.

"It's not a place you'd visit unless you're interested in Anglo-Saxon churches, and you're not." Alex pulled in beside two stone-built churches with square towers, surrounded by moss-covered gravestones and trees. It was quiet except for the rustle of the autumn wind in the trees and the babble of the River Tyne just behind the churches.

Jo puzzled as she peered through the windscreen. "But how come there are two churches so close together?"

"Nobody's absolutely certain. But they stand at the meeting point of two Norman baronies. It's logical to assume that these reflect the earlier Anglo-Saxon boundaries, especially as the churches originate in the Anglo-Saxon period. Two prominent families and two churches. Nothing else makes sense in my experience."

"Which church are we going to?" Jo's head turned left and then right.

Alex pointed to her right and the smaller of the two churches. "St Andrew's over there. It's no longer in use, but the vicar is there paying a visit to check everything is alright."

They walked up a path, past time-worn gravestones, and around the side of the church to the door. As they entered, the church was cold with a faint musty smell because it was no longer in use. But as she looked around her, it was a beautiful, well-cared for little gem with whitewashed walls and a steep wooden gabled roof. Light streamed in through the three stained-glass windows behind the altar. A dog-collared vicar was sitting in the front row of one of the unused choir pews, obviously waiting for them. Alex held out her hand

"Hello, ladies." He smiled and stood up, his nose crinkling in a benevolent manner, and his brown eyes grew warmer as he stretched out his hand. He was a man of medium height, with a shock of dark brown hair going grey at the wings. He gestured towards the pew opposite for them to sit down.

She sat down on the hard, cold wood, slippery from centuries of use, with Jo next to her. She regarded the man sitting opposite her and then said, "I'm trying to build up a picture of Helen Carter. What can you tell me about her?"

"She was a very good woman," he said, speaking in a soft baritone hum. "A pillar of the community as the cliché goes." He pointed with his left hand towards the flowers. "And gifted at flower arranging. She did all the flowers for the church, including weddings."

"And she did these flowers?" They had started to wilt. Flowers weren't of much interest to her, but her mother had been accomplished at flower arranging, and she could see that the arrangement Helen Carter had created was very good: white lilies cascading down from a stand in front of the lectern. It didn't surprise her that the woman they'd seen at the opera and charity event, and who enjoyed ostentatious display, was good at flower arranging.

His eyes saddened. "Yes, for an event here not long before she died."

"So, I take it she was a regular church goer?"

"Yes. Since your phone call, I've had a word with the bishop. He agreed that under the circumstances, I could divulge what I discussed with Helen because it wouldn't be regarded as a 'confession' but rather as 'confidential'. As you might already know, Helen and the bishop were friends. The bishop was supportive of Helen's work in Africa." He paused.

She knew nothing about Africa and would have to talk to the incident team. "I realise this can be difficult." She was much more used to dealing with the medical profession and the issues they had with patient confidentiality. 'We usually get a court order in cases like this, when we need patient information from the medical profession." She had never had to approach the Roman Catholic Church about information from an actual confession which she knew could be tricky, or impossible. But this was an Anglican vicar and confession wasn't such an integral part of the Anglican tradition as it was the Roman Catholic faith. "A court order isn't appropriate for this situation. And at the moment we don't know if Helen Carter has been murdered." She noticed he jerked his head at the word 'murder'. "I need as much information as I can get."

He took a deep breath. "Helen told me that as a youngster she'd been raped at a party. She was looking for forgiveness for the abortion and I tried to give her it." His head moved to the brass cross which stood on the altar. "We don't think about consequences when we are young," he spoke to the altar, "and yet we can create consequences which can last a lifetime."

Jo's eyebrows nudged up. "Did she forgive herself?"

"I told her that God was all-forgiving. She'd been a good mother to Rebecca, and a good member of the community."

"Did she say anything about the men who had been responsible?" Jo asked.

"She did seem to resent that they'd gone on to have happy lives. I tried to persuade her that this was a good sign and meant that they'd turned out good responsible men."

He clasped his hands and rested his elbows on his knees. He was a good man and if anyone could've got through to Helen Carter, it would've been this man with his kind brown eyes and soothing voice. Long before psychology and counselling, it had been priests who had fulfilled this role. Alex suspected that this man was good at counselling people in trouble. She liked him. He too, like the counsellor, Maggie Russell, had mentioned that the men who'd raped Helen Carter had gone on to have happy lives. But they now knew that Helen Carter had had a private detective look into them.

"Did she accept what you said?" Jo pursued.

"She seemed to accept forgiveness for herself but struggled with forgiveness for the men involved." His eyes strayed again to the cross on the altar. "But eventually, after we'd talked on a few occasions, she came to terms with forgiveness for the men."

Alex's heart skipped a beat. Her intuition told her to trust this man's judgement. He said that Helen Carter had come to terms with the abortion, and she'd forgiven the men she'd alleged had raped her. "Were you expecting to talk to her again?"

"No. As I said, she'd come to terms with the past." His voice was firm.

"And when did you have the last conversation?" Alex said. "I mean, was it recent?"

"Yes." He paused. "It must've been a couple of days before she died."

That was after the murder of Neil Thomson. "Was it only the abortion she sought forgiveness for?"

He shot Alex a glance. "She didn't mention anything else," he said in a low quizzical voice.

She wasn't surprised that Helen had unburdened herself to this man with his soft baritone voice and kind face. "And you didn't get any sort of impression that she may've been contemplating revenge on the men who raped her?"

His eyes widened with surprise. "None. Why do you ask?" His baritone voice rose to a higher pitch.

She watched him closely as she said, "Because one of the men has been murdered."

His mouth fell open. "I can't imagine Helen doing something like that." He shook his head slowly from side to side. "No. Not that."

She wondered for a moment if she should ask him whether he knew about Helen Carter's affairs? But she decided against it, she doubted Helen Carter would've told him, it wouldn't have suited her self image with this man. And she had enough information from Jane Simpson who was more likely to know more about the affairs. She remembered what Jane Simpson had said about Alan Carter being anti-social. "And did her husband attend church?"

"Oh yes, unless his work commitments stopped him. And their daughter, but not her husband."

She considered what she'd just learnt from the two old ladies at the charity shop in Hexham. "Apart from flower displays and attending church, did Helen have any other involvement with the parish?"

"She helped with fund raising. She did coffee mornings." He sat up straight, resting his back against the wooden pew. "And in the summer she got people to open up their gardens for a day for charity."

"So, I take it she was popular with the parishioners?" Alex was now expecting to be told that Helen Carter was well regarded.

"Very. She was a good woman, always smiling, who would help anyone with anything." The warm twinkle had returned to his eyes. "Helping the elderly and visiting them if they are on their own or ill, for example."

She wondered if there was anyone else in the area who knew Helen Carter well. "Did she socialise with anyone, or was she particularly close to anyone in the parish?"

"I don't think so. Her husband's work schedule made it difficult for them to socialise in the normal way... dinner parties. But they did join in our social events. And, of course, she organised a lot of events for charities which kept her very busy."

His eyebrows knitted together. "Do you think that Helen has been murdered?" He searched again for the cross sitting on the altar.

"All we know is that it is a hit and run and we haven't got anyone for it. So, we have to consider all possibilities... Did you know Helen had terminal cancer?"

He sighed. "Yes, I knew."

"And had she come to terms with the diagnosis?"

"She struggled at first. And she blamed the abortion for the ovarian cancer... But after the second opinion, she finally accepted she had terminal cancer. She intended putting her affairs in order." He shook his head.

"And do you think she might've been suicidal?"

His eyes widened. "I didn't get that impression." he said. "You mean, if I think she was suicidal because of the cancer diagnosis?"

"Yes."

"No. I don't think so."

She trusted this man's judgement. He'd probably helped a lot of people with terminal illnesses over the years.

They left the vicar in St Andrew's and as they walked back to the jeep she turned to Jo. "I'm even more confused than I was in the charity shop. The person we've just heard about appears a paragon of virtue – Mother Theresa again."

"I'm not so worried. What you must remember is that narcissists, for example, are very good at appearing 'normal', they often do charity work and are generally philanthropic."

"You're not suggesting that she was a narcissist?"

"No. Certainly not at this stage. Nor a schizophrenic, before you ask. But I do think she may have some of the traits. Based on what we've seen so far. Today we have seen Helen's own narrative about herself, the wonderful angel who would help anyone. She was definitely a 'man's lady'."

She raised her eyebrows at Jo.

"The woman's equivalent of a 'lady's man'."

"Your own invention, I see."

"Of course." Jo smiled.

Chapter 14

Alex got out of the jeep in front of the Gibson house. She was going to speak to Helen Carter's young lover, Aidan Gibson, who she'd been told about by Jane Simpson and *was* the son of Liam Gibson – Helen Carter's 'great love'.

DS Ian Turner stood in front of his car waiting for her.

As they moved towards the door of the house, in front of them, parked in an open garage, was a red SUV. They were looking for a red SUV for Helen Carter's hit and run.

"How many of these jeeps are there?" Alex pointed at the garage.

"SUV, ma'am," Ian corrected her.

Good looking, clean shaven, short brown hair perfectly blow-dried and well-manicured nails; he would have put a beauty-conscious teenage girl to shame. He was ambitious and she was monitoring him closely because she didn't want overweening ambition to disrupt the rhythm of her team. Although she conceded that his type of ambition was more common now, she'd never been sure if it had anything to do with the fact that many more young people went to university than in her day, and so the competition was stiffer.

"I'm beginning to wonder if we'll ever get to the bottom of this hit and run. Phone forensics and get someone here straightaway. I'm not leaving until they've arrived." Her mind started working on potential scenarios. Had Helen Carter finished with Aidan Gibson and he'd knocked her down in a fit of rage? Had he gone down to Waren Mill to meet her and knocked her down by accident? The sea fret had been extremely thick that day, the same as the day they'd visited Jane Simpson. She'd ruled out suicide because it didn't make sense. Evidence was pointing towards Helen Carter 'fighting on', to use her husband's words, but she still couldn't rule it out completely.

The door was opened by a dark-haired middle-aged woman with a bad-tempered countenance. "Hello, I'm DCI Alex Shaftoe and this is DS Ian Turner." She took out her warrant card. "Are you Mrs Fran Gibson?"

"That's right," she snapped.

"I'm here to speak to Aidan Gibson, your son?"

Fran Gibson's eyes darted to the SUV in the garage. She obviously thought that Aidan had got himself into some trouble with the vehicle. Not an unnatural assumption to make when the police arrive and ask to see a teenage son. "May I ask why you want to talk to him?"

"It's in connection with the hit and run accident at Waren Mill on Sunday."

Her eyes widened. "Surely you don't believe he did it!" Her voice was brittle.

Alex swept a hand towards the garage. "Your vehicle is the right colour and type. A forensic team is on its way to check it." She could see her stare and then swallow. "Can we come inside?"

Fran Gibson turned her back and they followed her into the sitting room. It was light and white, with large windows looking out onto the garden, and its whiteness reminded Alex of a friend's house on the Greek island of Santorini. They were invited to sit down. Another affluent household. Her eyes scanned the room and noticed the three white leather sofas. "Could we speak to your son?"

Fran left the room and returned with Aidan who sat on the chair to the side of them, whilst she sat down on a chair opposite them.

Alex began. "We're here about the hit and run at Waren Mill last Sunday and the death of Helen Carter." He looked down at his feet. "Could you tell me where you were at seven last Sunday morning?"

Fran raised her eyebrows. "He was where he always is at that time in the morning... in bed. Do you have any teenage children?"

Aidan was a minor, so she was going to have to put up with his mother answering questions for him. "How do you know he was in bed?" She addressed the question to Fran.

"Because I went to wake him up at ten," she clipped.

Her hair was dyed dark brown, too dark, and without any consideration for the fact that the skin tone changes when you go grey. "And how do you know he hadn't got up earlier and left the house, then returned later on?"

"Because I would've heard him leave. I'm a light sleeper and I would've heard the car starting up. And anyway, he couldn't have gone out in the car because his father had it out with him."

She watched as it dawned on Fran what she had just said. Her mouth dropped and she looked from Ian to Alex. "Do you know where your husband was at that time on Sunday morning?"

"He said he couldn't sleep and decided to take the dog for a walk. He said he had some stuff about work on his mind."

"And what time did he return?"

Fran thought for a moment. "Just before seven-thirty."

"That was a short walk."

"He said that there was a bad sea fret and it was impossible to walk. I can't believe that Liam would've knocked someone down and not reported it."

Alex could see that she was working through the events of Sunday as she was speaking. "And where is your husband now?"

"He's in London on business. He's due back tomorrow." She clasped her hands together.

She decided to cut to the chase. "Did your dad know you were seeing Helen Carter?"

Fran stared in disbelief between Alex and her son. "Are you sure you've got that right? Who is this Helen Carter?"

"She's the woman who was killed in the hit and run on Sunday."

Her mouth dropped open. "What are you saying? That he had an affair with the woman who was killed in the hit and run. But she was my age!"

Alex said nothing but held her stare for a few seconds. She then turned to Aidan again. "Did he know?"

He shuffled his feet and muttered, "Yes."

His mother's jaw dropped and she started to shake her head.

"You're not saying that Liam deliberately ran down Helen Carter?" she bit out.

"No, I'm not. But I need to speak to your husband as soon as he returns to the north-east." She turned again to Aidan. "When you met Helen Carter, did you go to a caravan in Waren Mill?"

He nodded, still looking at his feet whilst his mother shook her head in confusion.

"Would you mind raising your head when I'm talking to you?" The impatience at Aidan's immaturity had got the better of her. As he did so, she could see a marked similarity with Neil Thomson, or at least what he must've looked like as a young man. She'd seen a photo of a young Neil Thomson in a collage of photos on the kitchen wall of his house in Darras Hall. Did this mean that Helen Carter had never got over him? "Did your dad know that Helen Carter regularly visited her friend at Waren Mill?"

He shook his head.

"Did you know that Helen Carter regularly visited her friend at Waren Mill?"

He nodded.

This was proving to be hard work. "And you never told your dad that she regularly visited her friend at Waren Mill?"

He shook his head as he looked down.

"Did your dad threaten to confront Helen Carter if you didn't break off your relationship?"

He nodded.

"Do you know if your dad had already confronted Helen Carter about your affair?"

He looked across the room and nodded again.

"Was your affair with Helen Carter over?"

He shuffled his feet and nodded again.

She pinched her lips together. In front of her was an immature teenager who was behaving like a naughty child. So far, he hadn't spoken – only nodded or shaken his head. "Aidan, it would be helpful if you could answer my questions rather than just nod or shake your head. It will be easier for all of us." She'd managed to keep her cool; her initial instinct had been to ask him if 'the cat had got his tongue'. She noticed a cold stare from Fran. "When was the last time you saw Helen Carter?"

"I – I – I – c – can't remember." He glanced towards his mother, his cheeks bright red.

"Can you remember when your dad went to see Helen Carter?"

"B – before he went away."

"And do you know where he went to see her?"

"At her house."

"That is her house in Corbridge?" She saw him nod again. "And do you know how your dad found out about your affair with Helen Carter?"

"No. I don't."

"Where did you used to meet up with Helen Carter?"

"At Waren Mill."

"Do you mean in the area in front of the track that goes down to the holiday lets and the bay?"

"Yes. That's right."

That was the spot where Helen Carter had been killed. At least his mother hadn't been interrupting. She was sitting with her head in her hands. She was obviously struggling to take on board Aidan's affair with Helen Carter. "And you were definitely not there with your dad on Sunday?"

"No. I wasn't. I was in bed, as my mum has already said."

He'd managed a sentence at last. "We'll have to get your dad to confirm that."

Fran scowled. “He doesn’t tell lies.”

Alex observed Aidan closely. He seemed tied to his mother’s apron strings by the look of it. His cheeks were bright red with embarrassment. What reason could Helen Carter have for this affair? Was it power? Even Jane Simpson had been embarrassed about it. Or was she taking revenge on his father, Liam Gibson, because he wouldn’t leave his wife and son for her? Aidan Gibson couldn’t look at her, even taking into account that his mother was there and his shame at his affair with Helen Carter. “How did you first meet Helen Carter?”

“Walking the dog at Budle Bay.”

That confirmed what Jane Simpson had said. “Is there anything else you can tell me that might help with my enquiries?”

“No. I can’t think of anything.”

“Are you suggesting Liam went to Waren Mill to confront Helen Carter on Sunday?” Fran’s voice was hard.

“I’m suggesting nothing. We’ll wait outside for the forensics team and we’ll need to speak to your husband when he returns.” As they left the house Alex could hear Fran Gibson’s raised voice and a door slam. She turned to Ian Turner. “You were quiet.”

“You seemed to be on a roll and I didn’t want to butt in.” He tapped his notebook to let her know he’d been taking notes. “Besides, I was watching the master at work.”

She smiled wryly. “Smoothy. What do you make of that?” She nodded back at the house.

“I’m not sure Liam Gibson was going to confront Helen Carter on Sunday.” He paused. “How would he know she was there? She didn’t have a regular pattern of visits. I think what he said to his wife was right. He got up to walk the dog.”

“And what about the boy?”

“I think he was telling the truth.”

“Yep, I agree. I just can’t work out why a woman like Helen Carter wanted that boy.”

Ian smirked. “Maybe she just wanted a bit of young stuff the way men do?”

“It doesn’t add up. She used her affairs to try and get a husband. This affair doesn’t fit her pattern.”

Chapter 15

As they walked into the plush solicitor's office, Alex's eyes moved towards a large polished oak desk, remarkably tidy compared to her paper-strewn desk, behind which a woman was sitting. Lorna Godfrey's silhouette was framed in a large Georgian-style window overlooking Grey Street. It was hard to see her features because of the light streaming in through the window. Just then Lorna Godfrey stood up, came around the desk, hand outstretched to shake hers. It was a firm professional handshake. She introduced Jo.

Lorna turned to Jo and raised her eyebrows. "Doctor?"

"Yes, I'm a clinical psychologist," Jo said

She now turned to Alex.

She answered Lorna's unspoken question. "We're trying to build up a picture of your sister to help us. And in modern policing we often use psychologists to help us do this." She had mentioned Jo's inclusion to Lorna Godfrey's secretary when they'd spoken on the phone and there had been no objections. But a solicitor like her would know that she could object to Jo's presence at this interview.

Lorna smiled. "I see, so it's not just in TV dramas." She gestured with her hand to a dark brown leather sofa and two armchairs. "Would you like to take a seat?"

As they moved towards the sofa, Alex scanned the room. The walls were all taken up with bookcases full of legal tomes. The light in the room was subdued, and would've been even darker if it hadn't been for the light coming from the Georgian-style window characteristic of Grey Street. The only concession to modernity was the computer on the desk, but the office spoke of affluence and she suspected the furnishings were deliberately intended to give the sense of the gravitas of the legal profession. Lorna had done well.

"Can I offer you a coffee?" Lorna asked.

Alex glanced towards Jo. "Yes, please. If you have decaf."

Lorna walked towards the door. "I'm sure we have decaf but it might be instant?" She turned back to them and they both nodded. She put her head around the door to talk to her secretary and then returned to sit in one of the chairs next to them. "As I said to you on the phone, my information about Helen is more than twenty-five years old." She breathed in. "I saw her for the first time again at our mother's funeral three weeks ago. I don't know how helpful this information will be to you?"

"That's okay," Alex responded. "At the moment we just want as much information as possible about your sister. How about starting with what you know about Neil Thompson and his relationship with Helen?"

"But that was a long time ago." Her eyes widened.

"Yes, I know. But he was killed a few days ago," she said

"And you think it might be connected to Helen's death?"

"We don't know."

Lorna was thoughtful and then said, "I feel Neil was the love of her life, as far as these things go. And thinking back, I can see why. He was handsome and charming and she was beautiful. They made a stunning couple, a 'golden couple'." She breathed out through her nose. "After the abortion, Helen changed. But the extent of those changes was only clear later on."

"Can you tell us about these changes?" Jo asked.

"Helen started telling lies virtually pathologically, but neither my parents nor I realised this until later on." She moved her hand up and pointed a bent finger towards Alex. "You see, we were an honest and straightforward family and none of us could conceive that Helen was lying constantly."

"Do you feel losing Neil was the cause of this, or had you noticed her lying before then?" Jo asked.

"Yes, that and the abortion. I think Helen was romantically in love with Neil and it wasn't reciprocated. She was never a feet on the ground type, but I hadn't noticed this type of lying before then... These events destabilised her." She looked down. "You know, abortion can cause psychological damage to women."

"How can you be so sure?" Alex asked. She had been observing Lorna Godfrey closely and comparing her with her sister, Helen. Lorna was dark to Helen's blond, and she was bigger built than Helen, about her own size. The only thing the sisters shared in common was the same blue eyes, the colour of the summer sky, but whereas Helen's blue summer had clouds, Lorna's eyes were clear, bright and friendly. One aspect of the person which didn't change – the eyes – 'the mirror of the soul'. Lorna Godfrey's brown suit and russet blouse were warm like a cheery autumnal fire. Alex liked her, whereas she and Jo had taken an instant dislike to Helen Carter.

"I talked to a clinical psychologist...You see, Helen destroyed my marriage."

Alex and Jo's eyes met as Lorna's gaze lowered to the floor. Alex peered at Lorna's left hand where a plain wedding band and emerald engagement ring were visible.

"Would you mind telling us about that?" Jo asked.

"Not now, it's no longer raw." Her eyes moved from the floor to Jo. "Helen accused my first husband, John, of trying to have a relationship with her and trying to get her into bed. Unfortunately, I believed her." She rubbed her arm. "You see, my sister was my best friend, or so I thought, and Helen was stunningly good looking in her youth.' There was pain in her eyes. "It cast a shadow over my marriage and we subsequently split up and divorced. I was suspicious of my ex because the trust had been destroyed. He couldn't forgive me for believing Helen. By the time I had my doubts about Helen's story, John had remarried. But that I'd believed Helen, and not him, would've always stood between us."

Lorna's voice had depth without being deep, but it hadn't turned flat and monotonic as she had described what had happened to her first marriage. There was still pain there.

There was a tap on the door and the secretary, a youngster in her late teens or early twenties, dark-skirted with a white blouse, entered the room bearing a tray. The clothes were too subdued for someone of that age, so there must be a legal dress code in a law firm of this standing. Lorna handed them their coffees and signalled to the biscuits with an open hand gesture.

The aroma of freshly ground coffee percolated around them and all three of them reached for their cups. The decaf was fresh and not instant and massaged Alex's taste buds with a soothing smoothness. She must ask what the coffee is?

"Then how did you find out the truth? ' Jo continued.

"She did the same thing to one of her friends. But she didn't succeed on that occasion because her friend believed her husband. Unlike me." Lorna shook her head "Her friend told me what Helen had done and said that she suspected that was what had happened to me. Later, I discovered she had told a series of lies and I started to doubt that she'd had the affair with John. He'd always protested his innocence. And when I challenged Helen, she tried to protest her innocence by saying that she hadn't had an affair with John. That she told me he'd been making passes, that was all." Frustration was mounting in her voice. "What was worse was she was absolutely convincing when she said this. Almost as if she believed her own lies."

"So why do you feel she did it?" Jo asked.

"Jealousy. She wasn't happily married." She paused. "My problem was I loved my sister and couldn't believe she would do this to me." There was a stony expression on her face. "And she also relied on people not talking to each other and checking out her stories. She could lie her way out of anything," she said with disbelief. "It backfired because her friend came to speak to me and told me what she had done to her, and put doubts in my mind. I then talked to my mother and it came to light that Helen had been accusing me of a variety of things to our parents. Fortunately, they didn't believe her, but didn't say anything to me until I confronted them.... Then there was the case at work." She spoke rapidly. "She accused the senior secretary at the RVI where she worked of having an affair with one of the junior doctors and of losing some medical files. She was believed. The junior doctor was moved to another hospital and the senior secretary got the sack. Helen then took her job."

The facts were just tripping off her tongue and she needed no prompting. Perhaps it was her training as a solicitor, or maybe she'd gone over these events so much in the past they were burnt into her mind. "Can you give me the names of the friend whose marriage your sister tried to break up, and the secretary from the hospital?" Alex asked.

"I'm afraid after all these years I can't remember. Helen's friend wasn't someone I knew very well, but you should be able to find the secretary through the RVI," Lorna said.

It was a long shot, Alex thought. But the public sector did keep staff files until the person was seventy-eight because of pension rights.

"What do you feel was going on in Helen's mind?" Jo asked.

"I think she'd turned into a consummate liar who wouldn't take any responsibility for her actions. And then there were changes in mood. She would verbally attack you... and viciously, and then within minutes she was all smiles and charming again. She was completely convincing when she was telling her lies. But when she was directly challenged about her story, she showed unease and got very nasty. She was relying on plausible stories that went unchallenged. If she accused someone of something, she never challenged the person about what they were supposed to have done... because, of course, they hadn't done it. She would accuse them to other people behind their backs. And her character assassination of them was malicious." She shook her head.

"What do you mean about not accepting responsibility?" Jo asked.

"She was prepared to fabricate lies and tell any story rather than accept responsibility for anything if she'd done anything wrong or made a mistake. She became headstrong and stubborn. It was as if she couldn't get anything wrong or make a mistake." Her voice was slightly raised in her exasperation. "She wouldn't listen to anybody or take advice. And, believe me, she was getting a lot of things wrong. She wasn't the world's brightest person, and she wasn't a good judge of people or situations."

"Do you feel the abortion caused this?"

"Yes," she said emphatically.

"I discussed what had happened with my parents. They tried to make excuses, probably out of guilt about what had happened and their part in it. I made it clear that it was impossible for me to trust Helen again. What she'd done to me was malicious. I had loved John very much and it took me a number of years to get over it all." Bitterness marked her face.

"And now?" Jo asked.

"I'm happily married with two teenage daughters. I'm not sure if children make the difference, but I think so. Even if mine are currently going through those difficult teen years." She smiled.

Alex was making some quick calculations in her head. Lorna was older than Helen, who was forty-eight, which meant she'd had her children in her late thirties. There must have been quite a gap, between the end of her first marriage and her second marriage.

"You said you had talked to a psychologist?" Jo said.

"Yes, to make sense of it all."

"And what did they say?"

"She felt that my sister was showing narcissistic tendencies. Her conclusion was that she had a weak character prone to living in a fantasy world, and she hadn't been able to cope with Neil letting her down and the abortion. This led to the fantasy world turning into a world of lies. Or at least that is what she told me."

"How did the psychologist explain splitting up your marriage and trying to break up her friend's marriage?" Jo asked.

"She felt it was a combination of jealousy and trying to prove she was still attractive after what had happened."

"And the diagnosis of narcissism?"

"She ticked enough boxes in the definition which includes lies, self-centredness, self-aggrandisement, unable to take criticism or challenge... I can't remember all of it now." Her voice was beginning to sound hoarse and she took a sip of her coffee.

"And after this, you had no contact with your sister?" Jo asked.

"No, I couldn't stand the sight of her." Her nose wrinkled as she said this, as though she'd smelt rotten meat.

"But your parents stayed in contact with Helen?"

"Yes."

"That must have been difficult to manage?"

"We all got used to it over the years."

"You said the psychologist thought that your sister had a weak character before the events surrounding the abortion. What made her think this?" Jo asked.

"I went through events when we were children. Looking back, there were a number of tell-tale signs. She was unable to focus or concentrate on anything at school. She wasn't rated academically by the teachers. She had difficulty getting on with other kids and didn't forge any close friendships. And she was jealous of me."

"But that could account for a lot of kids, surely," Jo said.

Lorna drew back her shoulders and straightened her back. "I suppose what I'm trying to say is even as a child her feet were not planted firmly on the ground. It's the only explanation I can come up with for why some people recover from a serious blow, and others don't."

"You said she was jealous of you. Wasn't that just sibling rivalry?" Jo asked.

Lorna's posture stiffened again. "I'm sure it was when we were children, but you hope that someone will grow out of that when they get older. Helen was beautiful, blond-haired and blue-eyed like our mother, whereas I favour our father. No one could understand why beautiful Helen was jealous of me, particularly our mother."

Alex revisited the charity event and the conversation with Helen Carter. The way she'd regarded her and Jo with disdain and her analysis had been based on appearance. She'd backed off quickly when academic qualifications had come up. Yes, she could believe she'd been jealous of Lorna.

"I think when all the circumstances surrounding the breakdown of my marriage were analysed, I started to look back in anger and unpick events from our childhood."

"Can you give us any examples?" Alex asked.

"I was academically capable and did well at school and then went on to university. Helen had been very jealous of my academic ability and my friendships. I had a number of close friends and she was always trying to take them from me.... I realised later on, of course."

"Can you explain a bit more about this?" Jo asked.

"She tried to claim that my friends were her friends and would try to buy them birthday and Christmas presents which were better than the ones I had bought them."

She paused. She had been speaking at speed and Alex thought her brain might be trying to catch up with her mouth.

"And then there were the tales to my parents." She paused. "Not the type of tales which would get me into serious trouble, but which would undermine my relationship with our parents. For example, she said I was getting good marks at school because I was the teacher's favourite and was getting help with my exams. As I said, all this came out much later. It's the reason I realised I couldn't continue any form of relationship with Helen." She shook her head.

The portrayal Lorna had given of her sister was as good as any psychological profile Alex could've expected.

"At the time, it was devastating. I had lost both my husband and my sister," she continued.

"Can you give us some more information about your mother's relationship with Helen?" Jo asked.

"They were very close, or so I thought. Helen constantly tried to ingratiate herself with our parents when we were young. But she was much more of a 'daddy's girl'."

"Why was that?"

"Like Helen, our mother wasn't a feet on the ground type, and like Helen, she was a beauty. In fact, Helen looks very much like our mother. When I saw Rebecca at the funeral, the resemblance between the three of them was remarkable. My father, like many men, married for good looks and not brains. There was no badness in our mother but she wasn't a person you would turn to in a crisis. I think Helen turned to our father for support when she was a child, and she got it in much the same way as he supported our mother. I think he tried to support Helen after the rape and the abortion, whereas our mother just tried to pretend it hadn't happened." Her gazed flicked upwards. "My mother was 'old school', like many women of her generation. She thought you should be a virgin when you got married and brought us up to believe that. Which was, of course, at odds with the behaviour of our generation and what was expected in relationships. She was very much into how you looked, and clothes." She clenched her jaw and crossed her arms. "They should've got Helen proper help from a psychologist or a counsellor, but it wasn't the done thing back then. And I'm not sure the services were available in the way they are today."

Alex could see the combination of disbelief, frustration and annoyance in Lorna's body language. "Have you got any idea of Helen's life in the past twenty-five years from what your mother may've said to you?" This was the only way they might be able to access this information, or at least get an opinion that wasn't Alan Carter's or Rebecca Gray's, because they already knew that Helen and Lorna's father was in a nursing home with dementia.

"My mother did have to look after Rebecca a lot when she was young. It caused some awkwardness for me because I had to avoid visiting my parents if Rebecca was there. Which was a lot of the time."

"Are you saying this was more than normal for grandparents?" Alex asked.

"Oh, much more. Rebecca virtually lived with them. Helen showed no interest or patience with her when she was very young. My mother taught Rebecca to read and write and ride a bike. Any quality time she had was with my parents who used to take her walking on the beaches of Northumberland, and on holiday with them. My mother was complaining about it all the time, and she worried about the impact it was having on Rebecca."

Was this a consequence of the rape and abortion? Had Helen Carter rejected the child? She'd had difficulty bonding with her daughter, Lisa, because of Daniel's death, but her maternal instinct had re-asserted itself quickly and powerfully.

"And what about Rebecca's father? Where was he?" Jo asked.

"Flying all over the world with his job," Lorna responded.

"And how long did this go on?"

"Until she was about ten. My parents made clear to Helen that she needed to become a more active parent because they were getting older and, of course, the hard work had been done by then. Rebecca was no longer a toddler and needed less care."

Alex's mother had had to do the same when Lisa was growing up. But they were all living in the same house and she spent time with Lisa every day. "And did you learn anything from your mother about Helen's marriage?"

"My parents never complained about Alan Carter. He was a good provider and devoted to Helen. But they thought he allowed Helen too much of her own way. He did whatever she said and obeyed her slavishly." She smirked. "And this was coming from my mother who'd spent her life getting whatever she wanted from my father."

Why had Alan Carter allowed his wife to walk all over him, because this was what Lorna was describing? Her team were already looking into Alan Carter but she hadn't had any feedback yet. Was he capable of the murder of Neil Thomson because he'd harmed his wife? The team would be checking his alibis. The state he was in after Helen Carter's death showed his devotion. Or were they just dealing with a hen-pecked husband? "And did your parents think Helen was happy with her marriage?"

"In short – no. They thought Helen was bored with Alan Carter."

"And you can't elaborate on that?" Alex asked.

"Not really."

"I must ask you where you were on the day your sister died?"

Lorna raised an eyebrow. "If I was going to kill my sister, I would've done it a long time ago. When she destroyed my first marriage."

"Yes, but I need to eliminate you from my enquiries, and as a solicitor you must understand that."

"I was with my husband and children at home," she said.

"And they will be able to confirm this?"

"Yes."

***

As they left the office and walked onto the pavement on Grey Street, Alex turned to Jo. "What did you make of that?"

"I believe her."

"It seems schizophrenic. There are two Helen Carters. The one in Hexham and Bywell is a paragon of virtues. Today we have a liar who destroyed her sister's marriage."

"We all have a dark and a light side. It's like Dr Jekyll and Mr Hyde," Jo said. "Yesterday we had Dr Jekyll and today we had Mr Hyde."

"But Helen Carter is two extremes like Dr Jekyll and Mr Hyde. That can't be normal behaviour?"

"No, it isn't."

"And what about the diagnosis of narcissism?" She turned her head towards Jo as they walked past the grand sandstone buildings of Grey Street.

"I didn't hear anything that made me suspect that Helen Carter had developed narcissistic tendencies in childhood. Living in a romantic fairy story and being jealous of her older sister doesn't amount to narcissism. And anyway, our understanding of it is much better now than it was twenty-five years ago. I heard nothing that was not an average upbringing.... Narcissism can often pass through families."

"Are you saying it's genetic?"

"No. The jury's out on that. Narcissistic parents are more likely to produce narcissistic children because of the behaviour the children are subjected to. There's a greater chance that Helen Carter's daughter is a narcissist because of her mother's adult behaviour. But not necessarily Helen Carter herself."

"I'm confused!"

Jo smiled at her. "Psychology isn't an exact science."

She smirked. "Tell me about it."

"Helen Carter's conduct during the childhood of her daughter on the basis of what Lorna described... is likely to have affected her daughter's behaviour. But I doubt that Helen's mother had this affect when she was growing up... Helen's conduct in adult life is a direct consequence of what happened to her in her late teens. The breakdown of her relationship with Neil Thomson and the abortion. She may well be a narcissist because of these events... but when I've diagnosed narcissism the person has been alive, and I've been able to interview them. All I've got here is the night at the charity event and a brief conversation with her."

"So, you feel Neil Thomson and the abortion explain Helen Carter's adult behaviour?"

"Yes, on the basis of what we currently know."

"And twenty-five years ago, getting help from counsellors and psychologists wasn't the done thing, as Lorna pointed out."

Jo nodded. "Helen's adult personality has been changed by those events. Another person may've been able to get over the trauma and have responded differently. So perhaps we're back to the fairy princess. She couldn't cope with what happened and turned into a bad person. It happens."

"Do you think Helen Carter could've murdered Neil Thomson?"

"I don't know. It's one thing to turn into a nasty piece that breaks up her sister's marriage, but murder's in another league." Jo shrugged. "I'm sure that narcissists have committed murder. But that's your remit, not mine. It's going to be based on fact and evidence."

"Yes. I know, Jo. But if Helen Carter is in any way involved in the murder of Neil Thomson, we will need a psychological profile, more especially since she's dead."

CHAPTER 16

Alex was standing beside the coffee machine in her new interview room when Dave Bell came in to find her.

"I've had a report back from the uniforms who were doing the door to door on the streets where Neil Thomson, Peter Dodd and Terry Marshall live," Dave said as he entered the room. "There's no sighting of Helen Carter where Neil Thomson lives in Darras Hall. But she's been recognised on the streets where Peter Dodd and Terry Marshall live. Curtain twitchers." He remained standing near the door because he knew Alex was about to interview Rebecca Gray.

"What was she up to?" Alex muttered.

"Aye. Especially as it must have cost a fortune for a couple of weeks of George Hall's time."

"What about CCTV?"

"We've picked her car up in the area of the Dene early one morning. But nothing around Darras Hall or Gosforth where Terry Marshall lives."

"Do we know if the daughter was with her?"

"The CCTV picked up two blond women in the car. So, it looks likely."

Dave opened the interview door to leave just as Anaya Patel and Jo had reached it. Anaya was clutching some papers in her hand. Alex poured another two mugs of coffee, then placed them on the coffee table as Anaya and Jo sat down. "Tell me," she said to Anaya as she took a seat.

"Rebecca Gray went to a private school. She was expelled for bullying a girl for being 'ugly'. She then seems to have been tutored at home." She shuffled her papers. "She just scraped into Newcastle Uni to do Media Studies but she gave up after a year. She seems to have had a much higher opinion of her ability than the university did."

"And what about her marriage?" Alex had noticed Rebecca Gray's wedding ring when she'd been clutching her mother's jumper in the bedroom at the house in Corbridge.

"She's married to an orthopaedic surgeon. He's about ten years older than her. I've not been able to find out anything else," she said earnestly.

Alex wondered if Rebecca Gray was a 'lady of leisure'. "And does she work?"

"She has her own company," Anaya said.

Her eyebrows rose in surprise. "Tell me more."

"She audits the green credentials of companies working in Africa." Anaya looked up from her papers. "When I spoke to the company, she doesn't seem to be held in much regard. I was surprised at their candour. Seemingly, all she does is strut around looking good. All the work is done by her deputy."

"And do we know much else about the company?"

"Only that her father seems to have put up the money for it."

"Okay, let's bring her in for interview."

***

The door of the interview room swung open and the slim petite figure of DS Anaya Patel came into the room accompanied by Helen Carter. Alex started in surprise. She'd noticed the similarities between Rebecca Gray and her mother when she'd visited the Carter household in Corbridge, but then Rebecca Gray had spent most of the time hugging one of her mother's jumpers to her face. Like her mother, she expected to be noticed and admired, her head was held high and she strutted rather than walked.

"This is my colleague, Dr Jo Johnson. You don't mind her being involved in the interview?"

"No."

And you have already met DS Anaya Patel. Would you like to take a seat?" A twist of mockery was directed by Rebecca towards Anaya.

She then smiled vividly with a false sweetness whilst her bottom lip quivered slightly. "Doctor? A doctor of what?"

"I'm a psychologist." Jo had chosen to ignore Rebecca's behaviour, something she did in clinical interviews, Alex knew, when folk were being cantankerous.

"And you work full time for the police? "Rebecca asked with a broad smile across her face.

"No. I lecture at Newcastle University."

Rebecca got up and moved from the chair she was sitting in to where Anaya was going to sit, and then looked towards Jo. "I'm pleased you are interviewing me. Perhaps with your brains you will be able to work out what happened to my mum." There was a hint of distain in her voice. "It seems I'm being interviewed by the very best." She again smiled at Jo and moved back to the first chair she had sat in.

Alex had set up an unconventional interview room with the consent of the ACC and the help of Jo. The move to the new office had allowed them to do this. Instead of the usual police interview room with a table and chairs, there were comfy chairs in green, red, dark yellow and blue set around a coffee table. It looked more like a trendy break-out area in a modern office where executives went to brainstorm ideas. Apart from putting interviewees at their ease, which was one motive for the new set up, it allowed Jo and her to study the body language and she'd sold the room set up to the ACC on that basis: hyping up the use of body language techniques in resolving crimes – that always chimed with him.

Alex's jaw clenched. Was she playing musical chairs or was it a tactic to annoy them? If it was the latter, she was being stupid.

"Are you having a problem with the chairs?" Jo asked.

"I'm having a problem with the lighting." She peered up at the ceiling and grimaced.

"I'm afraid there's not much we can do about that. I hope it doesn't cause you too many problems," Jo said firmly.

"That's kind of you. My eyes are sensitive to light. Could I have a cup of coffee?"

Alex got up and went over to the coffee machine. "I'm afraid it's decaffeinated."

Rebecca got up and sat in the chair Alex had been sitting in. "That's better. Can I have a proper cup?"

Alex nodded to Anaya who put her head around the door to ask for some coffee.

Jo engaged with Rebecca again. "Can you tell us a bit about yourself?"

"What do you want to know?" She tilted her head to one side.

"How's about starting with your job?"

"Oh, it's very interesting and I can do a lot to help people, just like my mum. She came up with the idea for the company," she crowed. "She got the idea when she was in Africa arranging for my dad to help the people set up their IT. My mum had connections with important people, so I was able to get on board some companies who operate in the region. I'm now trying for business with the big multi-nationals."

Jo continued. "What is it you do exactly?"

"I audit companies to make sure they are operating 'green' policies, and that what they do is sustainable for the economy of that country." She licked her lips. "That is, they're not causing problems by destroying the land. And I make sure they are giving the producers a fair price."

"What type of produce do you usually deal with?" Jo asked.

She leaned forward towards Jo. "Mainly coffee and sometimes cocoa beans."

"And do you have many people working for you?"

"Yes. But it also depends on what is needed; sometimes a geologist or a soil expert or an expert on beans. I'm surprised we haven't met. I'm at the university a lot."

"But not in the area where I work." Jo said. "You must travel a lot?"

Jo was keeping her voice even and her body language neutral. They'd agreed beforehand that Jo would start the questions, much in the same way as she would conduct an initial clinical interview. After what they'd heard so far about Helen Carter, they were curious about how Rebecca had turned out. Alex's brief meeting with her, when she was in the first throws of grief, hadn't left her with much of an impression of her. She intended to take over with police procedural questions later.

"I check what's going on in Africa from time to time. Mum used to come with me sometimes."

The door opened and Anaya got up to take Rebecca's coffee and then placed it in front of her on the coffee table.

She took a sip of her coffee and winced. "I'm afraid I'm used to really good coffee. I've learnt about it as part of my job." She placed the mug back on the table.

Jo ignored what she had said about the coffee and continued with her questions.

"And your husband doesn't mind you travelling?"

"No, he's fine about it."

"He's a lucky man... brains and beauty."

Alex tried to keep her face straight at Jo's comment. She knew what Jo was doing. She studied Rebecca's appearance. She was wearing a black pair of expensive figure-hugging jeans, black leather ankle boots with a delicate silver chain across the ankle and then a tight-fitting black cashmere jumper – the woman in black. Helen Carter had been wearing black at the charity event. Was the black a gesture of fashionable mourning for her mother?

Jo smiled at Rebecca conspiratorially as she said, "Does your husband not find it difficult with all the men wanting to get their hands on you?"

"He hasn't called anybody out for a duel yet." She laughed.

"I see you did Media Studies at university. What made you change career?"

"I wasn't really happy with Media Studies. The work was boring." She smiled sadly.

"Didn't you think about changing course when you were at university?"

"No. University isn't for everyone."

Alex signalled to Jo that she was going to take over.

"Mrs Gray, you were with your mother in Chinatown the night of the gang fight and the murder of Neil Thomson. Was your mother with you all of the time?"

Rebecca crossed her arms across her chest. "Yes, that's right." She took her handkerchief out of her handbag and dabbed her eyes, her bottom lip quivered petulantly like a child whose toys had been taken away. "Could I have a glass of water please?" Alex saw Anaya get up.

She was determined to pursue this. "Well, the staff at the Chinese restaurant remember your mother leaving the restaurant for a period of time. It's in the statement they gave about the gang fight."

"She may have gone to the ladies. I really can't remember."

"We know you and your mother have visited that Chinese restaurant for the past few weeks."

A few seconds passed before she replied. "My mum was meeting up with people to do with her charity work."

Alex persisted. "You said that your mother stayed overnight with you."

They would need to check that out, if they could. "What about Friday morning?"

She shook her head. "I really can't remember."

"We know you and your mother were in Jesmond Dene... very early in the morning."

"Yes, you're right. I was in Jesmond Dene with mum, or at least there was one day I went to Jesmond Dene with her." She sat up straight in the chair.

"And what were you doing in the Dene?"

"Oh, mum wanted a walk down memory lane. You see she was brought up near the Dene."

"Whereabouts exactly?"

"One of the houses near St Gabriel's church... you know, behind the Corner House."

"Can you explain the dog bite on your mother's leg?"

Rebecca looked her straight in the eyes. "Yes, she was bitten by a dog when we were in the Dene."

"And were you with your mother when she was bitten?"

"Yes." She rolled back the sleeve of her jumper and showed Alex a plaster. "The damned thing bit me as well. You see, we had our dog, Brian, with us and the dog went for him first. Mum and I tried to stop it."

"And what about the owner of the dog? Where were they?"

"Nowhere. The dog bit both of us and then ran off... a dog like that should be on a lead."

"Do you know what type of dog it was?"

"A black Cocker Spaniel."

"Where were you in the Dene?"

"We were in a tunnel which runs under a road there. The dog must have heard Brian bark. It ran back into the tunnel... attacked Brian... and then we tried to stop him."

"Mrs Gray, I want to ask you what you know about your mother's movements on Sunday morning."

"She didn't stay with me on Saturday night, if that's what you mean." She leaned forward. "She was on her way to visit my Aunty Jane. She isn't my real aunt, but her and my mum have been friends since they were young. They were close."

Rebecca's body language and tone of voice were child-like. "It seems a bit early in the morning to go up the coast?"

She smiled. The look of contempt she had given Alex earlier on had gone. "Mum has always been a light sleeper and early riser. She had the dog with her. She would have taken him for a walk before going to Aunty Jane's for breakfast."

"So, was this a regular routine for your mother?"

"Yes. Every week, but not on the same day. It could vary depending on the times my dad was working. And of course, Aunty Jane isn't always at Waren Mill. When she's not, my mum and her often meet at each other's houses, though my mum usually visits her."

"So, your Aunty Jane has known your mother virtually all of her life?"

"Yes." As she said this, her eyes started to stray around the room.

She waited until her attention had returned and then said, "do you know why your mum and your Aunty Lorna were estranged?"

"Yes. Lorna had been jealous of my mum since they were children. It was because my mum was better looking." She uncrossed her legs.

"So, you're unaware that your mother caused the breakdown of your Aunty Lorna's first marriage?"

Rebecca held her chin high and was baring her teeth as she raised her voice. "No, she didn't. That's lies."

"But did you ever ask your grandparents about what had happened?"

She tilted her head back and looked Alex straight in the eyes. "No, why would I? I believe what my mum told me."

"Had you met your Aunty Lorna before your grandmother's funeral?"

"No, that was the first time we'd met." She said it in a very matter-of-fact way.

"And what was your mother's relationship with your grandparents like?"

"She got on well with them," she said nonchalantly.

"And what about your relationship with your grandparents?"

She shrugged. "It was okay."

"I noticed when I visited your parents' house that they have separate bedrooms. Was everything alright with their marriage?" There was no reaction to this question which some people might've thought impertinent.

There was a long pause before she replied as her eyes wandered around the room. "My dad works abroad a lot and when he's at home he can work into the night if there's a problem he is fixing.... My mum, as I've already explained to you, is a light sleeper," she clipped impatiently.

Alex stared directly at her. "So, you don't know whether your mother was having an affair or affairs?"

She sat up and straightened her back. "What type of question is that?"

"A reasonable one. I have to build up a picture of your mother. We know she was the victim of a hit and run, but at the moment we don't know if it was deliberate or an accident. As you've just explained to us, your mother regularly visited your Aunty Jane. Someone may have known her movements and have followed her."

She stared blankly at Alex. "Are you trying to suggest that my dad killed my mum because she was having an affair?"

Why had she suggested her father may have killed her mother? Alex's well-practiced response tripped off her tongue. "No, I'm not suggesting anything. I'm fact finding. Was their marriage happy? And do you know if your mother was having an affair?"

Rebecca flashed anger at her. “No, she was not.”

“And was the marriage happy?”

She shrugged. “It was alright... My dad doesn’t talk much... and isn’t the easiest person to live with.”

“What do you mean by that?” Alex had met Alan Carter when he was in the throes of profound grief, and so it hadn’t been easy to form an impression of his behaviour. But what Rebecca was saying confirmed what Jane Simpson had told them at Waren Mill.

Rebecca leant back in the chair. “Well, he can go all day without speaking to anyone and he often just locks himself away in his study. He doesn’t like socialising and can be a bore if we have company.”

Alex was surprised at her candour about her father. “Has your father always been like that?”

“For as long as I can remember. He was the opposite of my mum who enjoyed the company of people. In fact, my mum wondered if he was schizoid. A lot of IT people are, you know. She even got him help.”

Jane Simpson had said that Helen Carter had got her husband a psychologist. “What type of help?”

“I don’t know. A psychologist or a psychiatrist.” She moved around in her chair.

“That seems a bit extreme.” It wasn’t but Alex was trying to prompt her for more information.

Her gaze started to wander again. “Well, my mum is his second wife and the other one divorced him because of his behaviour.” She was speaking with her hands and as she gestured, the light flashed across the large diamond engagement ring on her left hand which was almost like a knuckleduster on her slender fingers. Her surgeon husband was obviously wealthy by the glitter of the ring. "But you have a good relationship with him?" She was beginning to question this on the basis of her candid revelations.

She shrugged. "Yes, it's okay, but I'm closer to my mum." Rebecca shifted in her chair and crossed her legs.

"And you knew your mother had terminal cancer?"

"Yes." She put her handkerchief to her eyes.

"And do you think that your mother could've been suicidal because of this?"

"No. She was not," she snapped.

"And you are unaware of your mother's abortion when she was young?"

"I know nothing about that." Her posture suddenly stiffened.

"And you are also unaware that your mother was blaming her cancer on that abortion?" Alex looked directly at Rebecca who refused her eye contact.

There was a momentary pause as she took in what Alex had just said. She stood bolt upright. "I know nothing about that," she screamed.

Alex waited for her to calm down. She slumped back into the chair, her head in her hands.

"And your mother has never mentioned a man called Neil Thomson to you?"

"No." Her head jerked up.

Alex noticed a flicker in Rebecca Gray's eyes. She continued. "He was murdered in Chinatown on the night you were there with your mother.... She had a relationship with him when they were young."

Rebecca said nothing.

"And what about two other men, Peter Dodd and Terry Marshall?"

Her eyes shifted about, but she said nothing.

"This interview is now ended. However, I would like to caution you that we will need to speak to you again. You're not to leave the area."

Rebecca got up and swivelled on her heels before storming out without a word or a backward glance, slamming the door as she left.

"She knows more than she's saying." Alex took her phone out of her handbag and showed Jo a photo of Peter Dodd. "Do you recognise him?"

Jo studied the photo for a few seconds. "It looks like the man who runs in the Dene every morning."

Alex knew Jo took Bernie for a walk in the Dene early in the morning. It was something Barry, her husband, used to do before he had died of cancer. "Have you noticed where he runs?"

"No. But we normally see him at the same spot every morning."

"Where's that?"

"Near Lord Armstrong's Banqueting Hall."

"You mean up at the top. Near the entrance?" This was located on the small road which ran along the west side of the Dene. It was a semi-circular entrance, built for the days when guests would've arrived in carriages.

"No. Down at the bottom. Near the ruins. Bernie generally likes to snuffle around there. We either see him running around the ruins or running up through the tunnel under the road. He has his dog with him, a black Cocker Spaniel."

"Have you or Bernie ever had any problems with the Cocker Spaniel?"

"No."

***

Rebecca's mind was in a turmoil as she walked down the corridor. She could hear her heels clicking on the hard floor and her cheeks burning with anger. How dare that policewoman talk to her in that way, and how dare she insinuate things about her mum. Her footsteps speeded as she thought of the questions she'd been asked. She didn't believe the police. They were trying n to pin a murder on her mum because they couldn't solve the crime themselves. She stomped on. They obviously didn't know what her mum had told her, or that nasty detective would've asked her. She knew her dad didn't know because her mum had told her that she hadn't told him – there was no need. She wasn't going to say anything either, she always kept her mum's secrets. She pushed the swing door open and walked out into the fresh air.

Chapter 17

Luke Richardson knocked on Alex's glass door just as she was readying to go up to the RVI. "Sorry to disturb you, ma'am. I've been looking into Alan Carter, ma'am. He has an alibi for the time of death of Neil Thomson and his wife, Helen Carter. He was out of the country. He's highly regarded internationally in the world of IT. He's got an interesting past with three marriages before Helen Carter but no other children except Rebecca Gray. He was adopted as a child It's sad really. Two sets of adoptive parents returned him because they said he was cold and didn't talk."

Luke had a little boy lost look about him as he waited for her approval, swaying slightly from side to side. She smiled at him. He was still relatively new to the job and he hadn't toughened up like the rest of them. It wasn't that they were hard, but they often handled the worst side of human nature and after a while they just stated things in a matter of fact way to protect themselves from emotional involvement. But that didn't mean a loss of compassion. This meant that what Jane Simpson had said to them about Alan Carter might be right. He did have problems and that could fit into the schizoid category – loner, detached from other people. But three marriages! Alan Carter was more than ten years older than Helen Carter and was probably in his mid-thirties when they married. That meant he'd managed three marriages in a short period of time – he definitely had a problem. She wondered why Jane Simpson hadn't mentioned it? She'd been very candid about Alan Carter. But then she began to suspect that neither Jane Simpson nor Helen Carter's parents knew about the three previous marriages before Helen. And Rebecca had said that Helen Carter was Alan Carter's second wife, so she mustn't know. "Have we got any record of any treatment he might've had?"

"The old records aren't very good, ma'am. And if he had recent private treatment, how are we going to find out about it?"

Alan Carter's alibis ruled him out. No point in a court order to pursue the psychologist. "Okay, Luke. Thanks."

***

Alex had decided to walk from the station to the hospital through the town because she needed the exercise – too much sitting on her bum for the past few days. She stepped back into the past as she took her final short cut through Newcastle University. She passed through the stone and brick arches of King's Court, mimicking Oxbridge colleges; it was a legacy from the days when Newcastle University had been King's College, Durham. A cluster of students hovered around the court whilst others moved across it, with the air of intent, clutching laptops rather than books.

She emerged from Kings' Court and looked over towards the RVI. It was still an affront to her eyes, the bulbous new wings in their white and green bolted in front and to the side of the brick building which bore the name of the then reigning queen – Victoria. To her left, St James' Park, home of Newcastle United and the 'Toon Army', loomed above the nineteenth-century stone-terraced houses of Leazes Terrace, once the residences of the affluent, but which were now student accommodation.

She entered the hospital and made her way along the corridors to pathology. The scent of hospital disinfectant turned to a more pungent whiff of formalin, and the sweet metallic smell of blood as she approached Chris Laidlaw's Charnel House – the domain of the dead. She could hear the strain of Vaughan Williams' *Tallis Fantasia* coming from the morgue – a good sign. She had learnt some time ago that she could measure the success of Chris' endeavours by the music coming from his room. If it had been Beethoven's 'Fifth', she would've worried more. And it wasn't always classical music. Meat Loaf's *Bat out of Hell* had, on one occasion, let vent to Chris' frustration at being unable to solve one pathology puzzle.

The metal gurneys had been pushed to one side as she walked into pathology. The red head of John Robertson stood above those of a man and woman she didn't recognise. They were both in uniform: the man in a porter uniform with some red sticky tape crosses placed across his chest. A young, slim blond woman dressed in a nurse's uniform was standing in the stiletto heels which she'd retrieved from Helen Carter's bedroom during her visit the Carter household in Corbridge.

"I'm waiting for Chris before we start," John said to her.

On cue, Chris came out of his office.

John moved the porter and nurse onto two crosses he had marked on the floor. He put a knife, whose blade had been bandaged with tape so it could inflict no damage, into the nurse's hand. He nodded at the nurse and Alex realised that the scenario had already been rehearsed. The nurse lunged at the crosses marked on the porter's chest. John caught her just before she went flying forward as she lost her balance on the stiletto heels.

"Do you regularly wear stilettos?" Alex asked. She knew she would've lost her balance if she'd been wearing them.

"I do," the nurse said.

Alex scanned her feet to see if Helen Carter's shoes were a good fit. They were.

"Now let's try it with the trainers on," John said.

The nurse removed the stilettos and put her feet into the trainers which Alex had purchased from the charity shop in Hexham. The nurse then lunged at the porter.

"She's not hitting the right places," Chris pointed out on the porter's torso.

John then took the knife from the nurse and lunged at the porter who was being murdered for the third time.

"The angle's wrong," Chris said. "You're too tall."

Chris took the knife and thrust it towards the porter.

"Not been committing any murders at Blackfriars?" John said with an eyebrow raised as Chris hit the spot on the porter's body.

"We're looking for someone my height," Chris said as he smirked at John.

"And there's no DNA on the trainers to link them to the murder at Blackfriars Gate." John shrugged his shoulders.

"So, what do you think happened?" Alex asked.

"Well, Helen Carter's stilettos definitely had Neil Thomson's blood on them." He paused. "At a guess, I'd say she walked into Blackfriars after Neil Thomson was murdered. Turned around and walked back out when she saw his body."

***

When her mam had been diagnosed with dementia, Alex's immediate reaction to her condition had been to take time off work to take care of her. But the doctors hadn't thought it a good idea. They felt that Alex trying to care for a mother with dementia, single-handedly and full-time, wasn't good for either of them. She would always regret the decision to put her mam in a nursing home. Her mam had been as much of a mother to Lisa as she'd been and she owed her so much. She deserved a much better end than this. Her dad's end had been quick, even though the speed of it all had shocked them: his body had continued after the massive stroke when his mind had gone elsewhere, but that had been measured in days. Her mam had a lingering existence in a shadow world between life and death.

She stopped at the door of the office of the nursing home where her mother had been a resident for the past six months. Doreen, who headed up the nursing staff, was at her desk. A large middle-aged woman, wearing a dark-blue uniform and sunny countenance. "Hi, how are things with the old girl, Doreen?"

"About the same, pet. She still has moments when she knows who she is and where she is." Doreen shuffled some papers on her desk.

"Has she been asking for me?" She said, her voice shaking slightly. It had been difficult to get in to see her mam over the past few days because of her cases.

"A bit. That is, when she realises where she is," Doreen said in a soft sing-song hum.

A nurse dashed into the room. "Doreen, we need some help with Mr Davis." He had a concerned expression on his face. "He's turned violent again."

"Right, pet." Doreen picked up her phone to arrange for assistance.

She left Doreen to deal with her emergency. She'd visited two hospitals recently and it had caused her to notice how much more pleasant the nursing home was. The corridors were wider than a hospital corridor with good quality beige carpet on the floor matching the cream walls, and no over-powering smell of disinfectant. On her way to her mam's room, she passed a hairdresser with the conical standalone hairdryers which served well her mam's generation with their perms and sets. To the right was the Common Room, but few people used it as most of the residents had dementia or Alzheimer's, with a couple of cases of Parkinson's disease. She'd visited a lot of homes with Lisa alongside her before they'd decided on this one. They thought it the best because the rooms and building were bright and cheerful, and the staff friendly and helpful.

It was lucky that her dad had been a successful businessman, and shrewd enough to build up a good pension pot, because it paid for her mam's nursing home which was expensive. He'd been clever enough to buy up property on the banks of the Tyne when it was run down warehouses going cheap, and he'd made a lot of money when the area had been regenerated: he'd done well for a lad born on the steep sides of the Tyne at Byker. She didn't need to work anymore because that money was now hers, but she wasn't prepared to make any decisions about her future at the moment.

She turned into her mam's room. The door was wide open as it usually was during the day so the carers could easily see what was happening inside. Both Lisa and she had tried their best to make it as homely as possible. Her mam had her own duvet on the bed, a couple of her favourite pictures on the wall and photos of her, Lisa and Dad scattered around the room. Her mam was staring blankly into the TV screen which had some game show on. "Hi, Mam. It's Alex." Her mam turned her head from the TV screen.

"Hi, Lisa. How was school today?"

She couldn't understand how she confused her with Lisa because Lisa took after her father, Daniel.

"Did they give you a lot of homework?" Her blue-green eyes were blank.

"No, not that much." She had learned to play along because there was no point correcting or contradicting her. It only upset and disorientated her. And lately she'd started to get aggressive.

"I miss John."

A moment of lucidity? Her mind often wandered to her husband who'd been dead for five years. "He'll be in to see you as soon as he gets better." She'd been allowing her mam to think her dad was ill when she asked this question. It was impossible to get across to her that he was no longer alive.

"There's been a really nice young boy sitting on the window singing to me. He always waves before he leaves."

"That's nice, Mam."

"And those cats on the roof are back again and fighting as usual."

She looked at her mam and remembered the younger woman: the smart, slim blond with blue-green eyes who had turned her dad's head. They'd had a happy marriage and she'd had loving parents, but her mam had always regretted that she was an only child because she'd been from a large family.

A distance had grown between her and her parents as she'd got older, caused by the thing they were determined she would have – an education. Her interests had become more academic and intellectual and she'd had little time for the things which occupied them. The same was true of her numerous cousins who she only ever saw at funerals and weddings. She suspected they thought her a snob, rather than the truth which is that she found it difficult to relate to the things that interested them. It was, of course, the inevitable consequence of being the first generation with a university education. The same void hadn't opened up between her and Lisa because they could understand each other's activities and passions.

Her parents had been children during the Second World War when the teachers had been enlisted and schooling had been at a minimum – reading, writing and adding up. Her dad had lamented his lack of a formal education, but she doubted her mam would've been interested in it, even if the opportunity had been there. As her dad's business became more and more successful, she'd noticed how ill at ease he'd been amongst the educated in the business community in Newcastle. When she suggested he do something about it he had responded, 'for another lifetime'. He'd been respected because of his honesty and helpfulness, making his money without shady deals or backstabbing. The church had been full to bursting point at his funeral, where she'd learnt for the first time about many of his good deeds. Her heart ached. She hated the fact that the lights were out in her mam's eyes. It was strange to be grieving for someone before they were dead, and she was grieving.

"Alexandra, where's Lisa?"

Only her mam used her full name. The lights were on in her mam's eyes; she was delighted even if it was only for a few moments. She'd learnt to keep eye contact with her to try and keep her in the present. "She's in America, Mam."

"What's she doing there?"

"She got a job and decided to go for the experience."

"It seems a long way away."

"It's a small world now and only a few hours away on the plane."

"Is she being careful? It's violent in that country."

"Yes, she's being very careful."

"I want to go home, Alexandra."

"I know." She took her mam's hand and her chest ached. "I'll get you home when you're better, but at the moment you need to stay here." She'd learnt that a white lie was easiest. She'd never leave here.

"Those nurses have been stealing from me again. Money has gone missing from my purse."

She didn't have a purse.

Alex's phone rang.

"Things seem to be on the move at Otterburn. A white van has arrived," Dave Bell said without any introduction.

"I'll go and get Jo in any case and go ahead with our walk as planned. That is, unless anything goes live in the next hour."

"Righty ho."

CHAPTER 18

Alex parked her jeep at one end of a country lane, not far from Otterburn, on the Northumbrian moors. "Let's get kitted out," she said as she stepped out of the jeep and walked to the boot. Jo got out of the jeep, opened the passenger door on her side, and let out her golden Labrador, Bernie.

They put on their walking boots and waterproof jackets, and Jo fastened Bernie's lead to his collar. As Alex put a camera around her neck, she checked again that she knew how to use it. "Smile," she said to Jo and Bernie as the camera clicked. She'd been given thorough instructions at the station, but like many women, she wasn't into gadgets and used her phone when she needed to take a photo. But today was different.

"Okay," she said as she looked at the photo she'd just taken, "let's walk slowly past the house. If you see me putting the camera to my face. Make it look like I'm taking a shot of you. Pose."

Jo gave a mock salute.

They had been monitoring Peter Dodd's house, here, near Otterburn, for a few days now. Fortunately, there was a clump of trees not far behind the house and they'd been watching twenty-four seven from there. But it didn't give them a good view of the front, and there was nowhere else about where surveillance could be mounted without it being obvious to the inhabitants of the house. It was too remote and the moors too barren. So, from time to time, they'd had one of their officers walking past, pretending to be a walker because fortunately there was a public footpath to the side. And they'd done this when shifts were changing for those doing the monitoring from behind the trees. Today, two middle-aged women and a golden Labrador, out for a walk, looked innocuous enough.

As they walked past the front of the house, there was no sign of life. But there was obviously someone in there because there was a white van parked out front. The house was old and built of stone, but the stone had been cleaned and there were new windows and a door. It had been refurbished and she didn't doubt that it had also been renovated inside as well.

She kept glancing to her right, but there was no sign of movement and no one came out. There was a large outbuilding behind the house and she reckoned it must've once been a farmhouse: sheep farming, there was nothing else you could do up here on the moors. They made their way up the public footpath to the side. Nothing. And then slowly up the incline towards the moors where she waited for Jo and Bernie at the top, both of their gaits slowed by arthritis, Jo leaning heavily on her walking sticks.

"I'm creaking," Jo said as she panted to a stop beside her. "I wonder how long it's going to be before I have to get my knees replaced?"

They began to walk towards the trees. It was a windy autumn day with clouds sweeping across a slate-grey sky which capped the moody green and brown of the moors. It was a barren beauty with rough grass and heather. To her left was the large swathe of Otterburn Military Camp, which had been established before the First World War, and had been the base for training many

British soldiers since then. It accounted for nearly a quarter of what was now the Northumbrian National Park.

"Heathcliff," Jo gasped out as she walked.

As she turned to Jo, the wind blew her hair in her face.

"Well, *Wuthering Heights* could easily have been set up here. It's the same type of country as the Yorkshire Moors," Jo said.

"I see what you mean. But the Bronte's were born in your native Yorkshire and not here."

They had walked past and to the side of the small, thin, copse of wind-beaten trees. They were now doubling back into the copse to talk to Ian Turner and Luke Richardson who were currently doing surveillance there.

She could see the blond head of Luke, at the edge of the copse nearest the house, crouched down behind a boulder. They didn't hear her approach, probably because of the howl of the wind through the trees. "You two would be dead if anyone had crept up behind you." They both jumped and turned around. "Keep your eyes on the house. We don't want to miss anything." They turned back. Bernie decided he wanted to make some new friends so he went across to Ian and Luke, tail wagging, pushing his nose up against first one of their faces and then the other. They both managed to pat him whilst crouched down and keeping their eyes on the house.

"Anything to report? We saw nothing as we passed."

"We got a shot of a Chinese man coming out of the back of the house about twenty minutes ago," Luke said enthusiastically.

"And?"

"I sent it across to Anaya. She's just come back and said it was the Chinese chemist who Neil Thomson recruited... Li Qi-ang. And who we think he saw with the Chinese Triad Chief and Peter Dodd in Chinatown."

Just then, the white van which had been parked at the front of the house came around to the back and a Chinese man got out of the driver's side of the van. Ian and Luke's cameras clicked. The Chinese man went into the back of house.

"It's not the same man as before," Luke said as he peered into his camera screen. "This one's taller."

Alex bent down and peered over Luke's shoulder at the photo. "Luke, take your USB out and put it into my camera."

She pulled her phone out of her pocket. "The reception seems to be good up here," she realised with relief.

"I think it's because we're near the Military Camp," Ian said.

"Dave," she said into her phone. "I think we might have some action up here. They've moved a van to the back. Have we got everything in place?"

"Aye. The uniform is on standby in Otterburn. The Military Camp knows. They will block any attempted escape along the country lane in their direction. They will lock the gate."

"We've just spotted a tall Chinese man. He might be the one we're after for the gang fight, Dave... If the van moves, we move. But I'd love to get Peter Dodd. Let's hold off to the last minute."

"Righty ho."

She turned to Ian and Luke. "You heard what I just said. If the second man is the Chinese man responsible for the gang fight, he's likely to be carrying a knife." She pointed to their bags. "Put your protective clothing on, just in case." She paused. "We might have the *Battle of Otterburn* on our hands."

Ian smiled. "Or perhaps the *Ballad of Chevy Chase.*"

He was a history graduate and was the only one around her who understood any of her historical references. She was impressed with his reference to *Chevy Chase* because he wasn't from around these parts. *Chevy Chase* was a set to between the English and Scots, not far from here in the Cheviot Hills. *The Battle of Otterburn* was fought between the Percy's, as Dukes of Northumberland, and the Scottish Douglas' in the fourteenth century – the Scots were victorious. "Then we'll have to pretend we're Scots," Ian smiled again whilst the other two looked blank.

Her phone buzzed. She'd switched it onto silent.

"Good news." It was Dave. "Peter Dodd has left Newcastle and is heading up towards Otterburn."

"Then we're ready to move."

"Aye."

"I'm heading down to my jeep with Jo. I'll wait there. You park your car past the house at the end towards the military camp. Get the uniform in place. Are the NCA ready to move in with their team?"

"Aye."

***

The police were all in place as Alex, accompanied by Dave Bell, knocked on the door of Peter Dodd's house near Otterburn. The door was opened by the Chinese chemist with Peter Dodd directly behind him. "We have a warrant to search these premises." She held up the warrant. Peter Dodd was trying to hide the worry which temporarily twitched across his face. He knew he had been caught. But before she entered the house, she noticed police officers running up the footpath to the side of the house. Someone was trying to escape. She signalled to Dave to continue and ran towards the public footpath. She drew breath quickly as she ran up the path at a pace, trying not to lose her footing on the uneven surface of grass and rocks. As she reached the top of the incline, she could see ahead of her the Chinese man being chased by two uniforms and Ian and Luke. They were gaining on him. She tried to run but slipped on some rock and put her hand down to steady herself. She ran on. Then suddenly the Chinese man disappeared and the four in pursuit came to a sudden halt. What had happened? She quickened her pace again as the wind lashed her hair around her face. She desperately wanted the Chinese man in custody to see if she could unravel the Neil Thomson murder.

She was panting as she approached but only the two uniforms were visible. Luke and Ian had disappeared. As she reached the edge of a gully and looked down, she saw Luke and Ian standing beside the Chinese man who was lying across the bottom of the gully. She scrambled down to join them as Ian put out his hand and took hers to help her down. The Chinese man was lying dead, a knife in his side. His eyes, in death, staring wide in surprise at what had happened.

"He's dead, ma'am," Luke said as if he needed confirmation.

She stood between Luke and Ian and put a hand on each of their shoulders. They both turned their heads towards her. Their faces were showing shock and Luke seemed particularly upset. She realised that their attempts to apprehend criminals hadn't, until now, led to a death; this was the first time for both of them. "This type of thing happens to all of us from time to time. You're not to blame." She squeezed their shoulders. "She scrambled back up the side of the gully and went over to the two uniforms. "You two alright?"

"Yes, ma'am."

They, too, were shocked by what had happened. She put her hand first on one of their arms and then put her hand on the other one's arm.

"He just tripped and went over the edge, ma'am," Luke said from below in the gully.

"Well he'd obviously pulled out a knife and fell on it. Although he could've tripped and broke his neck. It happens but fortunately, not often. I'm just pleased none of you are hurt. I want you four to go back down to the house and get a cup of tea. Send another two uniforms up here. I'll wait here."

She pulled out her phone. "Dave, I need a police surgeon up here. The Chinese man has been killed in the chase." She gestured to the four who were still standing at the lip of the gully to leave. "He tripped into a gully and has fallen onto his knife. I want another two uniforms up here to stand guard."

She watched another two uniforms come up the hill to stand by the body. She then walked back down the hill to the house. There was a hive of activity around the outbuildings, as white suited and booted members of the NCA team started their investigation. This meant that they'd found drugs. She didn't know any of them and so looked about her for the person who seemed to be in charge. She walked across to a man in his mid-thirties, middle build and mid-brown, short hair. "Are you in the lead?" she asked tactfully.

"Yes, I am. And you are?"

"DCI Alex Shaftoe. I'm in charge of the police side of this investigation. It's my officers who've had the place under surveillance for the last few days."

He nodded slowly. "Wayne Goodman." He took off his white glove to shake her hand.

"What have we got?" She looked around the room which had been set up like a laboratory. It reminded her of the chemistry lab at her school.

"It looks like they've been manufacturing fentanyl."

She knew about fentanyl. It was an opioid twenty times stronger than morphine. "I thought the fentanyl was coming in from China?"

"It is. But it's easy to manufacture if you've got the right chemicals. So, I suppose this was bound to happen."

"Is this the first time we've picked up its manufacture in the north-east?"

"Yes. Or it's the first place we've found up here."

"Have we found anything else?" She was thinking of other drugs like heroin or cocaine. The Chinese Triads had introduced these drugs into the UK through Hong Kong, decades ago now. And more recently they had been bringing cannabis into the UK through the Netherlands and Germany.

"Not so far," he said. "But we're going to check Peter Dodd's warehouse in Newcastle."

"When?"

"There's another team going in there now."

"I think I'd better go down and take a look. We're going to have to interview and charge the two we've got in there." She nodded towards the front room where Peter Dodd and Li Qiang were under guard.

She walked from the outbuilding to the back of the house and found Dave in a traditional kitchen. "I'm going down to Newcastle to see what the NCA find at Peter Dodd's warehouse."

"The police surgeon is on his way." He jerked his head in the direction of the moor.

"Get them two brought down to Newcastle. Let's interview them at the same time. I'll do Peter Dodd and you do the Chinese chemist, Li Qiang."

Chapter 19

Peter Dodd's warehouse was on the banks of the Tyne, near St Peter's and near to where Alex's dad had opened his first business. As she walked into the warehouse, the whole place was a hum of NCA officers in white suits, some with sniffer dogs. "Who's in charge?" she asked of one white-suited man. He pointed at a youngish woman, her blond hair pulled back in a ponytail. She walked across to her. "Hello, I'm DCI Alex Shaftoe and I'm in charge of the police investigation. I've just come down from Otterburn. We've arrested the owner of this place," her eyes surveyed the warehouse, "and I'm going to need to charge him. What have you got?" The warehouse was dingy with cardboard boxes piled up everywhere. It felt disorganised and didn't seem to be a fast-moving business.

"Hi, I'm Sheila Broadbent." She smiled. "We've picked up heroin and cocaine. But it's going to take a little while to find out exactly what's going on." Her white-gloved finger pointed towards an office at the end of the warehouse where her officers were at work. "Although from our initial look, it seems that he might have been selling fentanyl online using his legitimate business as a front. There's some fancy goods from China." She gestured towards boxes piled up against one wall which had been opened up. They had Chinese script written on them.

"There's fentanyl in the boxes over there." She pointed to another wall in the warehouse where there were newer looking brown cardboard boxes. "And there's a pile of padded envelopes in boxes just outside the office. There's four computers in there, so we suspect there's people in there putting fentanyl in envelopes to be posted out. But it's going to take a while to nail down exactly what's been going on?"

"Was there anybody here when you arrived?"

"No. The whole place was locked up."

"What about the heroin and cocaine." She was horrified at the thought that this had gone online as well.

"Couldn't say at the moment."

"How come you haven't picked up anything to do with Peter Dodd before now?" She raised an eyebrow. "He might've been at it for years." She was thinking of Peter Dodd's long friendship with Wang Wei Li, the Chinese Triad Chief.

"We had no intelligence on him." Sheila Broadbent shrugged.

"And what about Wang Wei Li?"

"We know about him. But nothing to do with him has led us to Peter Dodd... until now."

"Have you seen an operation like this before... selling online and using a legitimate business as a front?"

"I can't say I have. But it's known to have happened in America."

"Well, we've got enough already both here and in Otterburn to charge him."

"There's an NCA team about to check the Dodd residence in Jesmond," Sheila Broadbent volunteered.

***

An NCA team were already at Peter Dodd's house in Jesmond when Alex arrived. "Have you found anything?" she asked the nearest officer.

"No drugs so far."

She wasn't surprised that Peter Dodd had kept his home clean. "Has anyone spoken to his wife?"

"We were leaving the questions to you. But she knows why we are here."

The aroma of coffee wafted into her nostrils as she walked into the kitchen. They had become the main room of a house instead of the front room and a lot of time and money was spent on them. This kitchen was impressive but in a different way to the kitchen of the Thomson house in Darras Hall: one wall was bare bricks and the other walls were whitewashed. A breakfast-bar island stood in the centre of the room beneath triangular dark-wood beams and here a woman was slumped with a mug of coffee.

"Hello, Mrs Dodd. I'm DCI Alex Shaftoe. I think you've already been told why we are here."

Sally Dodd's eyes widened in surprise. "I don't believe that Peter's involved in drugs."

"So, I take it you know nothing about your husband's business activities."

"Yes. He sells fancy goods." She stared at Alex.

She expected that they might find that Sally Dodd knew nothing about Peter Dodd's activities, but they'd explore that later in detail. "So, you have no involvement in your husband's business."

"No. None."

"Do you work?"

"No."

“Am I right that your husband jogs every morning in the Dene?” Her eyes rested on another slim-built woman of her own age with hair colour much the same as her own, mid-brown.

“Yes, that’s right.” Sally looked at her with made-up eyes showing signs of stress.

“Did he always go out at the same time and did he always follow the same route?”

“Yes. Just after six every morning for about forty-five minutes and he always jogged down the same paths,” she clipped.

“And he took your dog with him?”

“Yes. That’s right.”

“Is your dog a black Cocker Spaniel?”

“Yes.”

Her eyes widened in a question. “Do you or your husband know a man called Neil Thomson?”

“No, I don’t think so. I’ve never heard him mention a Neil Thomson,” she replied without pause.

“And did you know your husband when he was at university?”

“No.”

“And how did you meet your husband?”

“He came into the hospital with a rugby injury. I was a nurse.”

She took a photo of the Chinese Triad Chief out of her handbag. “Do you know this man, Mrs Dodd?”

“Yes. He’s a friend of Peter’s.”

“Do you know how long he has known him?”

“Yes. They’ve known each other since they were students at Newcastle University.”

"And do you know this woman?" Alex took the photo of Helen Carter out of her handbag and handed it to Sally Dodd.

"No. I don't know who she is."

"We may need to speak to you again."

The Dodd household sat on the edge of the Dene and had one of the most expensive postcodes in Jesmond. It was on the opposite side of the Dene to Alex's home, but not far from Jo's house. It was still light so she decided to have a look at the area where Rebecca Gray said she'd been bitten by a dog. It was close to the Dodd house, and near the ruins of the Mary Chapel, which stood incongruous with the large residences around it. She walked down to the ruins. She had played hide and seek here as a child, but it had been later that she'd come to understand its significance in the medieval period: one of the main sites for pilgrimages, along with St Paul's and Canterbury. Pilgrim Street in Newcastle was named because it was the route the pilgrims took on the way to this shrine. A path from it led down to a stone tunnel underneath the small road which skirted the west side of the Dene. She walked through it and turned towards the ruins of Lord Armstrong's Banqueting Hall which had once housed his art collection. She thought again that it was criminal what had happened. The council had removed its roof after the childless Lord Armstrong had handed the Dene, and Armstrong Park, over to the city. She turned her mind back to the case. This was where Helen Carter and Rebecca Gray had been bitten by Peter Dodd's dog. The best place to confront Peter Dodd was surely the tunnel. He would have to slow down because he couldn't have run past them because it was too narrow. Helen Carter's attempt to confront Peter Dodd must've gone wrong. She'd got to the tunnel too late. Did she intend to confront him again? Have another go and get to the tunnel earlier? The current theory she had for Neil Thomson's murder was that he'd been removed because he'd seen Peter Dodd, Wang Wei Li and the Chinese chemist, Li Qiang, and may've been a threat to their operations. That was since they'd ruled out Helen Carter for Neil Thomson's murder because of the forensics and pathology. But what about Helen Carter? Had she posed a threat to Peter Dodd and been removed? Had she seen something when she had been following Peter Dodd? But she had her daughter with her. She wouldn't have done that if Rebecca hadn't known what she was up to. She had sensed that Rebecca hadn't told them everything she knew. There was a missing piece to this jigsaw puzzle and Rebecca knew what it was.

***

PC Darren Murray knocked on the door of one of the top floor flats in the block which overlooked Blackfriars Court. He'd been here before, a few days ago, with his colleague, Colin Ross, and DCI Shaftoe. They'd interviewed a Chinese woman who'd seen a cloaked figure at the time of Neil Thomson's death. He was here for a different reason today.

They were doing another sweep through Chinatown because they were trying to identify the Chinese man who had been killed at Otterburn. The other two they'd arrested claimed that they didn't know anything about him, except that he was called Johnny. They'd found no identification on him, only a set of keys – car and house. But they also knew that he might've been involved in the gang fight on Stowell Street.

The door was opened by the same young Chinese woman they'd met a couple of days ago, and who'd seen the cloaked figure. "Sorry to bother you, madam. I wonder if you could help us again?"

She smiled. “Of course, Constable.”

He showed her the photo of the Chinese man. “Do you recognise, or know who this man is?”

“Yes. He’s my next-door neighbour.”

CHAPTER 20

Alex arrived at the flats accompanied by DC Luke Richardson. She took the set of keys which they'd found in the pocket of the dead Chinese man out of her handbag and opened the door of the flat. She was never sure what might greet her as she entered someone else's house. She'd become accustomed to being surprised in her years in the police. Had she been met with an untidy mess of unwashed dishes, empty bottles and cans and the residue of drugs, it wouldn't have shocked her. But this flat was clean and tidy.

"Wow," Luke said. "I've never seen anything like it. The whole place is a *Star Wars* shrine."

She wasn't into *Star Wars*. Her daughter, Lisa, had been when she was young so she'd seen one or two of the episodes. "Into *Star Wars*, are you?"

"When I was young," Luke stuttered.

He was, she thought, worried that she may disapprove of his interest. "So was my daughter," she said to put him at his ease. On the walls, either side of her, were large canvas pictures of different views, which gave the impression that you were on the deck of the Millennium Falcon. In one corner was a life-size figure of Master Yoda, and in another corner a life-size replica of R2-D2. But it was the Darth Vader costume that drew her eyes.

It was life-size with the cloak and helmet and it dominated the room. "Let's have a look around."

She was looking through drawers in the bedroom when there was a knock at the door. She left the bedroom and went to the front door which she opened to John Robertson and another member of the CSI team.

As John walked into the front room, his jaw dropped. "This is amazing. You feel you're on the Millennium Falcon. I loved *Star Wars*.

"Another one," she said. "Well, Han Solo –"

"So, you know something about *Star Wars*," John smirked.

"I need a thorough check of Darth Vader over there... cloak... helmet... the full works."

"Okay, Princess Leah. But Chris isn't back until tomorrow, I think."

She raised an eyebrow and waited.

"He's abroad at a wedding."

"I've got enough from the drugs at Otterburn and the warehouse at St Peter's to charge the two in custody. And the owner of this place is dead. Can you get the DNA tests in motion?" she said whilst staring at Darth Vader.

John's eyes followed hers. "Will do. 'May the Force be with you.'"

She looked again at Darth Vader standing in the corner near the window and wondered?

***

The door of the flat in Alnwick was opened by Linda Vickers who smiled when she saw Alex.

"Come in," she said as she let her enter the flat and followed behind her.

The flat was new and bright and Alex was delighted that the Social Services had got Linda and Adam such a good place. She had worried that they might end up somewhere grotty. She had no doubt that Dave Bell had been behind this; he could be an old softy. "Are you happy with the flat?"

"Oh, yes," Linda said. "It's smaller than the maisonette in Byker, but it's much nicer. We have a new kitchen and bathroom. And the bedrooms have fitted wardrobes." She beamed.

But Alex could see that they still had the same tatty furniture that they'd had in Byker. The Social Services hadn't done anything about that. "And your new job?"

"I'm working on the till at Sainsbury's. It's fine. I'm enjoying it."

"And have you enrolled at night school?"

"Yes, I have. I'm doing GCSEs in English and Maths to start with." She looked towards her son, Adam. "So, we're both studying together."

"Are you getting help with your bills?"

"Yes, I am. We're managing better than we ever have."

She turned her attention to Adam. "I need you to take a look at a photo for me, Adam." He was sitting on the cracked faux leather settee, and she noticed for the first time that they didn't have a TV. At least he couldn't be distracted from his studies. She took the photo of the Chinese man from her handbag. It was the one Luke had taken of the man as he got out of the white van at the house near Otterburn. She handed the photo to Adam. "Do you recognise him?"

Adam nodded. "It's Johnny."

"And he's the man who was involved in the gang fight in Chinatown."

Adam nodded again.

"You're sure?"

"Yes."

She saw worry etch Linda's face. "Don't worry. He won't be causing any trouble. He's dead."

Shock replaced the worry on her face. "He fell on his own knife whilst trying to evade arrest. Don't worry, the local police are keeping an eye on you," she said in the hope that it would allay Linda's fear.

She made her way towards the door which led to a short corridor, and then the front door of the flat and Linda followed her. "Bye, Adam," she said.

As Linda closed the front room door behind her, Alex said, "How's things going with Adam?" She'd noticed that Adam hadn't said goodbye to her as she left.

"He's having a difficult time fitting in at school," she said. "He's got no friends and no one is bothering with him."

Kids could be cruel, Alex knew. But it wasn't just the furniture which was shabby, so were Linda and Adam's clothes. She realised that part of the reason he wasn't fitting in would be clothes, no computer and no TV at home. She started to hatch a plan in her mind to help out. "And how's he doing with his school work?"

"I think he's having difficulty with essays. It wasn't something they showed him at his last school. This school is a lot better than the one in Byker."

"I think I may be able to help you there. Do you mind if I call in again to see you?" Alex knew she would be able to show

Adam how to structure an essay. She guessed that this was the problem.

“Not at all.”

“And try not to worry,” Alex said as she left.

***

Alex walked into her interview room accompanied by DS Ian Turner. Peter Dodd was already in there with his solicitor. He had a top brief, and one the police knew because he made a good living from defending the guilty. It meant she wouldn’t be allowed to get away with anything, but she’d expected as much.

She sat down with her file on her knee and nodded at Ian who switched on the tape and then sat down on the remaining chair, notebook in hand.

She began. “You do not have to say anything. But, it may harm your defence if you do not mention when questioned something which you later rely on in court. Anything you do say may be given in evidence. Mr Dodd, you realise why you are here?”

“Actually, I don’t.” He smiled at her. “I’m at a loss as to what has happened here. I rented out the house to Li Qiang. I had no idea what was going on.” His voice was urbane and oiled to a treacly smoothness. He opened his palms in a gesture of surprise.

“Well, Mr Dodd, you may have got away with that at Otterburn, but we’ve been thoroughly examining your warehouse in St Peter’s.

He shuffled in his chair.

“How do you explain the existence of drugs at your warehouse?”

He shrugged.

“And what about the fentanyl at the house in Otterburn?”

"My client has already answered that. He has told you he was renting the house out to Mr Li Qiang," his brief, Karl Underwood, young in years but with a vast and wily experience at this type of defence, answered in an even voice and smiled at her as he finished. He was a small, thin man with black hair and pinched-in cheeks. His suit and Rolex watch spoke of the lucrativeness of his trade.

"It does seem a bit strange that illegal drugs have been found at a property you own near Otterburn, and at your warehouse in Newcastle," she said.

"Coincidences do occur," Karl Underwood stated.

"We are currently searching your house in Jesmond. So, we will see if there is a coincidence there as well."

Peter Dodd shuffled again in his chair. She studied him for a moment. He was about her age with dyed dark hair which made his skin appear sallow. As he spoke, he flashed dentist-white teeth. Her focus on him made him uneasy and he shuffled again in his chair.

"The Chinese man who escaped from the rear of the house at Otterburn has been positively identified as the man who started the gang fight in Chinatown last Thursday," she said.

Peter Dodd glanced at his brief and then spoke. "I have no idea who he is. He must be a friend of Li Qiang."

"So, what were you doing at the house in Otterburn today?"

"I was going to check on my tenant," tripped off his smooth tongue and must have been agreed with his brief beforehand.

"Then it's strange that there was a van full of fentanyl about to leave your house near Otterburn on the day you decided to visit your tenant."

"Another coincidence," Karl Underwood shrugged.

"You were in Chinatown on the night of the gang fight."

"Yes. You know I was. I gave a statement to the police. I was meeting an academic from Durham University for a meal."

"Another coincidence," She suggested.

Both men looked at her but said nothing.

"You were seen in Chinatown with Wang Wei Li, a known Triad Chief, last Wednesday."

"I have known Wang Wei Li since we were students. We see each other from time to time. I have no idea if he is a Triad Chief," Peter Dodd said with the best innocent countenance he could muster.

This wasn't even a game of cat and mouse. She knew they would be able to pin the drugs at the warehouse on Peter Dodd. As a consequence, they would probably be able to pin the drug production at Otterburn on him, particularly if they found fentanyl manufactured at Otterburn in his warehouse. But she knew the Chinese chemist would go to prison rather than shop Peter Dodd, particularly if a Chinese Triad Chief was involved. Prison was better than the alternative.

"We know that your dog has bitten a woman called Helen Carter." She saw Peter Dodd and Karl Underwood give each other a puzzled glance. This was obviously off their script.

"I know nothing about my dog biting anyone."

"Are you intending to arrest his dog?" Karl Underwood said coolly.

"No. Not yet anyhow." She attempted a smile at them. "But then you do know Helen Carter, although she was Helen Armstrong when you knew her." She waited and watched.

"I haven't seen Helen Armstrong in about thirty years." His smooth voice suddenly raised a pitch. He turned sideways to Karl Underwood.

She had rattled him. "But you are one of the men she accused of raping her."

"That was thirty years ago. It was refuted," he dismissed with a sweep of his hand.

"But Helen Carter got a private detective to follow you. And she was following you herself."

"I know nothing about that," he said adamantly.

"But Helen Carter was killed in a hit and run. And the car which killed her is a red SUV. You drive a red SUV, Mr Dodd?" She asked.

"I had nothing to do with that." His mouth opened as he swivelled in his chair towards his solicitor. "This is ridiculous, Karl."

"Is it, or did she see something she shouldn't have seen when she was following you?"

"No." His composure had gone.

"But that's what happened to Neil Thomson, isn't it?" She goaded them.

"I don't know what you are talking about?" He sneered.

"Neil Thomson saw you, Wang Wei Li and Li Qiang in Chinatown the day before he was killed. And you saw him."

"So?"

"You didn't want to take the risk that he would say something. He knew you and Wang Wei Li had been involved in drugs when you were students. And he had recruited Li Qiang for a company that you are involved with."

He said nothing.

She knew this was a likely scenario, but with the Chinese man dead how would they prove it? And as yet they hadn't any evidence that Chinese Johnny had killed Neil Thomson, only that he'd started the gang fight.

"You do realise, Mr Dodd, that if Neil Thomson hadn't died, we wouldn't have investigated you. He did tell his friend Rob Patterson that he had seen you. But he didn't intend to do anything about it. His death prompted Rob Patterson to tell us." As she said this, she noticed a flicker in Peter Dodd's eyes. Just the slightest flicker. She knew she had hit the mark.

***

Dave Bell sat in an interview room along the corridor from Alex. He had Anaya Patel with him. Opposite sat Li Qiang, the Chinese chemist they had arrested at Otterburn. He had a solicitor with him, a young Chinese man who they suspected might have Triad connections. The NCA knew about him.

Dave began as Anaya switched on the tape. "You do not have to say anything. But, it may harm your defence if you do not mention when questioned something which you later rely on in court. Anything you do say may be given in evidence. Mr Li Qiang, you realise why you are here?"

He said nothing but looked towards his solicitor. "Yes, he does."

"You have been arrested for manufacturing fentanyl illegally at The Old Barn, near Otterburn."

"What have you got to say to that?"

"My client is prepared to admit he was manufacturing fentanyl illegally."

"And was Mr Peter Dodd involved in the manufacture of fentanyl?" He asked.

"Mr Dodd knew nothing about it. The only connection between my client and Mr Dodd is that he was renting the property from him." The solicitor placed a tenancy agreement on the table for Dave.

"Mr Wang Wei Li, Mr Dodd and Mr Li Qiang were seen together in Chinatown last Wednesday." Dave said.

"My client doesn't know Mr Wang Wei Li. He only knows Mr Dodd."

"Then what was he doing in Chinatown with them last Wednesday?"

"He was meeting Mr Dodd, and Mr Wang Wei Li happened to be there."

"Is your client able to speak for himself?" Dave said. "I find it difficult to believe that as his solicitor you would be able to answer about his movements last Wednesday."

The solicitor said nothing.

Dave pushed a photo of the other Chinese man, now dead, in front of Li Qiang "This is the other man who was at the house in Otterburn. Can you tell us how you know him?"

"They met in Chinatown a few weeks ago. He agreed to help my client deliver the fentanyl," his solicitor responded again

"And how did they meet in Chinatown?" Dave asked.

The solicitor shrugged. "Chinese people meet each other in Chinatown."

"And have you been to Mr Dodd's warehouse in St Peter's?"

"No. He has not."

"Have you ever seen this man?" Dave showed Li Qiang a photo of Neil Thomson."

He saw Li Qiang shake his head.

"My client doesn't know him."

"You do realise, Mr Li Qiang, that you are likely to go to prison," Dave said, trying not to show his exasperation.

"My client understands."

"Then you will be remanded in custody."

Chapter 21

Ian Turner sat frowning into his computer screen. He couldn't find the file about the paint sample taken from Helen Carter's clothes which identified the car that had killed her. He now had two cars to check – Liam Gibson's and Peter Dodd's. He fiddled about for a few more minutes and couldn't see any obvious reason why it wasn't there. Unless, of course, Alnwick Station had forgotten to put it on the system in the first place. His left hand moved across his desk for his mobile whilst he continued to stare into the screen, his right hand continuing to click the mouse in the hope of finding a solution to his problem. "Hello, this is DS Ian Turner from Newcastle. I'm trying to access the file about the paint sample for the hit and run at Waren Mill."

"Hang on and I'll put you through to Paul. He's been dealing with it."

"Hi. Paul Franklin, how can I help?"

"It's Ian Turner from Newcastle. I'm trying to access the paint sample taken from the hit and run at Waren Mill. I've got two red SUVs I need to check."

"What y'on about? It wasn't a red SUV. It was black."

Ian's hand jerked from his mouse. "The record we've got here shows it's red." He could hear the click of Paul's mouse at the end of the phone.

"I'm looking at the record now, as I speak, and it definitely says black."

"It must be an IT glitch. Can you email the info to me?" Ian heaved a sigh. "I'll get our IT lads to have a look and see if they can work out what's happened." He ended one call and immediately began another.

"Hello, Jim. It's Ian. I've got a problem here. I need you to come across and have a look.

Five minutes later, Jim Dobson walked into the Incident Room. Like a lot of IT specialists, he hadn't yet seen his thirtieth birthday and had been playing with machines since his tiny fingers had been able to hit the keys. Dressed in jeans and a sweatshirt, the IT team got away with avoiding the dress code which governed the rest of them. The eagerness on Jim's face demonstrated that he was looking forward to solving an IT problem

"Well what ye got?" Jim said with enthusiasm.

Ian explained his problem as Jim sat down at the desk.

"We'll have to start by checking our log ons in the station, and cross check them with Alnwick. And then I'll have to check our terminals." He paused as his eyes scanned the screen. "We'll have to eliminate internal cock-up first."

"Will you be able to do it on your machine?" Ian asked. "I need to use mine."

"No problem." Jim said.

***

There was a knock on the door of Alex's office and DS Ian Turner came into the room. "We've got a bit of a problem, ma'am."

She looked up from her desk and waited for Ian to continue.

"We've been looking for a red SUV for Helen Carter's hit and run." He paused. "We should've been looking for a black vehicle and not necessarily an SUV."

"What the hell has happened?" Her voice rose.

"I've just been in touch with Alnwick. The record that went to forensics shows a black vehicle and that record is based on the samples taken from Helen Carter's clothes. Their records show a black vehicle and our records a red SUV. We've double-checked and we're not sure if it's a computer glitch."

"Have we got the computer lads looking to see how this happened? If it's a computer glitch, it may not be the only record with a problem." She paused. "This puts Liam Gibson and Peter Dodd in the clear."

"Yes, ma'am."

"And Ian, get all the CCTV cameras for the day of Helen Carter's hit and run re-checked... both north and south of Waren Mill."

"There's something else, ma'am."

Ian had a wooden box in his hands which he placed on her desk. She realised immediately what it was – it was the box Helen Carter had left at Jane Simpson's house. Damien had insisted on them getting a warrant for it when she'd bounced it off him after her visit to Jane Simpson's caravan.

"We've had to break into it because there was no key... the contents are very interesting."

He opened the box and she leaned over to look inside. Ian took out some letters and placed them on her desk. Beneath, there was expensive jewellery: an emerald bracelet and matching earrings, a ruby ring and a gold necklace with a single diamond. There was only one explanation for keeping the jewellery at Jane Simpson's house; they were presents from her lovers. But it seemed strange. Why keep mementos of failures? It must be because these men had professed their love and it boosted Helen Carter's ego. Ian put his hands on the letters and she took her eyes away from the jewellery. "Love letters?"

"All except one which seems to be a blackmail letter."

He handed the letter to her and she read it. She remembered the £10,000 that Helen Carter had in her handbag when she died. The letter alluded to events thirty years ago. This case had wormed its way into her psyche and she'd been uneasy from the beginning that events back then were caught up in this case. But what? There was something that had happened that they didn't know about. Something which had Helen Carter following three men because she wanted to speak to them. "Get Anaya onto checking this letter. I want a DNA analysis from it."

Ian pushed another letter in front of her and there was a smirk on his face. "Somebody's been a naughty boy," he said

She recognised the handwriting on the envelope and heat seared through her body at the shock. Ian now had a broad grin on his face. She felt like strangling Damien for not telling her about his affair with Helen Carter. She would've made sure that either Dave Bell or she had checked the box and not one of the team. And of all the team, Ian was the last one she'd have wanted to search it. She was watching his ambition already, and he still had a grin on his face like a cat that had got the cream. He now had something on the ACC. Time to wipe the smile off his face. "Ian, I will deal with this from now on." She gave him her sternest stare and watched the grin drop from his face. "The ACC is a good policeman with a distinguished career. I do not expect to hear you mention this letter again, or to tell anyone else about it. Am I clear?" She'd known Damien since they'd been young police officers and she didn't believe he'd had anything to do with the death of Helen Carter, even if she'd attempted to blackmail him. The letter was very old – too old to be of any consequence. He was happily married to Carole and he wouldn't want her to find out about his affair. But the marriage, she thought, was strong enough to survive if Carole did find out. And why would Helen Carter blackmail Damien? More to the point, why had she kept the letter? Had she been in love with him?

"Yes, ma'am."

"On my team, promotion is based on merit. Trying to use an incident like this for any advantage will result in the opposite." She intended to leave Ian in no doubt about her position.

"Yes, ma'am."

"Ask Luke to research the people Helen Carter had an affair with." She gestured towards the letters. "You focus on the SUV and the computer issues we have. Have you had a look at the letters?"

"Yes, ma'am. Most of her affairs seem to have been with professional people."

Her heart sunk. Damien wasn't going to be happy if they had to check alibis with prominent people.

***

Liam Gibson walked through the door of the interview room and Alex observed him closely. He was tall, middle build, a honey-coloured skin and heavy-lidded blue eyes. Anxiety marred his handsome face. He had arrived at the station and had asked to see her.

"My wife told me what has happened when I arrived home." His concern was evident in his voice.

She already knew that his SUV hadn't been involved in Helen Carter's hit and run. But as yet, they hadn't had time to communicate this to the Gibson family. "We know your vehicle wasn't involved in the hit and run."

She could see the tension leave him, his shoulders relaxed as he breathed a soundless sigh of relief. He knew he hadn't done anything so his relief must be for his son, Aidan. "I would like to talk to you about your relationship with Helen Carter... and your son's... We know from your son that he was having an affair with her and that you knew about it."

"Yes, that's right." His voice was stern.

She knew the answer to her next question but she wanted to hear what he had to say. "And did you intend doing anything about it?"

"I had already done that. I had confronted Helen about the matter," he said coldly.

"Could you tell me when and where this happened?"

"I visited her home at Corbridge, just under two weeks ago, and told her to leave Aidan alone."

He was attempting not to let anger get the better of him.

"And did she agree?"

"Oh yes, she broke it off immediately." His voice trembled with anger.

"Mr Gibson, we have evidence that you yourself had an affair with Helen Carter." She could see him gasp.

He looked at her anxiously. "It was a very long time ago and my wife knows nothing about it."

She smiled at him. "Will you tell me about it?"

He sighed. "It was about thirteen years ago. Aidan was a toddler and I was having a bad patch in my marriage. I met her at a charity do. I can't remember which one. She was absolutely stunning to look at and when she suggested we met for a coffee to talk about the charity, I jumped at the chance. I wasn't sure, of course, if she was meeting me to get money out of me for the charity. But when we met, she flirted with me. It began then."

"And why did the relationship end?"

"Helen started to get too serious." His body tensed. "She wanted me to leave my wife for her."

"And you had no intention of doing that?" She asked.

"No. It was an affair." He looked at her to gauge her reaction. "She was married and I was married and I didn't think it was anything more than a fling for both of us." He shrugged.

Helen hadn't been clever in her choice of men if none of them had been prepared to leave their wives for her. "And how did she behave when you broke it off?"

"She was absolutely furious and she started stalking me." He lifted his shoulders. "She was outside the nursery school when I picked up my son and standing across the road from the office." His voice was louder. "I started to get worried and so I confronted her and told her to leave me alone."

"And did she?"

"Not at first. I went out one morning and found the car tyres slashed." His face had turned to stone. "A few days later, Aidan's bike went missing." He rubbed the back of his neck. "I was beginning to get worried that I was dealing with Glenn Close in *Fatal Attraction*." He looked at her. "You know the film?"

She nodded and thought about the fact that Helen Carter had been following Neil Thomson and Peter Dodd.

He pushed his right hand across his forehead. "But then it stopped."

"And you didn't involve the police?"

His mouth fell open. "You must be kidding. I didn't want to smash my marriage and I bitterly regretted the affair with Helen." He stared at her. "And I haven't done anything like that since."

"And what was she like as a person?"

He paused. "I think it's fair to say that she wasn't the brightest person... she was interested in how she looked, clothes, shopping and so on."

She said nothing and waited for him to continue.

"She came across as very sweet and easy going at the beginning... but as time went on... she liked to have her own way in everything, there was no compromise... she had to be complimented all the time... looks mainly." He frowned. "She thought she was a kind and caring person and liked to be told this."

She smiled at him. "And was she a kind and caring person?"

"I think she appeared that way at a superficial level when she was dealing with her charity work... but she was quite a demanding madam when you got to know her better."

"Do you believe she knew Aidan was your son when she started the affair with him?"

"Yes. She admitted that to me when I confronted her... that is when she found out his surname and where he lived."

She recalled the one syllable responses she got from Aidan. "Can you give me some more information about what happened? Aidan wasn't very forthcoming." A polite understatement, she thought, as she remembered her interview with him.

"She'd suggested to him that they go for a cup of coffee to a caravan. He said she was just being very friendly and talking about the dogs."

"And then?"

"She got him to the caravan and they had a cup of coffee and she came and sat beside him and asked him if he thought she was beautiful." He scowled. "Aidan is a very young seventeen and I blame my wife for that. He says she put her hand down his trousers, then took his trousers off and got on top of him."

She rolled her eyes. "And no doubt he wanted to go back for more?"

He nodded his head slowly.

"So how did you find out about the affair?"

He rubbed his brow. "Helen rang me and told me. She laughed down the phone."

"So, you think she was taking revenge on you?"

"Oh, yes. What would she want with Aidan? And she was prepared to give him up too easily after I found out. Though I can't understand why she wanted revenge after all these years. I asked her why she was doing this and said that her husband would find out." He shook his head. "She didn't seem to be bothered."

His eyes were wide with surprise. He didn't know that when he'd met her, Helen was dying of cancer, and that she was taking revenge for the disappointments in her life. He hadn't realised that she was paying him a compliment. She had done this because he had mattered to her. "And Helen Carter didn't tell Aidan about her affair with you?"

"Yes, she did," he breathed out, his shoulders slumping forward, "but I denied it."

"And he believed you?"

He breathed a sigh of relief. “Yes.”

“My wife doesn’t need to know about my affair with Helen, does she?” He looked troubled.

“I can’t see any reason why she should. You are here to help us with our enquiries. You’re not being charged with anything,”

As she showed him out of her office, her mobile rang. “Hello, DCI Alex Shaftoe.”

“It’s Jane Simpson. I’ve found a phone in my caravan. It’s not mine. It must be Helen’s phone.”

The state Jane Simpson’s caravan was in, she wasn’t surprised the phone had only shown up now. “Where are you, Ms Simpson?”

“I’m at the caravan.”

“I’ll send someone up to get it.”

“No point. I’m just about to leave and come down to Newcastle.”

“ I’ll send someone to your house to collect it.”

“Okay.”

As she closed the call, she strode through to the Incident Room. “Dave, Jane Simpson has found a phone in her caravan. She thinks it’s Helen Carter’s. She’s on her way to Newcastle. We need to send someone around to her house to get it. And then check the numbers on the phone.”

***

Alex knocked on the door of the ACC’s office clutching the letter he’d sent to Helen Carter.

“Come.”

There were spreadsheets strewn across his desk. Like her, he'd never got used to reading on screen and still preferred to print out important stuff.

"It must be your 'famous' intuition Alex. I was just about to ask you to come and see me," he said, irritated.

As she approached his desk, the spreadsheets had row after row of numbers. He was checking finance which was never a good sign. They trained as detectives but once they reached the higher ranks, it was diplomacy and accountancy skills which were more useful.

"I've been checking over the finances and I can't believe what I'm seeing." His brow had gone red. "Why are you still monitoring Terry Marshall?"

"I still think he might be at risk," she said firmly.

"Are you suggesting that Helen Carter is trying to kill him from beyond the grave?" His cheeks had now gone red.

"There is a link." She tried to keep her voice calm.

He slammed the spreadsheet down on his desk and she jumped. "But there's no evidence." He stabbed the spreadsheet with his forefinger. "And I see we have overtime here for monitoring his house and movements," he shouted.

It was a long time since they'd had a set to like this and she could feel her blood begin to boil. She was furious that he hadn't told her about his affair with Helen Carter. She slammed the letter down on his desk. "And what have you got to say about this?"

He took the letter in his hand. "This was years ago," he shouted. "That's why I didn't mention it to you. It was irrelevant." He flipped his hand which was holding the letter dismissively. "Unless, of course, you think I killed Helen Carter?"

"But one of my team now knows about your affair because he checked the box the letter was inside. If I'd known about it, I could've made sure it was either me or Dave Bell who checked the box." Her voice had been getting louder.

He seemed contrite and there was a silence between them as they both calmed down. She took some deep breaths and Damien's eyes were no longer fixed on his spreadsheets.

"It was a long time ago. It must be fifteen years. I'd forgotten all about the letter." His voice was quieter but his face was still stern.

She lifted an eyebrow. "Bad mistake for a copper."

He nodded. "I'm sure you're more than capable of handling the member of your team who found the letter."

She stood up. "Helen Carter seems to have been a serial adulterer and she's had affairs with some prominent people."

"I want to know before you question anyone for alibis."

She'd expected him to say this and she could feel her muscles start to relax again. She turned to leave the room.

"Alex, call off the monitoring of Terry Marshall," he said from behind her.

Chapter 22

It was lunchtime and Alex and Dave Bell were sitting opposite each other at a two-seater table in a corner of a Chinese restaurant in Chinatown. It had the same familiar wall-paper with beige bamboo strewn across it, and a purple cloth on the tables topped with a white cloth changed after each customer. But it was the restaurant frequented by Neil Thomson and his friends and it didn't feel the same since the murder. Perhaps it was time for a change; the location wasn't as convenient since the station had moved. They'd come here for years to discuss cases or staff and the food was the best in Chinatown.

"Have you noticed if there's anything going on between Ian Turner and Anaya Patel?" She already knew his answer was going to be 'no' as she asked the question. Dave was not adept at noticing office romances, but she wanted to alert him to the possibility. She'd seen the way Anaya and Ian looked at each other.

He gave her a stare as he swallowed his food and then said, "What do you mean, 'going on'?"

She smirked at him. "I mean romance."

"Na." He looked down at his food. "But I'll watch now you've mentioned it."

This was his way of acknowledging that she was more astute at picking up relationship dynamics. He kept his focus on the work. She decided to move onto the thorny subject of Damien's affair with Helen Carter. "There's something I need to mention to you." She eyed the restaurant to make sure there was no one nearby or anyone listening to them. She lowered her voice to a whisper. "The ACC had an affair with Helen Carter."

Dave stopped just before shovelling another mouthful of Singapore Vermicelli into his mouth. "Bloody hell... the heed banger." His voice had risen.

"Sh... I know, I know –" She was about to continue but stopped herself as she saw he about to speak.

His jaw had dropped. "Have you confronted him about it?"

She breathed out as she said, "Yes." And before he asked her, she continued. "He was dismissive and said he hadn't mentioned it because it was so long ago it was irrelevant."

"When did you find out?"

"Ian Turner retrieved the box from Jane Simpson." She waited for him to acknowledge this because he would've organised it, and he did with an incline of his head. "He came to my room about it."

"Just what we need." He put his fork down on his plate noisily.

"It looks as if it was a long time ago. There's no way he has anything to do with Helen Carter's hit and run," she said, pointing to a positive.

"But he didn't mention it to you?" He countered in a low suspicious voice.

"No. But there's not many people keep mementos of ex-lovers over what seems to be a twenty year period. And Damien and his wife are happy, you know that." She waited for him to comment but he said nothing. "And anyway," she went on, "it looks as if her ex-lovers include some prominent people in the area and Damien wants to know before we interview any of them for alibis."

"It's not going to look good for him, is it?" He clipped. "I've seen more brains in a pan of broth, as my old granddad would've said."

"It's a long time since I've heard that one," she smiled. "I think he'll survive it if he has a word with the Chief and we can prove he was nowhere near Helen Carter when she was killed in the hit and run."

He breathed out loudly. "I'll get on to it."

"Dave, do it yourself and don't involve anyone else. I've had to put Ian in his place about his attitude to finding Damien's letter." She'd already had a word with Dave about what she perceived as Ian's ambition, and she'd asked Dave to keep an eye on him. "I'd rather have had any other member of the team open that box." She looked around the room again to check that she still had no one flapping their ears. "And Damien is in one of his tizzy's about finance. He wants me to call off monitoring Terry Marshall."

He eyes rolled. "And?"

"I want to continue monitoring him –"

He butted in. "Don't tell me you've got a feeling in you're watter again... it's a wonder you don't have kidney trouble." One bushy eyebrow climbed up his face.

She looked across the table at his empty plate which had been heaped high, and then at his growing belly that could've belonged to an eight-month pregnant woman expecting twins. She reached into her handbag and pulled out a leaflet for a gym close by the station and placed it on the table.

"What's this?" he asked as he examined the leaflet suspiciously.

She smirked. "It's for you." She gave him her best innocent look.

He stared at her, eyes wide open. "You've got to be having a laugh?"

She pointed at his belly. "You're looking unfit, Dave, and you're getting to that age where blood pressure can become an issue." She smiled at him with her eyes. "It's only because I care."

His jaw dropped. "Howay woman, man."

She started to laugh. Over the years the edge had been knocked off his Geordie accent and he'd stopped using words from the dialect, not least because not all of their staff were from the north-east. But when he was truly exasperated, he resorted to Geordie. One of the funniest expressions in Geordie was 'Howay woman, man'. It raised eyebrows every time from non-Geordies, 'man' being a Geordie expression of exasperation and nothing to do with the sex of the person to whom it referred.

Both their phones rang and Dave continued to eye her suspiciously as he answered his phone. As they both ended their calls, she said to him, "you first."

"Luke's been tracking down the numbers on Helen Carter's phone. She phoned Neil Thomson on the day he was killed."

"Do we know if they had any sort of conversation?"

"Na. But Luke's going to check with Neil Thomson's number."

"Anything else?"

"Na, not yet." He raised an eyebrow and waited for her to tell him about her call.

"That was the CSI team," she said. "The Darth Vader cloak is clean," she breathed out heavily. "I was sure that that was the cloak used on the night of Neil Thomson's murder. It's been thoroughly washed recently using Vanish."

"Vanish?" He stared at her.

"You know the stuff you buy at the supermarkets in the pink tub. Seemingly, if it's used, it breaks down DNA. Or so John Robertson has just told me."

"That probably means you're right about the cloak being used in Neil Thomson's murder. Otherwise, why has it been washed recently using Vanish?"

"I know. But we need some hard evidence, Dave. Chinese Johnny's shoe size is right for the footprints at Blackfriars Gate, but they haven't found the shoes that were used. We need Chris to check the knife now to see if it's a match for the stab wounds on Neil Thomson's body. John has suggested that after Chris' finished, they take it to pieces to see if they can find any of Neil Thomson's DNA inside. They are also going to do another fingertip search of Chinese Johnny's flat. We'll just have to hope they find something."

Just then her phone rang. "We're on our way." She turned to him. "Damien's wife, Carole, has been run off the road. She was driving his car."

Chapter 23

Ian Turner was waiting for Alex at the stairs leading up to the second floor and the ACC's office.

"Can I have a word, ma'am?"

"Can it wait, Ian?"

"No, I don't think so."

She halted on the first step of the flight of stairs and turned to him.

"Ma'am. The computer that changed the details from a black SUV to a red SUV is the ACC's computer. We need to take his computer to see what has happened."

Her jaw dropped. "You're sure?"

"Yes, ma'am."

"Okay, I'm going up to his office now. I'll tell him. Make sure you've got a replacement for his machine. You can come up after I've been in."

She continued up the stairs. This wasn't good. He'd had an affair with Helen Carter and his machine had changed the records.

She knocked on Damien's door.

"Come."

She walked towards him. “How’s Carole?” Concern nudged her voice to a higher pitch

“Shook up but not hurt.” His mouth quirked.” I wish I could say the same for the SUV.” His eyes flicked up in exasperation.

Her brow wrinkled. “Has she been able to tell you what happened?”

“She was on her way back from her sister’s and heading for the A1 when a white vehicle came up behind her and started to drive very close... he started tooting his horn at her... she couldn’t understand why because there was plenty of room to overtake.”

“It was definitely a man?”

“Yes. But he was wearing dark glasses and a hat. He kept driving close to the bumper and then braking. Then doing it again. Until he got her into such a state that she drove off the road into a dry-stone wall.”

Her mouth turned down. “I’m not sure this was random road rage.”

His jaw dropped and a shocked expression fixed on his face. She pursued her train of thought. “I think whoever has done this thinks you’re responsible for Helen Carter’s hit and run.”

He stared at her, his mouth now wide open. “How.”

She’d already guessed what had happened without checking with the team. She would confirm it later. “Because I think we’ll find that your black SUV was on the A1 in Northumberland early on the Sunday morning Helen Carter was killed.”

He paused to think before he answered, clasping his hands on his desk. “Carole was up at Alnwick helping her sister move house.” His voice pitch had risen.

"We've discovered that our IT records have been altered. We've been looking for a red SUV for Helen Carter's hit and run when we should've been looking for a black SUV."

He heaved. "We've never had anything like this happen before." He opened the palms of his hands on his desk.

"We've had our IT lads checking what's happened." She pointed at his laptop. "It seems the changes were made on your laptop." She watched closely for his reaction to what she had just said.

His mouth opened. "You must be kidding me?"

She said nothing for a moment. "The lads are coming up to collect your machine and give you a replacement."

"You can't think I had anything to do with changing the records?"

"I've known you too long. And I know you're no better than me with computers. And if you'd done this you wouldn't be stupid enough to use your own machine. But on the face of it, it doesn't look too good. You didn't admit to the affair with Helen Carter. Your black SUV was on the A1 on the morning Helen Carter was killed. And your machine is responsible for the change in records. We are going to have to play this by the book, as much for your sake as anyone else's. We need to eliminate your black SUV from our enquiries. And we need to find out what happened to your laptop."

"Do you think someone has set me up."

"It's more than a possibility after what has just happened... you're sure Carole didn't know about your affair with Helen Carter?"

"Yes, I'm sure."

The exchange between them yesterday had been bad-tempered because of finance and she now decided to ask what she would've asked then, if the circumstances had been better humoured. "I didn't get the chance the other day to ask you about your affair with Helen Carter... but I think it's now relevant." He didn't object or try to deflect from the subject so she knew he was going to answer her question.

He gestured to the seat opposite his desk. "I'm trying to remember where I met her. Yes... it was at a charity do at the Civic Centre."

"And you weren't interested in leaving Carole for her?" She had butterflies in her stomach about asking this question about a marriage which everyone regarded as happy.

"It did cross my mind. Carole had post-natal depression after our second and it went on for a long time. I was an ambitious DCI, working all hours, and she couldn't cope at home. I was regularly attacked and punched and we must've gone through a complete dinner service with what she had lobbed at me. And then I met beautiful Helen."

He was giving her more information than she expected, as if he was trying to justify himself to himself. She hadn't realised that Carole had had such serious post-natal depression, but then she and Damien weren't working on the same team at that time.

He gazed towards the window. "I think my main reason for not leaving Carole at the time was the kids. I think that's the case with a lot of men once there are kids. You think twice."

She decided to push her questions whilst he was in the mood to answer. "Were you aware that Helen wanted to leave her husband?"

"That was clear from early on."

She turned to her interview with Liam Gibson before she formulated her next question. She was curious about whether Helen Carter had been in love with Damien. "And you didn't have any problems with her when you showed no sign of leaving Carole for her?"

He stared at her. "No why d'you ask?"

"Well... one man had difficulties when he wouldn't leave his wife for her and described her as behaving like Glenn Close in *Fatal Attraction*."

He shook his head. "I didn't have anything like that to deal with."

Helen Carter mustn't have regarded him as a serious prospect. "If you hadn't had the kids would you have left Carole for Helen?"

"I've been happy with Carole, as you know. This was one very bad patch because she had post-natal depression. And for the record, I haven't been unfaithful to her since then." His face was pointed and his voice sharp-edged as he said, "And you will have realised that this conversation is between the two of us to help you with your enquiries and will go no further... even Jo."

Then why have an affair in the first place? Was her immediate reaction and she hoped her face didn't betray what she was thinking? But she wasn't surprised that the marriage had survived and prospered. Carole had supported him in his rise through the police ranks. And he was willing to help her because he was on the back foot because he'd stayed silent about his affair with Helen Carter. She could feel her pulse quickening. "I can't understand why she couldn't find anyone. Men do leave their wives and kids."

His eyes reflected his surprise. "They were all married?"

She puffed out. "It seems so."

"It's a difficult one." He rested his clasped hands on his desk. I think it was intuition. I know men aren't supposed to have good intuition." He quirked his lips. "There was something artificial about her sweetness; it felt like an act. She was too good to be true. I think there was something lurking behind that beautiful exterior. I'm saying this now, but I didn't think it through at the time. I just acted on instinct."

"But did she have problems?" She'd learnt long ago that building up a picture of a victim meant getting all the evidence she could. And as Helen Carter had emerged as a deeply troubled woman who was a serial adulterer, this was relevant.

He paused. "I think she probably did, although I didn't think about it at the time." He shrugged.

She knew that Liam Gibson had ended the affair with Helen Carter, but what about Damien? "Who ended the relationship?"

"She did," he responded immediately.

"Why? Did she give you an explanation?"

"She didn't give me a reason. I think she probably realised it wasn't going anywhere and judging by what you say about the number of men she had, maybe she'd found a better prospect."

She reckoned he was probably right about that. "How did you feel when it ended?"

"Relief. She'd started to get nasty. Not like the bloke you've interviewed, she was snappy and would fly off the handle at the least little thing. She liked to get her own way with everything... and she didn't like it if you weren't complimenting her all the time... telling her how beautiful and stunning she was."

She thought about the two faces of Helen Carter – Mother Theresa and the serial adulterer, the do-gooder and the narcissist. "Did she come across as unstable?"

"I don't know about unstable? You just had to agree with her all the time and she didn't like to be crossed." He paused and looked at her. "Are you focusing on Helen Carter? I thought the forensics had ruled her out for Neil Thomson's death."

"It does. But I've still got to resolve her hit and run. And I've got a cast list of men with whom she had affairs."

He gave her a stern glance. "Be careful, Alex, if it's anyone prominent. I don't want any complaints. And I want to know before anyone is interviewed. I told you that yesterday."

There was a pause. "Where are we with the gang fight in Chinatown?"

He had changed the subject and it was obvious that the discussion about Helen Carter was over.

She sat back and watched him fiddle with the papers on his desk. He avoided meeting her eyes. He was about to confront her with something and he was feeling guilty about it, she thought.

He began. "We're skint, Alex. I don't want to spend any more money on overtime. Not unless a new suspect comes into the frame. What I said to you yesterday still stands."

Her body tensed. "I want to continue the watch on Terry Marshall's house." She tried to keep her voice even. "We know from neighbours that Helen Carter was spotted on the street... and on the street where Peter Dodd lives."

"No, Alex. He can't be at risk. It's just a coincidence that they all knew each other thirty years ago."

"I don't agree." She kept her voice firm.

He gave her a sceptical stare. "I can't see how you can argue this on the basis of the evidence," he ground out. "I hope you're not going to argue your famous bloody intuition."

She could feel the heat building in her cheeks. "Helen Carter was stalking Neil Thomson, Peter Dodd and Terry Marshall. She was up to something. I know it."

"But she didn't bloody well kill Neil Thomson, did she?" He said firmly.

"But I don't know the part Rebecca Gray or Alan Carter have played... I do know they are lying about what they know." Her voice rose in frustration.

"I don't care," he shouted. "The DNA tests have cost a fortune. And I haven't got Jo's bill yet." He breathed in. "I mean it, Alex. No more observation of Terry Marshall's house."

She knew she would get nowhere when he was like this. He usually listened to her unless finance was involved. He was tasked to keep them on budget. His performance measured by the cases solved within budget. She knew he'd brought up the subject again because he didn't trust her to obey him. She did have a history of ignoring things when it suited her, but in those cases it had come right and her disobedience had been ignored. She could only hope that this was the case again this time because she intended to continue watching Terry Marshall's house.

Chapter 24

Ian Turner could see out of the corner of his eye, Anaya Patel glance sideward at him as he peered through the rear-view mirror of the car. He felt frustrated because this was the first time that he and Anaya had been alone, and now one of them was going to have to keep an eye on the rear-view mirror, which was going to make broaching the subject of romance difficult, if not impossible.

Anaya turned her head to the right towards him and asked, "Do single officers always have to do night shift?"

He kept his eyes on the mirror. "Usually. The boss has had this system for years. It's her personal way of keeping police divorce statistics down. She lets the married officers go home to their families at night, if she can."

"It's hard luck for the single officers if they've got a date."

He bristled. His spine straightened. "Supposed to be meeting someone tonight, are you?"

"No, no," she stuttered. "I was talking generally." She looked out of the passenger-seat window. They were sitting down the road from Terry Marshall's house, in a well-to-do suburban street in Gosforth, on the north side of the city.

He breathed out and relaxed back into the driver's seat. "At least we've got it easier tonight. We don't have to worry about our cover because it's Halloween." He looked out of the front window of the car at the kids dressed up to go around the houses playing trick or treat. He smiled at the memories of his childhood days but hoped none of the kids were cheeky enough to knock on the car door. He would have done that when he was young. "Did you ever play trick or treat?" He squinted out of the rear-view mirror and watched DS Jackie Palmer, whose surveillance shift had just finished, at the far end of the street. DI Dave Bell had worried that there might be a report of suspicious activity from one of the residents, so he and Anaya were parked on the same side of the street as Terry Marshall's house, but much further up. They were relying on the rear-view mirror to monitor the house, but he wondered how effective this would be now it was dark.

He saw Jackie draw parallel to the Marshall's house. She was signalling frantically. He pushed the car door open and jumped out, shouting at Anaya. "There's trouble at the Marshall house." He sprinted towards the house, adrenaline pumping through his body. As he ran, he could see a cloaked figure racing up the street in the opposite direction to him. He quickly glanced back as he kept running. Anaya was behind him. He accelerated his pace, his breath coming fast, to reach the Marshall house. He stopped suddenly because Jackie was slumped in the drive and another figure lying across the front door.

Jackie shouted, "I'm alright. You go after him." She pointed up the street.

He turned, signalled to Anaya by pointing into the house and accelerated again around a corner. He saw the figure racing well ahead of him, running towards the top of the street. He increased his pace again. He could feel his heart punching his chest. His lungs ached as he surged to round the next corner. Half way up the street a woman had started to chase the man. He puzzled about why she'd done this, as he kept his legs moving as fast as possible. He forced his body to speed up again as his lungs seemed ready to burst his ribcage. The figure stopped, just as the woman caught up with him and her hand grasped at his cloak. He threw a punch at the woman. She fell to the ground. He then jumped a fence. Ian pushed his body hard as his lungs smashed against his chest. He ground to a halt at the prostrate woman on the ground. The woman was sprawled across the pavement – it was the boss. The cloaked figure had gone.

***

DI Dave Bell, furrow-browed, walked briskly up a corridor in the RVI towards Accident and Emergency. DS' Ian Turner and Anaya Patel were waiting for him.

"The boss has got concussion," Ian volunteered as Dave arrived. "It's not serious but she's still unconscious... Jackie's alright. He just pushed her over... just a few scrapes. Terry Marshall was punched... he's unconscious, but the doctors don't think it's serious."

Anaya eyed Ian and then continued the story. "We're not sure exactly what happened. But Mrs Marshall said her husband went to answer the door because they thought it was kids playing trick or treat. They'd already had two groups of kids calling and had some sweets ready by the side of the door."

"And she didn't see anything?" Dave asked.

"No," Anaya said with frustration in her voice. "She arrived at the door at about the time I got there... she didn't even see the cloaked figure... only her husband unconscious on the doorstep and Jackie on the path."

Dave shook his head slowly. "And Jackie, what did she see?"

Anaya puffed out a breath. "She says the cloaked figure turned and ran down the drive when they saw her, knocking her out of the way. She obviously disrupted him."

"Too right, or Terry Marshall might've been worse," Dave butted in. "Does she know if it was a male or female?"

Anaya looked at the floor. "A male."

"I can confirm that, sir," Ian said. "That is, based on the way he was running and his height. And Jackie says it's a bloke as well."

"And no one saw him go into the Marshall driveway?" Dave asked.

"No, Jackie was walking up the street in that direction because we'd just changed shifts. She saw nothing." Ian shrugged.

"Which means our attacker was lucky and sneaked in as you were changing shifts," Dave grunted. "Or he was on to us and knew we were watching the house. He then chose his moment to sneak in." He'd been worried about them being detected right from the start because the street was too quiet.

"There were kids on the street playing trick or treat. He could easily have used them as cover," Ian suggested. "And if he was on to us, he chose a bad time to strike, just as Jackie was walking up the street."

Dave had to concede that Ian was probably right. Mebbees he'd been too worried about them being detected? The case was already a bugger's muddle and this was going to make it a bigger mess. Helen Carter couldn't have attacked Terry Marshall from the grave, and whoever it was chose to wear a cloak like the Neil Thomson murder in Blackfriars. "And what was the boss doing there?"

“We weren’t expecting her. She must’ve been coming to visit us. She was carrying three takeaway coffees,” Ian said.

Dave had questioned Alex’s decision to watch Terry Marshall’s house because with Helen Carter dead, there didn’t seem any point. It was one of her intuitions. If it was a bloke, then it couldn’t have been Rebecca Gray. All the same, he’d better find out where she was last night. More questions than answers.

CHAPTER 25

Anaya Patel heard a ping from her computer and looked to see what had come through. It was the results from the DNA test on the blackmail letter from the box which Helen Carter had left with Jane Simpson. DNA was usually John Robertson and the CSI team's domain, but it was easy to check if DNA matched anything on the police database. She put the results into the database and then there was a second ping. It had matched something.

She picked up her mobile and phoned John Robertson. The call was forwarded to another mobile. "Hello, Paul Burke."

"Hi. This is DS Anaya Patel. I was looking for John?"

"He's on a day's holiday. Can I help?"

"I've a DNA test here which matches DNA on the police database. I just wanted to double-check that it is a full match." She knew that there could be matches between family members and wanted to be absolutely sure about what she'd got.

"Push it through to me now. I'm sitting at my desk with my laptop in front of me. I'll check it for you while you're on the phone. She pressed a key and then waited. After what seemed ages of silence.

"They're a match," Paul said.

"By that, you mean a full match? These people are related?"

"Yes. They're related."

"Thanks, Paul."

Her eyes moved back to her screen and to the information about the person whose DNA they'd identified. His name was Douglas Blake. He lived in Edinburgh and he was thirty years old. She paused to think. She'd been expecting someone older which was hardly surprising; the box the letter had come from was full of mementos of Helen Carter's lovers – men her own age. She stopped. Her next port of call was the database with birth certificates, an initiative by the Home Office which the police had access to. Her mouth dropped open. The birth certificate said, 'father unknown', but the mother was named as Helen Armstrong. She next looked up the mobile number for Douglas Blake.

She got up from her desk and walked across to Luke Richardson who was concentrating on his computer screen. She told him what she had just found. "Luke, I need you to check this phone number." She handed him a piece of paper with the number scrawled on it. "Has this number called Helen Carter or has she called this number?" She perched her hip on Luke's desk and waited as he scrolled down his screen.

"Bingo. He has called her and she has called him."

"What about on the day of the hit and run?"

There was a pause. "Bingo."

"Can we tell if the calls were made from the Bamburgh area?'

"I'll have to check with the mobile providers to find that out."

"Let's do that. But first, let's have a look at the CCTV. You've been looking at that haven't you?"

Luke nodded.

Anaya went across to her desk and pulled her chair across. She sat down beside Luke and they both studied his screen and the CCTV cameras for north Northumberland on the morning of Helen Carter's hit and run. They knew already that they were looking for – a black SUV.

"Bingo," Luke said. "Let's see who the owner is."

A swift move onto the DVLA site produced an owner for the black SUV – Douglas Blake.

***

Dave Bell pushed open the door open of the Incident Room.

"What's the latest?" Ian Turner asked Dave. The team then grouped at the front sitting on desktops.

"Jackie's been released from hospital and she's at home now. The boss has regained consciousness but they are keeping her in for observation, although they don't think she has any serious damage." He didn't mention he'd had to stop Alex from discharging herself from hospital. He'd had to get Jo's help to do that. "She doesn't know much. It all happened too fast." It suddenly crossed his mind that Alex's famous intuition might've been at work and that is why she'd turned up to see Ian and Anaya. He'd quizzed her about this in the past and she had told him that she didn't know why she did things herself. She just had a knack of turning up, just as things were about to happen. "Terry Marshall is still unconscious."

"Sir, I've got some interesting information just through this morning," Anaya piped up as Dave paused for breath. "We've got the DNA from the blackmail letter in Helen Carter's box. It's on our database and it's from a man called Douglas Blake who lives in Edinburgh. He had some small-time trouble with drugs when he was young – nothing serious.’ She moved across the room to her desk and studied the computer screen. “I’ve just got a birth certificate for Douglas Blake who was adopted when he was a baby and his natural mother is Helen Carter.”

Dave was just about to speak and compliment Anaya on her initiative when she continued.

“There’s more. Douglas Blake was driving the black SUV we picked up on the A1 driving north towards Scotland on the morning of Helen Carter’s death.”

Dave puffed out his cheeks and then breathed out slowly. He knew what he was going to do. Mebbees the bugger’s muddle had started to unravel at last. “Luke, I want Douglas Blake down here for an interview. I don’t want anyone to give anything away until we get him here. I want forensics to crawl all over his vehicle... Anaya, keep digging about the connection between Helen Carter and Douglas Blake. See what we can find out from the sister and if she had any inkling that it was a birth and not an abortion... and check with the counsellor again and make absolutely sure Helen Carter didn’t mention an adoption... and the priest at Bywell who the boss spoke to.”

He turned to Anaya. “Get a photo of Douglas Blake and ask uniform to go through Chinatown and the taxi ranks again.” He paused and rubbed his stubbly chin. “They had better take a photo of Helen Carter with them as well, just in case they were together... and a photo of Alan Carter.”

Dave slumped down at his desk, opened his drawer and took out a packet of chocolate biscuits. He looked down at his belly. Then he took out a biscuit and scoffed it. After he swallowed the last bite, he picked up his mobile phone and phoned Chris Laidlaw. “Hi, Chris. Have you heard the news?”

"No. I'm just in for the first time in a few days, I've been at a wedding."

"Have you caught up with anything?" Dave said, reminding himself that Chris was entitled to a life. "We picked up a cloak at a flat in Blackfriars. It belonged to the Chinese man we were trying to find for the gang fight. He's now dead. And probably in your morgue. The cloak is clean – no DNA. It had been washed recently in Vanish. We need to know if he's responsible for the Neil Thomson murder. It's going to be based on the knife... and DNA on it." Dave paused. "It's got more complicated." He heard Chris give out a deep sigh at the end of the phone. "A cloaked figure attacked Terry Marshall last night. You know, the third bloke accused of raping Helen Carter. He got away. So, you can see the problem."

"Yes. I can."

"Can you get onto it straightaway? I need these results yesterday. I'm just about to go up to the hospital to get Alex. She was hurt in the chase last night."

"Nothing serious, I hope."

"No. Concussion. The same for Terry Marshall, although Alex is conscious but he isn't yet."

"Give Alex my best when you see her."

"Will do."

Dave scoffed another chocolate biscuit before he made his second call. "Lindsay, it's Dave Bell."

"Hi, Dave. How's Alex?"

News always got around the station fast. "Concussion, but she'll live." Lindsay was the Press Liaison Officer. "You've obviously heard what happened last night. I need to know if there have been any press articles about the cloaked figure in Blackfriars?"

"You're worried about a copycat?"

"I need to rule it out."

"Okay. But I haven't seen anything in the press. And I monitor the press releases every day. But I'll double-check. Tell Alex I'm asking after her."

"I'm going to phone the Chinese woman who reported seeing the cloaked figure in Blackfriars," he said as he ended the conversation.

He raised his head from his desk and shouted across the room to Luke Richardson. "Luke, I need a number for the Chinese woman in Blackfriars who saw the cloaked man."

Luke consulted his computer screen, scribbled something down, rushed across the room and put the number in front of him on a stick-it note.

He made another phone call. "Hello, Mrs Smith. This is DI Dave Bell. I wonder if I could ask you a question?"

"Fire away."

"Have you told anyone about the cloaked figure you saw at Blackfriars, the night of Neil Thomson's murder?"

"Well, my husband obviously knew because he was in the house that night. And I mentioned it to my sister and mother."

"What about the Chinese man who was your neighbour?"

"No. I didn't know him. We just said 'hello' if we bumped into each other in the corridor."

"And you haven't spoken to the press?"

"No."

"Thank you, Mrs Smith."

***

Alex was on the ward where she'd been monitored since last night and the curtains were drawn around her bed. She'd just finished dressing. Her head felt like a piece of dough which had been thoroughly kneaded and her mouth as rough as sandpaper. The doctor had agreed to discharge her on the understanding that she wasn't left alone at home, so Jo had agreed to stay with her. Both Dave and Jo had spent all night at the hospital, sitting in the waiting room. Her vision was blurry and she knew she wasn't capable of driving a car.

She'd had one of the strangest nights of her life because whilst unconscious, she'd been with Daniel and the dream was so real she hadn't wanted to wake up. They'd been on the beach at Alnmouth, Daniel as he was when he died, Lisa and her as they are now. They'd walked along the beach but as she remembered it in childhood with concrete blocks – now long gone – scattered along the edge of the sand; a precaution during the Second World War against a German invasion. She'd introduced Daniel to his daughter and they'd all spent time walking and talking on a beach empty apart from the three of them. They'd bought an ice-cream from a van parked at the edge of the beach just past the golf course. After they'd married, Daniel and she had often taken weekend breaks at the house her parents had bought in Alnmouth. They loved to walk the Northumbrian coast and so it was little wonder they'd gone back there, this time with their grown-up daughter. She'd treasured every moment of the dream and felt sad now she'd woken up.

She could hear the familiar footsteps of Dave Bell coming down the ward. He was here to take her home. He'd clucked around her like an old hen after she regained consciousness and before going to the station to check on the latest with their cases.

She smiled. Jo and Dave had insisted on her staying in the hospital when she'd wanted to discharge herself this morning. She slowly stuck her head around the curtain.

Dave gave her an anxious look. "How ye feeling?"

"A bit rough. And there's a big bump on my head." She put her right hand up towards the right side of her head and touched her hair gently. "I'm desperate for a shower and a decent cup of coffee."

He looked at her closely, no doubt trying to measure how good she was. "I've just heard that Terry Marshall has regained consciousness."

"Is he able to speak to us?" She emphasised the word 'us' to let Dave know that she intended to be involved if they did speak to Terry Marshall.

"I don't know but we can ask before we leave the hospital."

***

"Hello, Mr Marshall. Can we talk to you for a few minutes?" Dave said as he pulled out his warrant card to let Terry Marshall know they were friend not foe.

They'd got permission from the doctor because Terry Marshall, like Alex, had been concussed but otherwise no other injuries. He'd been lucky because they'd found a knife on his street which they suspected his attacker had dropped, and which was currently being analysed.

Terry Marshall opened his puffed eyes and nodded slowly. A grimace spread across his face. She realised that he was having the same difficulty as she was having if she moved her head – a searing pain and nausea.

"Mr Marshall, can you remember anything about your attacker?" Was it a man or a woman?" Dave asked. He'd insisted on asking the questions and she'd agreed because she'd felt wobbly just walking down the hospital corridor.

He stuttered, "A man." He kept his head very still whilst he spoke.

Dave gave her a quick glance. "Are you absolutely sure?"

He nodded without thinking, went pale and looked like he was going to be sick. He took some deep breaths before he continued, "I saw his hands... they were a man's hands... I saw a ring on his little finger... I could see it glisten. I think it had a small diamond in the centre. When I put my arm up, I pulled down one of his gloves."

Her heart jumped and it made her feel momentarily sick. She'd been right about her suspicions.

"Anything else you can remember?" Dave said with a note of optimism.

"No... he was wearing a mask... a Halloween mask. And a cloak...with a hood over his head."

The cloak and mask were a perfect disguise; so easy to take off and completely change appearance and, of course, it was Halloween, the one night a year when nobody would've thought much about someone wandering about in a cloak and mask.

"Thank you, Mr Marshall. We'll leave you in peace," Dave said.

They left the room. "Dave, I can remember when I met Alan Carter he had a ring on his little finger. With a diamond in it." She paused to take a deep breath before proceeding further down the corridor. "I thought we hadn't gone public about the sighting of a cloaked figure at Blackfriars?" She frowned and immediately regretted it as a stabbing pain shot through her brow.

"I've asked Lindsay at the Press Office, and she's pretty sure there's been nothing in the press. But she's double-checking. I've spoken to the Chinese woman who saw the cloaked figure on the night of Neil Thomson's murder. She's not spoken to the press."

She was glad to see she didn't need to say anymore because she wanted to concentrate on getting to the car.

As they set off in the jeep, Dave said, "Are ye going to tell me why you wanted Terry Marshall's house watched?"

She took a deep breath. She'd been expecting this. "Deduction based on the information we had, my dear Watson." She cautiously gave a wry smile. "I believed that Helen Carter may've killed Neil Thomson. We knew early on that she had a motive. We now know she didn't kill Neil Thomson, but she'd been stalking all three men for reasons we still don't know." She paused and looked out of the car window to keep her head steady as Dave turned a corner. "But what if someone else believed that Helen Carter had committed the murder of Neil Thomson and knew she had been stalking these men? Someone who also knew Helen Carter was blaming her cancer on the abortion but didn't know about the forensics which we've got, which puts her in the clear for Neil Thomson's murder."

"Aye. I think I see what you mean." He gave her his 'who's a clever girl' look.

She continued. "There were three people who loved Helen Carter – Alan Carter, Rebecca Gray and Jane Simpson." She took some deep breaths as her head started to feel light again. "When I interviewed Jane Simpson, she was genuinely shocked when she heard about Neil Thomson's murder. And she didn't know Helen Carter had cancer. In the interview with Rebecca Gray, it wasn't clear what she knew about the three men, but she did know about her mother's cancer, and she was with her in

Chinatown and Jesmond Dene. When I interviewed Alan Carter, I thought he recognised the names Neil Thomson and Peter Dodd. He also knew about Helen Carter's diagnosis of cancer. Alan Carter was devoted to her. And as we found out more about his background... his failed marriages and childhood... I reckoned he might try and take a pop at Terry Marshall to finish the job for Helen, and because these men had ruined his life as well as hers."

He smirked. "And who's a clever bugger?"

"We still need to prove it. The ring is going to be crucial."

He nodded. "There's been another twist in our tale," he said to the windscreen of the jeep.

"Tell me," she said, although she wasn't sure she wanted anymore complications.

"A man called Douglas Blake's DNA was found on the blackmail letter we found in Helen Carter's box. He's Helen Carter's natural son. He's about thirty."

Her mouth opened and she turned her head slowly towards Dave to avoid a stab of pain knifing her head and eyes. "You're bringing him in?" She finally had the missing piece of her picture.

"Aye, there's more. He was in a black SUV travelling north on the A1 the day Helen Carter was killed. We've picked him up on CCTV." he quickly glanced in her direction before fixing his eyes on the road again.

She forgot about her injury and quickly turned her head towards him. She could feel the searing pain in her head and eyes and the nausea rising in her stomach. She leant forward.

Dave slowed the jeep. "Are you alright?"

"Yes. I just turned my head too quickly." She could feel the nausea subsiding in her stomach and her vision clearing. She took a deep breath. "Does Douglas Blake have the type of IT capability to have altered our records and to have got into the CCTV?"

"Na. But Ian's double-checking now."

She remembered Alan Carter's study in Corbridge and the computer screens. "Alan Carter's got the technical know-how. Do our lads know about him? Let's find out where he was last night?"

His head inclined. "I'm already onto it."

"And check where he was the day Carole Sutcliffe was run off the road."

They'd arrived at her house and he moved around the car to open the door for her. He put out his arm so she could take it and steady herself. She stumbled but his steady hand caught her. Jo was waiting for her, the front door open. "I'll be in tomorrow for the Blake interview and I want Jo and Chris behind the glass."

He looked sceptical. "Are you sure?"

"Positive. I'll be a lot better after a night in my own bed, and I'll get Jo to drive me over."

***

Jo had bought them a Chinese take-away but the smell of it made Alex's stomach turn. "I'm not sure I'm up to a Chinese tonight. My head's throbbing and making me feel sick."

Jo's jaw dropped. "You'll have to eat something, Alex. There was nothing except milk and bread in the fridge."

"I'm dying for a coffee. I'll try and eat some of the rice and spring rolls, even if I can't manage anything else."

Jo moved towards the coffee machine as she sat down at the kitchen table and took a spoon, shovelling some rice and spring rolls onto her plate. "I need to bounce something off you."

Jo flicked the button and the coffee machine started to gurgle. "Okay."

"We've just found out that Helen Carter had a baby which she put up for adoption. He's about the right age to fit in with the rape allegation and so it casts doubt on the abortion. It turns out he sent a blackmail letter to Helen Carter which we found in the box she'd left with Jane Simpson. He's now the prime suspect for the hit and run. Do you think she could've been lying about the abortion and in fact gave birth to a baby boy?"

Jo put her mug of coffee on the table in front of her, and then sat down at the table, putting her hand to her chin. "I find it hard to believe. Unless she convinced herself that she'd had an abortion when she hadn't... then we'd be talking ... delusional... and we haven't seen any evidence of that." Jo shook her head and put her hand back on her chin.

"Of course, there's another alternative," Alex said. "That she had both an abortion and then a pregnancy which went to full term."

Jo started to scoop some food onto her plate. "That seems more likely. And we're sure about the adopted child?"

"That's what it says on the birth certificate." She took a sip of her coffee and stood up. "I'm dying for a shower."

Jo glanced towards her plate and a half-eaten spring roll. "Will you be alright?"

"I'll call you if I need any help."

Chapter 26

It was late morning when Jo and Alex arrived at the station and immediately went their separate ways: Jo to the interview room and Alex to the Incident Room. As she walked through the door, Anaya Patel gaped at her.

"Are you alright, ma'am?"

They obviously hadn't been expecting her to come in today. She smiled. "Yes, thanks. A bump on my head but I'll live." As she made her way towards the glass board, the team swivelled their chairs around to watch her. She nodded at Dave. "Tell me."

He gestured towards Anaya.

She cleared her throat before speaking. "Alan Carter is out of the country so we haven't been able to bring him in to interview him. And we don't know if he was out of the country on the day the ACC's wife was run off the road."

She felt herself going into automatic pilot despite the bump on her head. "Get onto the Border Agency and check his passport for yesterday and the day Carole was driven off the road... and get onto the passport office and check if he holds more than one passport." She saw surprise register on Anaya's face. "It's not unusual for people who travel a lot to have more than one passport." It was clear that Anaya hadn't thought about that, but why would she? She'd had another case where two passports had been involved. They were needed for business people because of the time it could take to get visas for some countries, particularly in Africa. And there were also some countries which would not let you cross their borders if you had a stamp in your passport from a hostile country: the Arab countries of the Middle East and Israel were a case in point of the latter.

"Right, ma'am." Anaya seemed a bit flustered. "But we haven't picked up his vehicle on any CCTV cameras in the area at the time of the incident with the ACC's wife."

"That just means he may've used side roads... which he would've done if he had any sense. And anyway, it was a white vehicle that tried to run Carole off the road. He told me when I visited him in Corbridge that he had a grey SUV," she said. "Check the hire companies and see if a car was hired out on that day or around that time. And see if any of them recognise Alan Carter." She put her hand to her head. She felt woozy.

"I've checked Douglas Blake's background and he definitely isn't capable of the IT job on our systems," Ian said with a concerned expression on his face as he saw her struggle as she sat on the edge of one of the desks.

She straightened her head. "Thanks, Ian. That means we're back to Alan Carter. Have we got a search warrant for the house in Corbridge?"

"We're expecting it any time now," Ian replied.

"And his car?" She moved her eyes to Ian without shifting her head.

"If he didn't take it to the airport, we'll pick it up when we search the house."

"Let's find out where Rebecca Gray was last night." She could see scepticism on the faces around her and she knew what they were thinking. "I know it was a man who attacked Terry

Marshall... but if it was Alan Carter, his daughter might be involved as well."

She turned to Dave. "Let's go and interview Douglas Blake." Out the corner of her eye she caught disappointment settling on Luke's face. He'd gone to Edinburgh to get Douglas Blake and obviously had expected to be involved in the interview. But she wanted Dave with her because she was feeling fragile. She opened her mouth to speak to Luke but changed her mind. She didn't want to focus attention on the fact she wasn't feeling up to par. She would smooth things over with Luke when it was all over.

***

In her interview room she saw a nervous Douglas Blake sitting beside his solicitor. She glanced towards the glass where she knew that Jo, Chris Laidlaw and Mark Walker, the pathologist from Alnwick, were watching them. She'd wanted the pathologists there because she intended to challenge Douglas Blake about the death of Helen Carter and their opinion about what he said could be crucial. She sat down opposite Douglas Blake. His height was difficult to judge because he was sitting but she reckoned he was a couple of inches short of six feet. She scrutinised him for some resemblance to Neil Thomson, Peter Dodd or Terry Marshall. But she saw only his mother, Helen Carter – the same shaped face, same nose and same sky-blue eyes. If he'd been introduced as Rebecca Gray's brother, there could be little doubt of it except he had ash-blond rather than light-blond hair. Helen Carter couldn't have failed to recognise he was her son if she'd met him.

"Mr Blake, you are under caution and your solicitor will have already explained to you your rights." Steve Davies, the duty solicitor sitting in a crumpled navy-blue suit, inclined his head to let her know he'd spoken to Douglas Blake. "You do not have to say anything. But, it may harm your defence if you do not mention when questioned something which you later rely on in court. Anything you do say can be given in evidence." She saw out the corner of her eye Dave switch on the tape as she began to speak. He now moved and sat down beside her. "Mr Blake, are you the author of this letter?"

"The witness is being shown a letter," Dave stated in a monotonic voice.

"Yes, I am... and so?" he stammered out.

His feet were constantly taping and he kept shuffling in the armchair. He was nervous, probably because he didn't understand why he'd been brought down to Newcastle on the basis of the letter. "Could you please tell us why you decided to contact your natural mother now... why not earlier?"

"I'm getting married shortly," he replied without referring to his solicitor for advice.

People often wanted to reach out to their families and needed a sense of who they were during major life events like marriage, deaths and births. She'd come across this before and no doubt Jo would give her chapter and verse later. "Then why did you attempt to blackmail your natural mother?" Apart from the problems in his teens, he'd had a good relationship with his adopted parents and had gone to the University of St Andrews where he studied physics. He ran his own small business in Edinburgh.

"Getting married is expensive and I reckoned she owed me. And I wasn't sure she would meet me if I didnae threaten her." His face pinched. "She hadn't shown any interest in finding me in thirty years."

The soft Scottish lilt, characteristic of Edinburgh, became apparent as he spoke. He was being candid and his nervousness was showing only in his body language and not his speech. "And how many times have you met your natural mother?"

His eyes darted to his solicitor at his side. "Once... she didnae show up the second time."

"Did your natural mother tell you who your real father is?" Helen Carter appeared to have lied about the abortion, although she was still uneasy about that because it didn't make sense. And whether she'd been raped had been questionable since the beginning of the case.

"She told me she'd been raped at a party when she was young and she didnae know who my natural father was."

"Did she give you the names of the men who raped her?"

He stared at her. "No."

Back to the story of rape. She moved on. "Could you tell me where you first met your natural mother and what happened?"

His gaze continued to move around the room. "I met her in Berwick... at a restaurant."

The blackmail letter had hinted at money. "And did she give you any money?"

He inclined his head and then said, "Yes."

This was like drawing teeth. Had his solicitor briefed him well or was this another symptom of his nerves. "Could you tell me how much money?"

His feet started to tap again. "£10,000."

"That's a lot of money." Helen Carter must've felt guilty about what had happened. "Did she offer to give you any more?"

"Yes."

That would account for the £10,000 in Helen Carter's handbag when she died. "Did she offer to tell her husband and daughter about you?" Helen Carter had had enough time to talk to them both before she died. But would a woman like Helen Carter come clean about her past, even with death approaching.

He moved uneasily in the chair. "She told me she had terminal cancer and only had a few months to live... she said she'd tell her daughter about me and introduce me."

"And what about your mother's husband?" How would Alan Carter react to this revelation? And if he'd known, was it enough to tip him over the edge – Helen Carter dying, the rape allegation and a son he didn't know about?

"She said she couldn't see the point. He wasn't my father and as she was dying there was no reason to have contact with him."

"Did she intend coming to your wedding?" Curiosity had got the better of her as she wondered whether Helen Carter's behaviour meant she had regretted giving her son away. But then a narcissist could show no regret because they couldn't have done anything wrong in the first place.

He gazed at the floor. "She said she would probably be dead before then."

So, Helen Carter had come to terms with her imminent death and the vicar at Bywell had been right. "How would you describe your mother's reaction to you contacting her?"

"If she was shocked then she'd got over it before we met. She said she was sorry for what had happened, but it wasn't her fault. She'd been very young. She said she was pleased that she'd met me and that there was no doubt that I was her son. She promised she would help me as much as she could before she died." Douglas Blake looked her in the eyes. "She showed an interest in me. She asked me if I had had a happy childhood... and about my parents... my company... and my fiancée."

It sounded like Helen Carter had taken a genuine interest in her son. "And the second time you were supposed to meet your mother?"

"We didn't actually meet. We were supposed to meet but she didnae show up. I tried to call her, but I got no answer from her mobile." He shrugged. "I assumed she'd changed her mind."

She could see the disappointment in Douglas Blake's face. She signalled Dave who understood that he was to take over the questioning.

"Could you tell me where you were supposed to meet?" Dave asked in a flat voice.

Douglas Blake started tapping his feet again. "At a place called Waren Mill, not far from Bamburgh."

Dave continued. "And what time had you arranged to meet your mother?"

"It was very early in the morning. I complained because it meant I had to leave Edinburgh at five on a Sunday morning. But she said it was the only time she could meet me because she had hospital appointments in Newcastle during the week."

"And then what happened?" Dave asked.

"There was a thick haar when I got to Bamburgh and I crawled along the road to Waren Mill. I couldn't see her anywhere so I pulled in and tried to call her. No answer."

This made sense, she thought. They knew Douglas Blake had tried to phone Helen Carter on the mobile phone Jane Simpson had found in her caravan.

He continued, "I waited around for about ten minutes and tried her phone again. Nothing. Then I got in the car and drove a bit further down the road. I saw a place where I could turn the car around, so I pulled in, reversed the car and headed back to Edinburgh.

"And did you see any other vehicle when you were turning the car around?" Dave asked.

Douglas Blake paused to think. "Yes, I saw a cream mini parked where I turned."

He said this in a matter of fact way. She observed that there were no signs of deception on his face and body language, He hadn't realised that it was Helen Carter's car, but then he had only met her once.

"And did you bump anything while you were turning the car around?" Dave had asked a leading question.

Douglas Blake's mouth opened. She could see he didn't know where the questioning was going

He frowned. "I bumped something. I noticed a yellow sand grit bucket when I drove in. I assumed I'd bumped that."

"And did you stop the car to take a look?" Dave asked in an even voice.

"I realised I was going too slow to have done any substantial damage. I stopped later on when I'd driven through the haar. At a quick glance I couldn't see any damage... where is this going?"

She nodded at Dave.

Dave drew a deep breath. "I would like to propose an alternative scenario to you. That you went to meet your natural mother at Waren Mill and you argued. She'd refused to give you any more money or to introduce you to your sister. So, you ran her over with your vehicle."

There was silence. She watched Douglas Blake carefully as first his mouth opened and then his eyes widened into a stare. "What the hell are you talking about?"

Dave responded. “Your mother was found lying dead at the spot in Waren Mill where you admit to turning your vehicle around. She’d been the victim of a hit and run incident. She was found there by a friend less than half an hour after you left the area.” Dave had kept constant eye contact with Douglas Blake.

Suddenly Douglas Blake stood up and shouted, “I didnae kill her... I had no reason to... and you’re no pinning this on me.” Shock was written on his face.

She noticed Douglas Blake’s disbelief and that he’d spoken with the Scottish habit of saying ‘no’ instead of ‘not’.

Dave continued calmly. “We’ve tested your vehicle and the forensics show that it was responsible for the hit and run that killed Helen Carter.”

Douglas Blake slumped back down into his chair, his head in his hands. She watched him. He had believed he had hit the sand bucket. But why hadn’t he come forward? Of course, the accident hadn’t been reported in Edinburgh. Borders and rivers produced a strange psychology and the only thing marking the border with Scotland was a sign, ‘Welcome to Scotland’. Events in next door neighbour, Northumberland, were not necessarily reported in the Scottish media. Whoever had attacked Carole Sutcliffe had made the mistake of looking in Northumberland for the black SUV. They hadn’t thought about Scotland. They would need to check out Douglas Blake’s alibis for the death of Neil Thomson and the incident with Carole Sutcliffe. She turned her head to Dave to let him know she would take over the questioning again. She knew that if Dave believed Douglas Blake’s story, he would complain to her that he always got to play the ‘hard man’ in their double act during interviews. She turned towards Douglas Blake who still had his head in his hands with his elbows resting on his knees. “Mr Blake, you may be facing a charge of manslaughter.” She had said ‘may’ because she thought there was a good chance that this might be successfully argued as 'accidental death'.

"But if I killed her, I didnae know I had done it." His eyes were filled with tears. "I thought I'd hit a yellow sand bucket." he pleaded.

"And you didn't see or hear any reports of the hit and run?" She would get the team to check out whether it had been reported north of the border.

"No, nothing." His voice was quivering.

She turned her attention to Steve Davies, the duty solicitor acting for Douglas Blake, because she knew what she was about to say would shock him. But she didn't want this young man put in any danger. "We'll be keeping you in custody, Mr Blake."

"Is that really necessary?" The usually lugubrious Steve Davies was shocked.

"I think Mr Blake may be in some danger because we have reason to believe that someone may be attempting to kill whoever killed Helen Carter. It will be as much for Mr Blake's safety as for anything else." She turned back to Douglas Blake. "You need to get yourself a good solicitor."

She knew what she believed had happened. Helen Carter had shown up to meet her son but she didn't have her mobile with her and so hadn't taken his call. The sea-fret was so thick that Douglas Blake had got lost and had killed his natural mother as he had turned around to head off back to Edinburgh. She cast her mind to the day she'd visited the scene of the hit and run. Everyone, including the pathologists, believed it was an accident and on the basis of this interview it looked like they were all right.

CHAPTER 27

DS Ian Turner was just about to walk back through the door of the Carter house in Corbridge, when he heard a car approach and turned. He'd just finished putting Alan Carter's computers into the car to take them back to the station. A taxi was pulling up to the gate of the house. It must be Alan Carter coming home. But then the taxi set off again. If it was Alan Carter, he must've seen the police car. He ran across to his car and jumped into the driver's seat. He started the ignition and then slammed his foot on the accelerator pedal. The car skidded and crunched down the gravel drive towards the gate. He turned down the road to pursue the taxi. It had gone. He slowed and continued down the road, his head turning left and right, surveying the driveways of the houses. Nothing. Alan Carter couldn't have gone far. He pulled into the side of the road and took his mobile out of his pocket. "Can I have Rebecca Gray's address in Corbridge?"

He punched the address into the Sat Nav and set out for Rebecca Gray's house. It was nearby. Alan Carter, if it was him, now had a few minutes start as well as the advantage of knowing Corbridge. He pressed his foot down on the accelerator. He turned left down one street and then right down another. He skidded into Rebecca Gray's drive as the driver of a white Mini

Cooper was pulling out. For a split second they looked at each other through their windscreens – it was Alan Carter. He must've got the taxi to drop him off and taken his daughter's car. The Mini Cooper sped off and Ian moved into the drive, swung around sharply and followed the car down the road. Alan Carter accelerated. He wasn't going to let him get away this time. He could feel the adrenaline rushing through his body. The Mini Cooper screeched down the centre of Corbridge, ignoring the one-way sign. It mounted the narrow pavement to avoid an on-coming car. The car hooted ferociously. He switched on his police siren. The Mini Cooper turned towards the narrow bridge which crossed the Tyne. It swerved out of control. He wasn't a good driver. Ian followed. He could hear his heart beating in his ears. Up a road, Alan Carter accelerated again. A car came out of a side road. The Mini Cooper twisted to avoid it. There was the crunch of metal against wood. Alan Carter had driven into a tree. Ian pulled in and then jumped out of his car and ran over to the Mini Cooper. Alan Carter was slumped over the steering wheel. He looked at the car engine, no sign that it was going to explode. Better not move him in case it made any injuries worse. He took his phone out of his pocket and called for an ambulance.

CHAPTER 28

Anaya Patel knocked on the door of Alex's office and she signalled to Anaya to come in. One of the advantages of the glass, and the only one she thought, was that she didn't have to get up to answer her door

"I think I've sorted out the Alan Carter passport problem, ma'am," she said and sat down opposite her. "You were right, ma'am. He has two passports."

She noted how she hadn't had to invite Anaya to sit down. She'd taken the initiative which was a good sign. She wasn't surprised at the confirmation about the two passports. That's once they'd realised that it had to be Alan Carter for the Halloween attack and for running Carole Sutcliffe off the road.

"On both occasions, that is Halloween and Mrs Sutcliffe's accident, he was supposed to be working in Ghana," Anaya said. "He left the country using one passport both times. But then he returned using the second passport. I've spoken to the Ghanaian Embassy. They've been computerising the airport recently and they've been having some difficulties. So, they've had to continue with getting passengers to fill in forms. Filling in a form when they enter the country and keeping a section of it which they hand in on exit. But the computerisation of the forms hasn't worked.."

"What did he do?"

"He could've just said he'd lost the exit part of the form when he left the country with his second passport. That's what I expect he did. If the computers had been working properly two passports would've helped. It would probably have caused some confusion. As he left with his second passport, he could probably have argued that the computers hadn't worked when he had entered the country. At least, that's what I expect he was planning to do. But it doesn't seem to have been a good plan." Anaya paused to take a breath. "The thing is, there's only one flight in and out of the UK to Accra, and that runs daily to Heathrow. It's with BA."

"In other words, we could've found out from BA with or without him using two passports?"

"Yes, ma'am."

She paused to think. Obviously, they would've had to be suspicious about Alan Carter to check. All of Alan Carter's actions seemed to have been rushed and not well thought through. But then he was in grief for his wife. When Luke had checked on Alan Carter, he had established his whereabouts on the night of Neil Thomson's murder and on the day of Helen Carter's hit and run. They'd have to re-check the information and make sure he wasn't trying to play the same trick then. "So, what have you established he did?"

"He flew here from Accra and arrived on the morning of Halloween. And then he flew back to Accra the following day."

"And he did the same on the day of Carole Sutcliffe's accident?"

"Yes, ma'am."

"With the identification of the ring by Terry Marshall, that should be enough to prove he was responsible for Halloween. And Terry Marshall has identified Alan Carter's ring?"

"Yes, ma'am. From a photo."

"But we still need to find the car he used for Carole Sutcliffe's accident. That he was back in the country won't be enough."

"We're already onto that, ma'am."

***

Alex opened the door of an interview room which had been temporarily turned into a computer hub. The IT team had had a word with Dave Bell when she'd been in hospital and they'd called the National Cyber Security Centre – NCSC – for help. They'd been set up a few years ago to help the public sector deal with the cyber threat and were staffed by experts from GCHQ. "Tell me," she said. They were currently trying to find out if Alan Carter was responsible for what had happened to the ACC's machine, and the hack into the CCTV cameras. They had two members of the NCSC working with them now.

"It was definitely him," a fair-haired young man with his hair tied back into a ponytail said.

"You're sure?"

"It's a botnet," he said as he turned back to his machine and his work.

She looked blankly at Jim Dobson who headed up their own IT team. "You'd better explain."

"That's where a number of internet-connected devices are running more than one bot."

She raised one eyebrow. "English, please Jim."

"This is where someone from the outside takes control of the machine," he replied.

She felt relief sweeping through her because this put Damien in the clear. "So how did it happen?"

"We're trying to work out the kill chain now."

She stared at Jim.

"In IT we use the same terms and system as the military. It means Reconnaissance. Weaponization. Delivery. Exploitation. Installation. Command and Control. Actions and Objectives."

She rolled her eyes. "Can you just tell me what you think happened to the bot thingy-me-bob and the boss' machine?"

The faired-haired ponytailed man from the NCSC raised his head from his machine. "Usually the perp... sorry, perpetrator, ma'am... disables the anti-virus on the machines and then downloads malware. This allows them to take control of the machine. It's a big problem internationally. You can hire bots on the Dark Web."

She knew about the Dark Web and had seen a presentation about it. It was a free-for-all for criminals who could buy any service from contract killing to drugs. The Americans had brought down a site called The Silk Road which was like an Amazon site for criminals. You could buy anything from sawn-off shotguns to drugs. And like Amazon, sellers were given a star rating. "And do we know where Alan Carter got this bot from?"

"Not yet, ma'am."

Her mind moved again to Alan Carter and the computer screens in his study. "And does it require a lot of know-how to be able to do this?"

"It does. But it's not extremely sophisticated."

"You mean it doesn't require someone of your expertise to do it?"

"No."

"And when was it likely to be set up?" She was wondering if it had happened after Helen Carter's hit and run?

"They can be set up months in advance and left dormant until needed."

"But it could've been set up in the last week or so?"

"Yes. But we'll need to do more research to be sure."

"As quickly as possible, please. This information is going to be key in one of my cases." She turned back to Jim Dobson. "We need to check if anyone has been into the DVLA systems to check who owns the boss' black SUV. If you need any more resource, let me know."

"I'll get onto the NCSC and see if they can assign someone else to look into that."

She walked towards the door and then turned back. "Do any of you know Alan Carter?"

The pony-tailed man lifted his head again. "Yes, we all do. He's internationally respected. Really knows his stuff. And he's really good fun to work with."

This wasn't the Alan Carter they'd learnt about. But then she wondered what counted as fun in the world of IT geeks.

***

The interview room door opened and Alex saw Rebecca Gray come in the room with Anaya Patel directly behind her. She was accompanied by a young dark-haired slim-built man in an expensive suit, and no doubt an expensive fee, with an arrogant swagger and air about him. It was her solicitor, Jack Robson. Rebecca Gray was well-dressed again in figure-hugging blue jeans with a white silk shirt tucked into them, her coat neatly drawn across her arm. There was no head held high strut this time; her head was bowed and her step uncertain. She felt sympathy for her because one of her parents was dead, and the other in serious trouble. But she hoped that this changed demeanour didn't mean she was going to have to put up with the 'little girl lost' today, like on the first occasion she'd met her at her parents' house.

"Would you like to take a seat? I hope you don't find the lighting too troublesome today." She remembered the 'musical chairs' during their last interview when she'd switched chairs at least three times. She tried not to let sarcasm creep into her voice, but nonetheless was hoping she wasn't going to have to put up with a similar performance today. Rebecca Gray sat down and looked at the floor.

Her analysis of her was that she was a coward and she would point a finger at her father rather than take any blame herself. At their previous interview she hadn't shown the same love and devotion for her father as she'd had for her mother. She was hoping to provoke her into 'shopping' him to get herself off the proverbial hook. "You do not have to say anything. But, it may harm your defence if you do not mention when questioned something which you later rely on in court. Anything you do say can be given in evidence. You know why you are here?"

Rebecca said nothing and continued to stare at the floor.

"We know that your mother accused Neil Thomson and two other men of rape. One of these three men is now dead... Neil Thomson. Another, Terry Marshall, has been attacked at his house and injured."

She paused. There was still no reaction from Rebecca, but her upper body had started to shake. Her solicitor Jack Robson, was staring with his mouth open. He had a lot to learn about not showing body language, even if his client hadn't properly briefed him, which judging from his reaction seemed to be the case.

"Mrs Gray, we know your mother hired a private detective to follow these three men."

"You don't have to answer that," Jack Robson said.

"Yes. But she didn't kill anyone," Rebecca screeched and then coughed.

"Mrs Gray, you and your mother were in Chinatown on the night Neil Thomson was killed." She waited but there was no reaction. "We know that your mother followed Neil Thomson to Blackfriars Gate because we have a pair of your mother's shoes which have stood in Neil Thomson's blood."

"Yes, but she didn't kill him. She found him dead," she said emphatically whilst Jack Robson's eyes widened.

"Why was she following him?"

"She wanted to speak to him. That was all." She stared down at the floor.

"After nearly thirty years?" Her voice rose slightly.

"She had tried to call him. But he didn't reply to her calls. So, she followed him to speak to him."

"And why didn't she call the police or an ambulance when she found Neil Thomson dead?"

"She panicked," she mumbled to the floor. "She was worried that she might be blamed for killing him."

Her eyebrows rose. It wasn't much of an excuse. "But she'd hired a private detective to follow these three men. Why?"

"Because she wanted to contact them."

"It seems a bit extreme. Why didn't she just try and phone them?"

"She wasn't sure they'd want to speak to her."

"Was that because she accused these three men of raping her when they were students? Something which they denied."

"They did rape her," she shouted and looked at her with eyes that had turned as dark as a sudden thunderstorm.

"Then why would she want contact with three men who raped her?"

"My brother," she mumbled as she gazed into the corner of the room.

"Your brother? Would you like to explain?"

"My mum got pregnant after she was raped. By the time she found out it was too late for an abortion, so she had the baby adopted. He made contact with my mum recently."

"And..."

"My mum wanted to speak to the men to tell them one of them was his father."

She waited because she knew there was a bit more.

Rebecca looked her in the eyes. "You know my mum had cancer. She wanted to tell the three of them about my brother."

"And was she going to tell your brother?"

"Yes. After she'd spoken to the men. She was going to tell him that one of them was his father."

"And this was the reason you were in Chinatown?"

"Yes. She thought that Neil Thomson was most likely to be his father." There was a flash of anger in her eyes. "But my mum wouldn't kill anyone. She was a good person. Even though he'd done the dirty on her."

"And what about Jesmond?"

"She was hoping to stop Peter Dodd when he was out jogging. But we missed him. So, she decided to call him instead. She was hoping he'd call her back."

"And did he?"

"No." Her eyes started to wander around the room.

"And have you met your brother?"

"No. Not yet."

"And what about the third man?"

"She hadn't got around to contacting him before she died," she sobbed into her handkerchief and then burst into tears. Jack Robson moved closer to her and put his arm around her. This seemed a bit cosy for a professional relationship.

She waited for the tears to subside. "Mrs Gray, your mother was blaming an abortion for her cancer. What can you tell me about that?"

"She had an abortion before my brother was born."

"And who was the father of that baby?"

She looked at her coldly. "It was Neil Thomson, of course."

"And she was sure about that?"

Rebecca stared blackly at Alex. "Yes. She told me it was about a year before she fell pregnant with my brother. Neil Thomson was in the middle of his studies and he didn't want to get married at that time. He promised to marry her later," she guffawed.

"And when she fell pregnant a second time?"

"He refused to marry her because he said that he didn't know that he was the father." Her voice was cold. "But he was responsible for plying her with drink and drugs and letting the other two sleep with her." Her face set in an icy stare. "But she said that he was still most likely to be my brother's father."

She stared back. "And the cancer?"

"She was very upset at first. And she thought it might be the abortion. Particularly as it was ovarian cancer and there's a link between that cancer and miscarriages. She was sure it was to blame, despite what the doctors said. But when she got the second opinion, she came to terms with the fact that... she was going to... die." There were tears trickling down her face.

"How?"

"Our vicar. He was really good. He talked to her and helped her."

"So, you're saying that the only reason your mother was trying to contact Neil Thomson, Peter Dodd and Terry Marshall was because of your brother?"

"Yes," she shouted. "After she met him, she wanted to help him. My mum was a good person. She gave him money. But because she knew she was... dying, she thought it was time that whoever was my brother's father paid up and helped him."

She wondered how easy this was going to be, if the men decided not to play ball. And, as Helen Carter thought Neil Thomson was the most likely candidate to be Douglas Blake's father, what she intended to do after he'd been killed? "And does your father know about any of this?"

"No... he knew about the cancer and the rape."

"And did he know who the three men were?"

"I didn't think so until yesterday... my mum must've told him because I didn't."

"And what do you know about the attack on Terry Marshall?" She stared calmly into Rebecca's eyes.

"Nothing. Until I spoke to my dad." Her voice lightened.

"And?"

"My dad explained when he came to take my car... he only stayed a few minutes... he said he thought that my mum had killed Neil Thomson... he attacked Terry Marshall to finish the job for her... and he tried to kill the person who had run her over." Her unemotional voice moved through the information in a matter of fact way.

"And you didn't try to tell your father that you knew your mother hadn't killed Neil Thomson."

"He rushed in and grabbed my keys... and then ran out. I didn't get the chance. And I had no idea of what he was planning to do... otherwise, I would've stopped him."

She could feel her heart racing. Rebecca had confirmed her assumption.

Her heartbeat slowed as she considered her. She was an immature, pathetic figure. A storm had erupted when she'd attacked her mother. But she squealed liked a packed pig on her father without thought or remorse. Jo was right. Helen Carter must've pumped Rebecca with her own narrative since childhood, and this included her disappointment about Alan Carter. She didn't seem to register that Alan Carter had also loved Helen. "To summarise, Mrs Gray, you're saying that your father told you he believed your mother had killed Neil Thomson. That he attacked Terry Marshall and tried run Mrs Sutcliffe off the road?

"Yes," she said calmly.

"But you yourself don't believe your mother killed Neil Thomson."

"That's right." It was the first time she'd deferred to her Jack Robson who had been as much use as a chocolate fireguard. He nodded at her.

"Mrs Gray, if you had told us all of this when you were first interviewed, you may have saved us all a lot of time and trouble. We have pursued a line of enquiry which we didn't need to pursue. And your behaviour amounts to obstructing a police enquiry."

Jack Robson stared at her with steel-grey eyes. “I’m not sure that’s reasonable.”

She gave him one of her sternest stares which Jo had once told her would wither flowers.

“Mrs Gray, we may need to talk to you again. You are not to leave the country or the area for that matter.”

Chapter 29

Alex stood outside her interview room. Inside, Alan Carter and his solicitor were waiting. Anaya Patel came dashing along the corridor, clutching papers and hopefully the information she'd been waiting for.

"Alan Carter can't be responsible for Neil Thomson's murder," Anaya puffed out. "Luke and I have just finished all of the checks. He was definitely out of the country on that day."

"And he hasn't been playing any games with his two passports?"

"No. He came in and out on the same passport. He was in Kenya on the day Neil Thomson was killed." She grasped the papers in her hand more tightly. "I've spoken to the company he was working for. They've confirmed he was there. And Luke has checked with all the airlines who fly in and out of Kenya to make sure."

She nodded. It was what she'd expected. She opened the interview room door and they both walked in. As she sat down, she signalled to Anaya to turn on the tape. "I'm DCI Alex Shaftoe." She gestured to Anaya. "And this is DS Anaya Patel." She stared firmly at Alan Carter. "You do not have to say anything. But, it may harm your defence if you do not mention when questioned something which you later rely on in court. Anything you do say may be given in evidence. Mr Carter you realise why you are here?" She was sitting with Anaya beside her whilst Alan Carter, sporting a black eye and some other facial bruising, sat opposite them. A suited man in his sixties, about the same age as him, was sitting beside him: his solicitor. "We intend charging you with the assault of Mr Terry Marshall, of one of my police officers, Jackie Palmer, and of myself." He was avoiding eye contact with her. "You also tried to evade arrest."

She'd asked Jo about what the NCSC team had said about Alan Carter being good fun at work. Jo felt that his childhood answered the conundrum. He was ill at ease in family and social gatherings which made him reticent. However, as IT was his forte, he was comfortable in that context. She considered whether a schizoid diagnosis would have been given to the Alan Carter of the workplace? And she pondered whether Helen Carter had made a play for him because she'd met him at work, not realising until later on that he was uncommunicative at home? "And there is a charge of hacking into police computer systems and altering records."

"I think the charges of assault on your police officer and you, are harsh. I knocked you both over as I was running away." He deferred to his solicitor. "It wasn't deliberate."

"You threw a punch at me, Mr Carter... that's not an accident as far as I'm concerned." She kept her voice even. "And the attack on Mr Marshall. You're not denying assaulting him."

"There's not much point," he said in a defeated voice. His shoulders were slumped forward in a world-weary poise.

"Well, I'm glad that you're admitting it. It will save us all a lot of time. She paused. "Can you tell us your reason for the attack on Terry Marshall?"

His chin lowered to his chest. "He harmed my wife," was all he said.

This was vague but she guessed he must be referring to the rape. But she needed to be sure. "You're suggesting he attacked your wife?"

He shook his head. "He raped her when she was young."

"That's a long time ago," she said. She thought about her interview with Lorna Godfrey which seemed a lifetime ago and remembered her telling them that Helen Carter told different stories to different people, and then used it to play people off against each other. It would seem that he knew about the rape and abortion.

He stared at his feet.

"And what about Neil Thomson?" They wanted to corroborate what Rebecca Gray had just told them. "You know who he is?"

"He was one of men who raped my wife when she was young." His voice thickened. "I had nothing to do with his murder."

"And by that, you mean you didn't ask or hire anyone else to murder him?" Luke and Ian were currently investigating everything to do with Alan Carter, and in particular any foreign contacts he may have. They wanted to be absolutely sure that no-one else had acted on behalf of the Carters. She expected to draw a blank but she wanted to cross all the t's and dot all the i's.

"You do realise that we don't think your wife had anything to do with the death of Neil Thomson." She watched him closely. His head jerked back. Alan Carter had thought that his wife had murdered Neil Thomson, otherwise he wouldn't have been shocked when she'd said that she hadn't done it. He was trying to finish the job off for her, but they would never know if he would've actually killed Terry Marshall if they hadn't disturbed him. They had been unable to match his DNA to the knife found on Terry Marshall's street.

"We will also be charging you with dangerous driving and deliberately running Mrs Carole Sutcliffe off the road. Are you denying this?"

His solicitor piped up, "And what evidence do you have for that?"

They hadn't yet come up with the car Alan Carter had used, but she felt sure they would find it as they continued to dig. "Mr Carter's daughter, Rebecca Gray, has confirmed to us that her father admitted to her he had done this."

Alan Carter sat motionless and silent. It was hard to work out if his daughter's betrayal had upset him. "You do realise that it wasn't Mrs Sutcliffe's vehicle which was responsible for the death of your wife?"

Again, he remained still and silent. His bruised eyes emotionless.

She could see no point in mentioning the existence of Douglas Blake, Helen's son, nor her many affairs. It served no purpose other than to satisfy her own curiosity. It would be cruel to inflict this on a beaten man. She felt more sympathy for him than she did for his wife or daughter. He'd had a bad start in life and three failed marriages before Helen. He must've felt that this was his only chance at family life. But he had a wife and daughter who didn't love him, even though it seemed he loved them. She would finish off charging him with what he had done.

"You seem to have got an awful lot of things wrong, Mr Carter," she said quietly. "We will also be charging you with hacking into the police computer systems and changing police evidence. I'm referring to changing the description of the vehicle that killed your wife. And we will be charging you with hacking into CCTV cameras on the highways. I'm referring to you obtaining information about vehicles on the A1 on the day and at the time your wife was killed."

He remained silent.

"Could you explain why you were wearing a cloak and mask when you attacked Mr Terry Marshall?"

His eyes widened and his facial expression said, 'stupid question'. "Because it was Halloween."

"And there's no other reason?" she asked.

"What other reason could there be?" he said, puzzled.

It had crossed her mind that Alan Carter may've used the cloak because he knew about the Blackfriars murder. He had an alibi for that night, but as he'd believed that Helen had been responsible for that murder it could've diverted attention away from her. "You will be remanded in custody for the time being until a judge decides whether bail is appropriate."

She knew now that she had everything nailed except Neil Thomson's murder. But as she watched Alan Carter, her mind returned to his wife whom she'd disliked from the moment they were introduced. The only difference between her and the narcissists who had dominated world history, was the level of power. Helen Carter hadn't been able to harm on a large scale – only those who'd come into her immediate circle. As she regarded Alan Carter again, she realised that neither he nor Helen had had anywhere left to run and that was what had kept them together. He didn't want another failed marriage. Helen had tried hard enough to leave him, but none of her married lovers would leave their wives for her. She felt conflicted about Helen Carter. If she hadn't got involved in the student party scene too young would things have turned out differently? But then another person may've been able to rise above the experience and go on and have a happy life. And if it hadn't been the student parties then maybe something else going wrong may have destabilised her? Jo was tougher than her in these situations because she dealt with them regularly. And she was adamant you got nowhere with narcissists; they were incurable, like psychopaths. All you could do was limit the damage they did to the others around them.

There was a knock and then Dave Bell stuck his head around the door. She got up and left the room, shutting the door behind her.

"I've just had a call from Chris." Dave punched the air with his fist. "They've found Neil Thomson's DNA inside Chinese Johnny's knife."

She breathed out a sigh of relief. They now knew what had happened to Neil Thomson. Chinese Johnny must have left his flat in Blackfriars ahead of Neil Thomson and waited for him. It would've been easy for Chinese Johnny, after he killed Neil Thomson, to have taken off his cloak and walked up Friars Lane and then into Stowell Street and back to his flat. Despite the fact that they'd found no evidence on the Darth Vader cloak, she was sure he had used it and that what the young Chinese woman had seen was right.

CHAPTER 30

Alex was just about to pick up her handbag and leave the office to meet Ewan for dinner. She looked up and saw Douglas Blake about to knock on her glass door. She knew he'd been granted bail and that the charge was 'accidentally killing' Helen Carter. But she was puzzled about why he wanted to see her. Had he remembered something else about the hit and run? But she was certain they had wrapped everything up. She knew that they were never going to get Peter Dodd or the Chinese Triad Chief for Neil Thomson's murder, but they must've given the order to Chinese Johnny. Nothing else made sense.

She opened her office door. "Come in, Mr Blake. How can I help you?" She gestured for him to take a seat.

He sat down nervously and then cleared his throat. "DCI Shaftoe, I'm here to ask you if you can help me find out who my natural father is?"

She looked across at him in surprise. She hadn't really thought about this; she'd been too busy tying up the final pieces of her cases. But she supposed if he'd gone as far as tracking down his natural mother, he would want to know about his father. "And your mother gave you no hint at all."

"Only what I told you at the interview. That she'd been raped by more than one man."

She knew who the three men were, but there was no way she could tell him. She thought for a moment about what was likely to come out at Alan Carter's trial and realised that if he waited until then, he'd probably be able to work it out for himself. "Mr Blake, I can't tell you what I know. You must realise that."

He looked down at the floor and sighed.

"Have you tried contacting your sister to see what she might know?" She knew for a fact that Rebecca Gray knew the truth. They'd established that at her last interview.

"I tried to contact her. She slammed the phone down on me, screaming that I was a murderer," he mumbled quietly.

"She may change her mind once she's got over the shock." She wasn't taken aback at Rebecca's reaction to him. It was in character with the woman they'd interviewed. And she had been devoted to her mother. "Are you really sure you want to know?" She was thinking of Peter Dodd as she said this. But then she remembered the lengths to which Helen Carter had gone to find his father. One of the candidates was dead, another was a drug dealer facing prison and she didn't know much about the third, apart from what had happened at Halloween.

"Yes, I'm sure."

She'd hoped by asking him if he really wanted to know, it might've hinted to him to let sleeping dogs lie. But it hadn't worked. She wasn't going to suggest Alan Carter to him, although she knew he knew. "I'll see what I can do, Mr Blake. However, I'd be grateful if you didn't contact me again about this. If I find anything out for you, I'll contact you. Is that clear?"

He smiled at her. "Yes." It was Helen Carter's smile.

It was ironic that she was being asked to finish off what Helen Carter had started and which had led them a merry dance in trying to unravel what had gone on. Had they known about the man sitting in front of her earlier, it would've made it much easier. "Mr Blake, we have your DNA, but we can't use it for anything except police purposes. If you would have a word with one of my officers as you go out, you can sign to say you are giving us permission to use it for a paternity test." She raised her eyebrows. "But I can make no promises." She glanced at her watch. "If you'll excuse me, I'm going out to dinner."

She took her handbag from her desk. She'd already decided on a plan of action. Neil Thomson was dead and so she would have to ask Sarah Thomson for permission to test his DNA. And she wasn't sure how she'd react. Peter Dodd, she thought, was unlikely to help. So, Terry Marshall seemed the best place to start.

She wasn't sure what legal rights Douglas Blake had, or if he had any at all in these circumstances. The birth certificate said, 'father unknown'. And Helen Carter wasn't alive to make a statement that she thought his father was one of three men. And if she had made this statement, would that have given Douglas Blake any rights? Had Helen Carter checked out the legalities? If she had, she couldn't imagine Rebecca Gray or Alan Carter being helpful about it. She closed her office door and noticed that Dave Bell was still at his desk. "Dave, do we know if Terry Marshall has any children?"

"No. I don't think so."

***

The taxi dropped Alex outside an Italian restaurant on the Quayside in Newcastle. As she walked through the door, the main room of the restaurant had soft lighting and tables strategically placed for intimacy. She spotted Ewan at a table in a corner and smiled at him. He stood up as she approached, took her coat which he gave to a waiter, and pulled her chair out for her. His manners were certainly good. She wasn't used to this type of treatment.

"I'm glad I'm no longer a murder suspect," he said mischievously, wrinkling his nose in a smile which exposed his even, white teeth.

She rolled her eyes. "I'm sure a man of your intelligence realised the difficulty of my position?" As the waiter came over to their table, he greeted Ewan and it was obvious that he frequented this restaurant. As she surveyed the room, its ambience and the other couples sitting at the tables, her wariness returned as she wondered how many other women Ewan had brought to this restaurant. "Do you come here often?"

"I live in a flat nearby."

"I had wondered. I thought you might live in Durham?"

"I prefer living in Newcastle. I can jump on a train at the Central Station and be in Durham in twenty minutes."

"Shall I order?" He said. "Can we have a bottle of Pinot Grigio?"

She was now sure he'd been talking to Jo, his choice of wine too much of a coincidence otherwise. She ordered pate for a starter followed by sea bream and Ewan ordered a mozzarella salad followed by steak.

"I was going to tell you a bit about my past since you haven't asked." His palms turned upwards in an expressive gesture.

The waiter returned with their bottle of wine. "Just fill the glasses," Ewan said.

He was watching her to see how she reacted to his suggestion. She waited for him to continue and took a sip of her wine. She'd taken a taxi to the restaurant so she could have a drink. She'd reckoned she might need it.

"I divorced five years ago and I've two grown-up children, neither of them living in the north-east. My son is at university in Cambridge and my daughter now works in London."

Jo had already told her about this when trying to pique her interest in Ewan. He hadn't been responsible for the marriage breakdown; his wife had been having an affair with someone for a couple of years when he found out. She'd refused to give up her lover and so Ewan had left her.

She decided to intervene. "I know, Ewan. Jo told me. It's normal 'girl talk'. No doubt Jo has told you about my background?"

The waiter arrived with their starters.

"I know about your husband and your daughter," he volunteered.

She met his eyes. "Tell me about your children?"

"My daughter, Nicola, studied economics at the London School of Economics and she's now a deputy finance director for a company in the city. My son's studying history at my old college, St John's, in Cambridge."

"I studied history and archaeology at St John's." A brief laugh broke from her lips. "I'm surprised we didn't come across each other."

"We might've done." He tilted his head to the side. "But you know what it's like if you're in different years. What about your daughter? Lisa, isn't it?"

She smirked. “Another history graduate from St John’s. She loves everything to do with books and she now works as a junior editor for a publisher in New York.

He focused his gaze on her. “I’m surprised you didn’t take up a career in history, even though as we all know, there aren’t many jobs.”

“I ended up studying Roman Greece.”

“Well Roman Greece is unusual.”

She agreed. “It is because most people who study in Greece do classical Greece or prehistoric Greece – the Minoans or Mycenaean’s.”

“Did you finish your studies?”

“No, unfortunately I didn’t.”

“That’s a pity.” He turned his attention to his food.

She realised the butterflies had gone from her stomach, she’d relaxed and had started to enjoy the evening. And she hadn’t dropped any clangers. She wasn’t sure how or why, but he’d managed to put her at her ease, maybe because he’d opened up about himself. It was strange, but many men didn’t do that.

“To change the subject.” His eyes widened with anticipation. “I was wondering if we could start to meet more regularly? To take you out, to use an old-fashioned term.”

Her heart missed a beat. She was trying to think about what she was going to say. She could feel her cheeks start to burn and she lowered her head. Then she felt annoyed with herself for behaving like a teenager. For twenty-five years she’d dealt with every type of crime and had interviewed murderers, yet she was dumbfounded because someone had asked her out. She swallowed and hoped he hadn’t been observing her closely. She met his eyes which had a twinkle in them. Was he amused at her panicked reaction? "I'm really out of practice, Ewan," she stuttered. "I've been on my own a long time... probably too long." She could feel her cheeks burning again.

"I know." His voice was low and soft. "Jo has explained."

Jo must have guessed at how she would react. She wasn't sure whether to thank her or throttle her. She took some deep breaths.

"We're both mature adults with a lot in common. Let's do this the old-fashioned way and meet for dinner or go to the theatre or cinema."

Her chin dropped to her chest. He really understands. She knew she would cringe tomorrow at the way she had reacted. She would be candid with him. "I was never one to jump into things, even when I was young." She gazed across at the window. "You see, I met my husband at work... and the two relationships I've had since then were with colleagues I knew from work... I was familiar with them before I went out with them." She pinched the skin at her throat.

Ewan took a sip of his wine. "The one thing we've got in common is archaeology. Why don't you come up and visit the excavations at Holy Island?" He paused. "My circumstances are different from yours. I'm divorced and it wasn't a pleasant experience," he sighed, "and now I'm feeling a bit lonely."

She could see his point. When a relationship went badly wrong it left a different feeling, a bad taste in your mouth even if you had once loved the person. Losing someone you love suddenly to death was very different because they'd left you when you still loved them. She'd experienced both; she'd had a bad relationship that had gone wrong before Daniel – a man she'd loved and thought she'd marry. She smiled at Ewan. "I just wanted to put my cards on the table... I'm rusty, that's all," she laughed. "I have a daughter in America and a mother in a nursing home... and my life feels like it's on hold at the moment."

He moved his head up and down slowly. He really was being very reasonable and she could see why Jo liked him – she liked him. He was a good listener and there was sympathy in his reaction to her reticence. She thought about what she found attractive in a man. Intelligence was the most important thing to her. The body of a Greek god was very nice but only when it was inhabited with brains. Intelligence was visible in body language. But there had to be more than that. A rapport, and there must be a similar outlook on life – liberal humanism, compassion and not an overriding materialism. She guessed he had these qualities otherwise Jo wouldn't have tried to push them together. But what about chemistry? There was a theory it had something to do with smell. She did like Ewan and found him attractive, and Jo was right, he was her type. She laughed. "And I haven't gone into the unsociable hours I work... obsessing with a case..."

He laughed. "Well, you've certainly laid the negatives out on the table but what about the positives?"

She hadn't thought about that in her anxiety. But a trip to the excavations on Holy Island was appealing. "You'll have to work them out for yourself as you get to know me."

He raised an eyebrow. "That almost feels like a challenge."

She smirked. "It probably will be."

Epilogue

Alex was driving through Darras Hall where the houses jingled with money. She was on her way to the Thomson household. They'd had a last twist to the case. She'd decided to ask Terry Marshall if he'd be prepared to take a DNA test to see if he was Douglas Blake's father. He *was* Douglas Blake's father which had shocked them all. She suspected that in their heart of hearts, they'd all thought Neil Thomson would be his father. Terry Marshall was delighted. He and Douglas Blake had met each other and Terry had arranged a good solicitor to help him with his charge of accidentally killing Helen Carter. Terry Marshall and his wife had subsequently met the couple who had adopted Douglas Blake and they were going to attend his wedding

She turned into the Thomson drive and breathed in deeply. She was going to tell a grieving widow that they knew who had killed her husband, although he was never going to be brought to justice because he was dead. She took another deep breath and rang the doorbell.

After she'd spoken to Sarah Thomson she was going to go to Alnwick and call in to see Adam and Linda Vickers, the county line boy and his mother. She intended today to show Adam how to structure an essay. Then finally she was going to head north up her beloved Northumbrian coast, to the Holy Island of Lindisfarne, and Ewan's excavations there.

If you have enjoyed this book would you consider leaving a review.

Amazon UK
Amazon US
Goodreads

If you would like to connect with the author
JJThomasauthor.com
Facebook

ACKNOWLEDGEMENTS

There are small group of people who have walked the path with me as I have learnt to write a novel – it has been a steep learning curve for me. Arl and Jacques were with me from the start as I formulated ideas and they read early drafts. The final read rested with my friend, Cat. Invaluable support also came from Rabia, Lisa and Mary.

I would also like to thank Sam Hook and Laura Race of the Blackfriars restaurant which inspired this book. I asked them if I could commit a murder at their restaurant entrance.

Last but not least my mother who has visited with me many of the sites in the novel. To her this book is dedicated with my love.

About the Author

Born in Newcastle upon Tyne, JJ Thomas is a history and archaeology buff like her detective Alex Shaftoe, and is happiest when she is visiting historical sites. Her other two passions are reading and travel. And she often combines all three.

She is currently trying to visit as many countries in the world as she can.

She has worked in government for a long time and travels abroad regularly with her job, most recently in the Caribbean and Africa. She has found this fascinating because you see the countries from the inside, something you don't always get to do when you are a tourist.

Printed in Great Britain
by Amazon

36902280R00174